—•••—

Murder
In the House of Beads

—•••—

MARY JANE FORBES

Todd Book Publications

Murder in the House of Beads

A Mystery in Paradise

ISBN: 978-0615954271 (sc)

Printed in the United States of America
Todd Book Publications
Port Orange, Florida

Website: www.MaryJaneForbes.com
Author photo: Ami Floyd

—•••—

To Noah Cohen who planted a seed bead*

...may the seed continue to germinate!

—•••—

Seed beads: tiny beads available in numerous colors and finishes. When used as spacers they resemble knots between beads.

Crystal Fantasy
Necklace & Earring Pattern
Designed by Pat Gathmann

58mm Rounds
166mm Bicones
164mm Bicones
164mm Rounds
46 mm Cubes
10Bead Caps
2Crimps
Seed Beads
Clasp
214" pieces of fine wire

Strands crisscross through 6mm cubes creating loop effect. String seed bead between each Bicone, Round, and Cube bead.

Hold the two wires together and insert through small fluted cap then 8mm Round. Separate wire. String a 4mm Bicone on each wire then a seed bead. Continue with a 6mm Bicone, seed bead, 4mm Round, seed bead.

Cross the strands through the cube by inserting the wire on opposite sides. Continue with a seed bead, 4mm Round, seed bead, 6mm Bicone, seed bead, 4mm Bicone, 8mm Round.

Repeat.

Crystal Fantasy
Jewelry worn by Catherine to the
Chamber of Commerce Charity Ball

Acknowledgements

First, let me thank my family for their support. Every author needs a few cheerleaders. My daughter, Molly, was especially helpful from the first draft to the final period.

The NSERB (North Side Editorial Review Board)—Vera Kuzymak, Lorna Prusak, Jean MacFarlane and Adele Fatigate—thank you for your editorial reviews, but most of all for your encouragement to go forward with the publication of this book.

A big thanks to Roger and Pat Grady who read the *rough* first draft. Your critique helped to make it a better book.

Thanks as well to my long-time friend, Geri Rogers, who suggested an additional chapter tying up loose ends.

Captain Miller, Port Orange, Florida, Police Department, gave me valuable insight into the workings of the police across the state. Deputy Chief of Police Stephen J. Beres and Investigator Jimmie Flynt, Daytona Beach Police Department, were very helpful regarding guns and drugs.

Thanks to Bill Heiser, President, Southern Hills Kennels, a K9 training compound. This particular organization trains dogs for police departments across the United States, Homeland Security, and military service around the world, including Iraq and Afghanistan. Mr. Heiser gave me a demonstration of a trained dog taking out a bad guy. After the culprit was brought down the German shepherd returned to his handler tail wagging and ready to play.

My two instructors, Barbara Rogan and Alice Duncan, WritersOnlineWorkshops.com, were especially helpful in the beginning stages of the manuscript and for urging me to *keep writing*.

Peaches' namesake lives in Michigan. After meeting her I knew she would be an integral part of a future story. Ted Wurschmidt's son, Lief, is her master.

Thank you Carolyn and Scott Fitzwilliam, managers of the bead shop Imagine That!® where it all began. They taught me the finer points of crafting jewelry.

Of course, there is always the person behind the scenes, the editor who polishes a manuscript. Thanks to Adele Brinkley for taking on this task. You did a great job.

Thank you, IUniverse! I received more help along the way than I expected, especially from the "manuscript evaluation."

And now, for Noah. While visiting my daughter in Michigan, her neighbor, Noah's mother, invited us and another neighbor for a ladies lunch. Noah, then eleven, fashioned a pair of earrings for each of us. Mine was a dangle with three small crystals—ruby red, dark blue and light blue. The pair immediately became my favorite.

When I returned to Florida I visited the bead shop so I could learn how to create earrings. On entering the shop, I was mesmerized by the display of the crystal beads in a rainbow of colors. Driving home from the shop, a story idea germinated about a murder in the house of beads. The next morning I began writing. A few weeks later I lost one of Noah's earrings. I searched everywhere with no success. A month later I stepped on something embedded in the carpet. To my delight it was the earring. Of course I wrote this discovery into the story. It became the linchpin clue nailing the killer. Thank you, Noah Cohen. You never know from whom an inspiration will spring.

—•••—

To all of you who savor a cozy, beach-chair or fireside mystery, enjoy!

–•••–

Murder
In the House of Beads

–•••–

Chapter 1

THE SUN ROSE OVER Daytona Beach, warming the day to a delightful seventy degrees. A soft breeze carried the scent of the ocean. Catherine Hainsworth stepped out of her silver BMW, breathing in the salty air as she entered the little bead shop on Granada Avenue. The antique clock on the building's cupola displayed the hour of four, time for class to start.

The soft tinkling of the shop's silver bell announced Catherine's arrival. Talking on the phone, Tillie, the proprietor, waved her on into the classroom. Tillie Brown had owned the bead shop for nearly six years. Her customers could always count on the latest in beads for color, quality, and design. She was especially proud of her unique stock of chains. They were sold nowhere else up and down the Florida coast.

The sun beamed at the perfect angle to strike the wall of beads through the store's front window, a wall sparkling with delicate chains of silver and gold. The array of beads also included strands of multi-colored gemstones of various cuts and weights, and creamy pearls of all sizes. The sparkling Austrian crystal display of reds melting into oranges, yellows, blues, violets, and greens seemed to dance to Vivaldi's "Spring" playing on the radio.

The sight of the colorful beads heightened Catherine's excitement and anticipation for today's class, the fourth in a series of five. Today they were fashioning dangle earrings. She rarely allowed herself to spend time away from her architectural design studio, but her friend Julie had pleaded with her to sign up so they could attend the bead class together.

Catherine hoped to create a pair of earrings with Swarovski peridot crystals to complement her lime green gown, the one she designed specifically for the upcoming Chamber of Commerce Charity Ball.

Catherine hummed to herself as she passed the mirror, positioned just outside the classroom where students could admire their latest creations. She took a quick appraising look at her trim five-foot-four image. Her hand automatically smoothed her blonde hair tied back with a black grosgrain ribbon. Not too bad for thirty-five, she thought. She didn't tarry at the mirror and entered the classroom. The aroma of Tillie's favorite hazelnut coffee permeated the air. Catherine helped herself to a cup, adding a thimble of cream, and settled into her spot. As always, she was the first to arrive.

The classroom's soft yellow walls provided a warm, cozy feeling. A long table covered with a pale yellow tablecloth stood in the center of the space, circled with five chairs, making room for four students and the instructor. The room, similar to a little artist's studio with a picture window at one end, allowed lots of light for the miniature tasks at hand.

In a rush, the instructor, Barb Wilson, mother of two, scooted in with two other students. She was thankful for a couple of hours out of the house for some adult creative activity. Wendy, a skinny sixteen, entered on Barbara's heels. Wendy was given the class by her mother who hoped to instill a bit of fashion in her baggy, blue-jean covered daughter.

Right behind Wendy came Susan, a snippy, "I dislike everything and everyone," thirty-seven-year-old, childless housewife. Her sour outlook on life marred an image of what some would say was a pretty woman. Stylish wisps of brown hair framed her face, making her brown eyes appear large and lovely. Susan lowered herself into her seat next to Catherine, a seat she didn't like and never would.

They were now waiting for the last member of the class, Julie, a pretty, petite redhead. An immigrant from Ireland, Julie married well. She was thirteen years younger than her prominent architect husband.

"Dangle earrings today, ladies. Did you pick out your favorite beads in the shop?" Barb asked. She placed a gray-felt bead board with grooves and indented squares to hold the beads in front of each student and also at Julie's place. Julie, late again.

Catherine and Susan dug into their totes, emptying their beads from little plastic bags onto the soft felt boards. Wendy dumped her beads on the board, flipping her head as she did, sending her blonde ponytail flying. "I really love these. The little pink hearts are just so cute, don't you think?" she said, popping her gum.

At the sound of the shop's bell, they all looked up expectantly to see if Julie had arrived.

"I'm sorry I'm late. Hope you didn't wait for me," Julie said, walking slowly to her chair.

Catherine immediately noticed that the usually vibrant woman looked pale. She was blinking her eyes erratically. "Julie, are you okay?"

"Yes…actually, no. I'm feeling a little nauseous…dizzy…a little faint," she said, wilting into her chair.

"Tillie, can we have a glass of water in here?" Barb called as she moved quickly to Julie's side.

"Sure, hon. Be right with you," Tillie called back.

The water was too late. Julie made a gagging sound as she went face down on her bead board. Her fingers clutched the yellow tablecloth, pulling it away from the table, causing the boards and all the gemstones to crash to the floor scattering throughout the room. In a very slow, graceful motion, her red curls slithered out of sight under the table as she hit the tiled floor.

Jumping up, Catherine jerked the chairs away. Kneeling, she tried to find Julie's pulse. "Someone call 9-1-1. Wendy, help me turn her over on her back, will you? Quickly, dear." Catherine lifted Julie's chin, tilted her head back, and put her cheek next to Julie's nose hoping to feel a breath. None. She pinched shut Julie's nose, covered Julie's mouth with hers, and exhaled a breath of air into her lungs. Again she checked for a breath. None.

Catherine scooted down on her knees stopping opposite Julie's chest. Placing one hand on top of the other over Julie's breast bone, she began giving compressions, counting out loud, "One one-thousand, two one-thousand, three one-thousand." She counted, just as she had done many times in her CPR classes, but never, dear Lord, had she performed the real thing. She scooted back up to Julie's head checking for her breath. None. Again pinching Julie's nose, covering her mouth with her own, Catherine gave her two breaths, causing Julie's chest to rise and fall. Still no response.

"Does anyone know CPR who can help me?" she rasped as again she took her position to administer compressions on Julie's chest.

Staring at the limp form, "No," they all said in unison.

Undaunted, Catherine continued with the cadence.

"Are the paramedics on the way?" Catherine shouted again, switching back to Julie's head.

A siren was heard in answer to her question. Doors slammed, the shop bell clanged, and the EMTs quickly entered the room.

Not missing a beat, Catherine filled in the two men and a woman on what happened. "I never felt a pulse," she said, as she quickly stood, backed away.

The EMTs took over. One checked Julie's vital signs, another set up a defibrillator, and the third one positioned the rolling gurney. Within seconds, Julie was on the gurney, out the door, and on her way to Halifax Memorial Hospital with a medic on either side never stopping their ministrations. As the EMT van turned the corner out of sight, nobody in the bead shop was sure if Julie was alive or dead.

Chapter 2

❧

AT 5:45 IN THE AFTERNOON the Daytona Beach Police Department received a call from Dr. William Tredwell, Halifax Memorial Hospital's Emergency Center. Hospital policy dictated that the police department must be informed when a death seemed out of the ordinary, and Julie Stone's death was certainly not ordinary. A young woman doesn't *usually* drop dead.

The police department routinely forwards such calls to the Criminal Investigation Division. CID then contacts the county medical examiner who checks the body to determine, in his judgment, whether or not there was foul play. Captain Manny Salinas, head of CID, was about to leave for home when his telephone rang. It was Dr. Tredwell.

"Captain Salinas, our EMT crew arrived with a woman thirty minutes ago. Her age is somewhere between twenty-five and thirty-five," Dr. Tredwell said. "She was dead on arrival. After a quick examination of the body, I could not determine a more specific cause of death other than cardiac arrest."

"I'll be right over," Manny said. He gave his dog, Peaches, a pat on the head. "Come on, girl. Just one stop and then it's steak time for you and me." Peaches, a three-year-old black Labrador Retriever, happily joined her master. She accompanied Manny everywhere and even enjoyed a cedar-filled pillow alongside the captain's desk.

Manny and Peaches climbed into his plain wrapper, black SUV, and drove to the hospital. The car did not have *Police* emblazoned on it outside, but inside it was an electronic communications marvel, with all the latest technology to aid Manny when and where he needed it.

Traffic was heavy on Clyde Morris Boulevard, but it didn't take Manny long to navigate to the hospital. He turned into the parking lot, slowing over the speed bump. Nonetheless, Peaches lost her footing and leaned into her master's arm. She gave him a slurp on his cheek before resuming her post at the window.

Manny entered the hospital emergency center and immediately spotted the doctor in his green scrubs standing behind the receiving desk checking patient charts. The waiting area held six people in various states of distress. All inhaled the cool antiseptic air from the hospital's air conditioning system, staring sightless at the pale-yellow, concrete-block walls—some decorator's idea of bringing sunshine into an area of blood and pain.

"Dr. Tredwell, I'm Captain Salinas. We spoke on the phone about a dead woman your EMTs brought in earlier."

"Captain Salinas," the doctor said, shaking Manny's hand. "Thank you for coming so quick. Follow me, please."

The doctor escorted Manny into an examination room. On the metal table lay a form covered with a white sheet. When Manny pulled back the covering he was surprised at who lay on the table. "This is Julie Stone, Russell Stone's wife," he said, to the doctor. "Have you heard of her?"

"Only her name from the driver's license in her purse."

"The Stones are quite well known in the community. Have you done anything to the body?" Manny asked.

"I did a cursory examination. There are no marks on her. No blood. No apparent blow to the head. Her death seemed a bit strange to me. She's rather a young woman. That's why I called the police."

"Reporting her death was the right thing to do, Doctor," Manny said, popping a Nicorette in his mouth. Manny, thirty-six, had been in the department for fifteen years, the last three as head of CID. The stress of the job interfered with the breaking of his smoking habit.

Pulling the sheet back over Julie, Manny said, "I'll call our medical examiner. He'll send a van over and take her back to the morgue. If we're lucky, he may know the cause of death by morning.

Otherwise it could take a while as he has several cases in the queue. Doctor, where did the EMTs pick her up and who called?"

Reading the intake form, Dr. Tredwell said, "The call came in from a Tillie Brown. She's the owner of the House of Beads over on Granada Avenue. Mrs. Stone just arrived for a class when she collapsed. A Catherine Hainsworth was administering CPR when the EMTs arrived and took over."

"Catherine Hainsworth administered CPR?"

"That's what it says here," Dr. Tredwell said. "Do you know her?"

"Yes, I do. Ms. Hainsworth is another prominent woman in our city."

The hospital paging system cut into their conversation.

"Excuse me, Captain. I'll be back shortly. I'm expecting Mrs. Stone's husband."

— •••—

THE DOCTOR HEADED DOWN the hall to the receiving area. He surmised that the man standing at the counter was Russell Stone, the deceased woman's husband. He had called Mr. Stone after notifying the police.

"Mr. Stone?" Dr. Tredwell said, extending his hand.

"Yes. I came as soon as you called. I doubt the woman you admitted is my wife. I haven't been able to reach her on her cell, but the body you have can't be Julie." Russell Stone nervously ran his fingers through his salt and pepper hair.

"Please come with me, Mr. Stone. I'll take you to the examination room."

Manny, finishing his conversation with the medical examiner, snapped his cell phone shut as Stone and the doctor entered the room. "Russell, I'm so sorry," Manny said.

"I guess you two know each other," the doctor said.

"It has to be a mistake," Russell said. Seeing the cold metal table holding a body covered with a stark white sheet sent a shiver down his spine.

"Dr. Tredwell, would you let Mr. Stone identify the body?"

The doctor pulled back the sheet. Russell Stone stepped to his wife's side. "My God, it is Julie." He put a hand to her cheek but instantly pulled it back, her flesh ice cold. His legs went rubbery as he grasped the table trying to regain his balance. He staggered to a nearby chair. "How can this be? Doctor, what happened? Manny, why are you here? My dear, beautiful Julie," he said. Again he went to her side, slowly bent over lifting her into his arms. Cradling his wife, he rocked back and forth willing her to wake up, tears slowly filling his eyes.

"Russell, the medical examiner is on his way to transport Julie to the morgue," Manny said. "Dr. Tredwell doesn't know the cause of death so the ME will determine how she died."

The word "morgue" brought Russell out of his trance. "Why the morgue?"

"When the cause of death is not obvious, the hospital reports it to the police. We notify the medical examiner who must perform an autopsy," Manny said. "I'll call you in the morning if we have the results. However, we may not know anything for a few days."

Julie's dead body lying on the table was too much for Russell Stone to take in. He once again held his wife in his arms. "Julie, Julie, what happened to you?" he murmured, clutching her lifeless body to him.

Chapter 3

❧

NEITHER MANNY NOR PEACHES slept that night. Manny paced the hours away, stopping now and then to add some ice to his glass of scotch. Sensing his distress, Peaches followed her master around the rooms.

"Peaches, why would a beautiful, seemingly healthy woman suddenly die?" he asked, repeatedly.

The sun finally came up, and Manny and Peaches left for the morgue located about two miles from the police department. The two went directly to the ME's lab. Peaches wasn't allowed in the lab, so upon her master's hand signal, she flopped down on the floor outside the door, put her head down on her paws, and watched her master enter the medical examiner's world.

The lights were blinding. A strong odor of bleach filled the very cold air, and Manny detected formaldehyde and a suggestion of something like curdled milk.

"Hey, Manny, you're in early," Sam said.

Sam Houston, employed by the county as its Medical Examiner for twenty years, was still enthusiastic about his profession, not in a maudlin way, but because of all the scientific breakthroughs which seemed to happen every day.

"Couldn't sleep," Manny said. "Have you had a chance to look at the Stone body?"

"Yup. A fatal dose of a drug," Sam said. "Probably a derivative of digitalis. It doesn't take much over the prescribed dosage to have a lethal effect. I'll know for sure after I do some more testing. There were traces of alcohol in her stomach, as well as lettuce, tomato, and bread. I'll get you the exact drug later this morning. There was no sexual assault."

"Sam, you're the best and thanks for the rush job. Once the press catches wind of this, I have a feeling it will be chaos around here. I'd like to keep ahead of them."

Manny and Peaches left the morgue and went on to the police department. Barging through the entrance, he asked the morning clerk for his messages. Finding none, he climbed the stairs to his office. The second floor of the department was a product of the open-office concept. No walls. Just cubicles with desks and cabinets.

However, Manny didn't want individual cubicles for his team. He created an open, octagon-shape bullpen to foster communication. Desks were placed against five of the eight-foot wide walls, one for each team member plus a spare. There was an opening, a doorway of sorts, on either side of Manny's desk. He obviously was the leader.

On the three walls directly opposite his desk hung three eight-foot long by five-foot tall electronic whiteboards. These boards provided space for diagrams, clue mapping, suspect lists, case status, and team assignments. The electronic boards provided the capability of storing the information, written or drawn, into a computer file.

The most important piece of equipment in the bullpen was invisible—the wireless network connection from each team member's PC to a computer hub in Tallahassee. There the data of all Florida crimes was stored, including past, present, and DNA samples for future use.

At the moment, the boards were full of lists, pictures, and assignments displaying the chronological history of the case they were wrapping up. Manny ordered the board's information to be stored and wiped clean for the next investigation—the death of Julie Stone.

Fred Watson and George Anderson, his two lead detectives, were already at their desks in the bullpen when Manny and Peaches arrived. Fred and George joined Manny's team at the same time Manny was promoted to head up the Criminal Investigation Division.

Manny chose Fred, thirty-seven, African American, on the basis of his law-enforcement knowledge. His experience with illegals crossing the border into the States was also a major factor in Manny's decision to hire him. He selected George, twenty-nine, Caucasian, for his youth, or, as Manny told him, "someone with fresh eyes, the better to see the unexpected." Fred and George were perfect foils for each other.

Dani, the fourth member of the team, entered the bullpen and flopped down on her chair, trying to smother a yawn that her morning jolt of Dunkin coffee couldn't stifle. Sergeant Dani Trotter, twenty-four, Caucasian, Manny's Research and Lab Technician, loved her job and looked at every assignment as a puzzle. Her shoulder-length black hair, tucked behind her ears, with streaks of blonde framed her cherubic face.

Anyone passing the bullpen would have seen the team of four dressed in black—the men in short-sleeved shirts, and Dani in a long-sleeve turtleneck T-shirt. Her forensic lab was always cool.

"Okay, guys, listen up," Manny said. Peaches remained asleep on her pillow still tired from last night's pacing. "We have a potential media-circus before us. Julie Stone, Russell Stone's wife, died yesterday. Sam believes she died of an overdose of some form of digitalis. She collapsed at the House of Beads over on Granada. EMTs were called and they transported her to Halifax Memorial Hospital where she was pronounced dead.

"Any indications of foul play?" George asked.

"Not that Sam could see from his preliminary examination," Manny replied. "Unless you can think of something else, I'd say there are three options. One, she accidentally overdosed. Two, she killed herself. Or three, she was murdered."

Manny walked to his desk, grabbed a bottle of cold water. He twisted the cap off downing a long swallow to soothe his parched throat. "I saw Russell Stone at the hospital when he ID'd the body," Manny continued.

"How'd he react when he saw his wife lying there?" Fred asked.

"He appeared to be dazed, upset, and distraught. Couldn't believe what he was seeing."

"Did he want to know how or when she died," Fred asked.

"Not specifically. When I told him she would be transported to the department's morgue, he wasn't happy about a potential autopsy."

"I can understand that," George said. "After all we're talking about his wife."

"Yes, I know," Manny said. "Stone's a big architect and builder in the area. Julie Stone was also fairly prominent in the community, not only because of her husband but in her own right."

"I've read about her in the newspaper," Dani said. "She was active in various big charities, and I understand she was quite a bit younger than her husband."

Moving to the left whiteboard, Manny addressed his team. "We'll assume all options are plausible until each is eliminated. The substance was probably administered yesterday. Dani, check with Sam as to how quickly the dose he found would kill her. We need a timeline of her whereabouts yesterday and a list of everyone she saw. With what we know so far, here's a list of people to get statements from this morning."

Writing the list of names on the board, Manny gave orders to his team. "Russell Stone. Fred, I want you to take this one. You'll probably find him at home. Tell Stone what the ME found and the probable substance that caused her death. Watch his reaction. Read him his rights. He's a smart man and will understand that he could be a suspect. Ask to search the house, particularly the bedroom, bathroom, and wherever else you feel drugs might be stored.

"George, you go to Stone's office. I believe he has an assistant. Check where Stone was every minute yesterday and verify the information. Get some input about the Stone's relationship. Take the assistant's statement and find out where she was all day yesterday."

Manny went to his desk for a fresh marking pen and a drink from his bottled water. "Dani, keep checking with Sam for the exact substance Mrs. Stone ingested. When you have the information, and if it is a drug, start the search of pharmacies within a fifty-mile radius that filled a prescription for it in the past year. Get a list of buyers. Also, pick up her purse. Sam has it. See if she used a cell phone. If she did, start checking the numbers, names, and dates."

"I'm on it," Dani said, grabbing her car keys.

"I'm going to the House of Beads where Mrs. Stone collapsed and to visit Catherine Hainsworth," Manny said. "I was told she administered CPR trying to revive her. That's it. Let's get going." At the word, *going*, Peaches got up and nuzzled her master's hand with her wet nose, letting him know she was ready.

"Keep in touch and plan to regroup here at the end of the day. Let's dig up some leads."

Chapter 4

❧

AT EXACTLY 10 AM Fred entered the driveway of Stone's property. The huge home sat on the banks of the Halifax River in Ormond-By-the-Sea, an affluent community. Onlookers might guess Stone was an architect and they would be right. He designed the home for the love of his life, Julie, and had poured his heart and soul into the project.

The home's style displayed a strong Spanish influence—red tile roof, delicate pink stucco walls, and balconies guarded with exquisite wrought iron filigree. The circular drive leading to and away from the front entrance was lined with white impatiens interspersed with pink begonias and purple Mexican petunias. A lush green, well manicured lawn gave way to beds of various colors of hibiscus, bromeliads, and groupings of the tropical Bird-of-Paradise. The warm spring day enhanced the brilliance of the flowers, drawing their fragrance into the morning air.

Fred pressed the doorbell as his gaze took in the beauty of the home and its setting. The door opened a crack.

"Sir, may I help you?" asked a woman.

"Yes. I'm Detective Fred Watson. I'm here to see Mr. Stone. I believe he's expecting me."

"Yes, sir," the woman said, opening the door wide. "Mr. Stone is expecting you. Please come in."

If Fred thought the outside was beautiful, the inside was almost palatial. A sweet scent of roses lingered in the air from a fresh bouquet on the gleaming cherry console table.

"Excuse me, sir. Please come with me," the woman said. Fred had lagged behind, his eyes lingering on the splendor of the home.

"Yes, of course," Fred said, focusing his eyes back on the woman.

She opened a door and entered Stone's library and office. Russell Stone sat at his desk, but his chair was turned, his back to the door. He appeared to be staring out the ceiling-high windows. The view through the glass panes followed the expanse of lawn down to the sparkling water of the Halifax River. A sailboat skittered by, but Russell apparently saw nothing but his grief.

"Excuse me, Mr. Stone. Detective Watson is here to see you."

Russell slowly turned his chair back to his desk and stood up. "Thank you, Annie."

"Hello, Mr. Stone," Fred said, extending his hand. "I'm Detective Fred Watson, Daytona Beach Police Department. I believe Captain Salinas told you I would be stopping by?"

"Yes, he did. Do you know anything yet about my wife?"

"Yes, but let me first say we are all sorry for your loss."

"Thank you, but tell me what you believe happened to Julie."

"The medical examiner found a form of digitalis in her system. The dose was large enough to kill her," Fred said.

"What do you mean? She died of a drug overdose? There has to be a mistake. It's absurd. Who would give Julie such a drug? Everyone liked her."

"Could you tell me, sir, was she depressed or distraught over something? Could she have wanted to harm herself?"

"Are you asking me if she killed herself? Good Lord, no."

"Do you know of anyone who might want to harm her?"

"No. No. I said everyone liked her. She was very active in the community, loved doing charity work, and retained a few close friends. No one would want to hurt Julie."

"Sir, forgive me, but I'm going to have to ask you a few personal questions."

"If you want to know how my wife and I got along, go ahead and ask," Stone said, drumming his fingers on the desk.

"Sir, did you and your wife have any personal problems, marital issues?"

"No, only the usual husband and wife squabbles. She felt I spent too much time at the office or at my various construction sites, but we were working through the issue."

"Please tell me everything you can remember about yesterday. From the moment you got up in the morning until you saw Captain Salinas at the hospital. Before you start, I must inform you that the spouse is always considered a person-of-interest until he can be eliminated as such. Do you understand?" Fred asked.

"Let me tell you what I understand. This is all a big mistake."

Fred pulled out a recorder and placed it in the middle of Stone's desk. Russell looked at the recorder and then up at Fred.

"It's standard procedure, sir. Are you okay with it?" Fred asked.

"Yes, I'm okay with it. Get on with your questions," Stone replied, his voice clearly showing his frustration.

"Please tell me about yesterday."

— ••• —

RUSSELL STONE STOOD, walked to the window, and slowly turned around. He didn't see Fred. He saw Julie sitting up in bed, sliding her slender legs over the edge...

"What are you going to do today, my love?" Russell asked.

"I'm going to run over to the coffee shop for my usual cup of Irish coffee, do some shopping, lunch, more shopping. Nothing important, nothing as interesting as your day, I'm sure."

"No meeting for the charity ball?"

"Not today. I do have my bead class. That'll be fun I suppose. How about you?"

"I have a meeting with the Tower Project Board this afternoon. With the information I get from them, I'll meet with several contractors and my design team."

"So, Russell, it'll be another night you won't be home for dinner. In fact it sounds like you'll be very late. When do you think you might return home, midnight, one, two?"

"Julie, you know this is a major project. If I'm awarded the bid, it will put the firm of Stone & Associates on the map. It will give us the money to retire early and travel the world together."

"Interesting that you put the firm first and me second."

— • • • —

"JULIE DRESSED QUICKLY and then stormed out of our bedroom. She shouted at me as she left, 'Have a prosperous day, Mr. Stone. Please don't wake me up when you decide to come home.' Those were the last words I heard from her lips. When I got out of the shower, she was gone."

"Then what did you do?" Fred asked.

"I was very unsettled because of our argument. Annie, our housekeeper, whom you met when you came in, called from the stairs that the coffee was ready."

"Did Mrs. Stone typically skip coffee with you in the morning?"

"Sometimes yes. Sometimes no. Lately she's been going to the coffee shop a few blocks from my company's building."

"Did Annie hear your argument?"

"I don't know. She could have, I suppose," Stone said.

"Did you go downstairs and have your coffee?"

"Yes, and Annie fixed my breakfast. After breakfast, I came in here to work on the design for the tower project, but I couldn't get into the job, so I left for the office."

"You went to your office in town?"

"No, I didn't. I found myself driving up Interstate 95. Next thing I knew I was in the outskirts of St. Augustine. I pulled into a roadside bar and drank a couple of beers."

"Did you plan to meet someone?"

"No. I was trying to think of a way to resolve the differences between Julie and me. The quarreling was getting me down. I thought they would stop eventually, but her complaints seemed to be getting worse."

"How long were you in the bar?"

"A little over an hour, I guess. I ate a couple of burgers and then left. I arrived back at the office about four o'clock. Maggie, my assistant, told me Bill MacFarlane, the contract award chairman, called while I was gone. He wondered where I was. He asked Maggie why I had missed the meeting and to call as soon as possible."

"So you didn't attend the meeting that day?" Fred asked.

"No. MacFarlane told Maggie the designs from some of the firms submitting bids had been received by the committee. He wanted to confirm the deadline for the financial part of the process. I had completely forgotten about the meeting."

"Did you call him?"

"Yes."

"What time was that?"

"As soon as Maggie relayed the message, so a little after four. I apologized to MacFarlane and asked if I could come by tomorrow. He said he was disappointed I had missed seeing him, but yes, we could meet tomorrow."

"Then what did you do?"

"I went home. I wanted to be there when Julie returned from her bead class. I wasn't home long when I got the call from the hospital. I left immediately. I guess you know the rest."

"When you were in the bar, did you talk to anyone?"

"Only the bartender."

"Do you have any receipts?"

"No, I paid cash for everything, gas, beer, burgers."

"Where exactly was the bar?"

"I don't know, off of Route 95, just before St. Augustine."

"Do you remember the name of the bar?"

"No, all I saw was the bar and I wanted a drink."

"Thank you, Mr. Stone." Fred reached over and turned off the recorder.

"Sir, Annie, your housekeeper, I'll have to interview her as well."

"Yes, yes, go ahead."

"Please understand we have to check all options on how Mrs. Stone came to have the substance in her body. I would like your permission to search the house for the drug. To your knowledge, does anyone in the household take digitalis? This drug is often prescribed for heart patients."

"No, at least not that I'm aware of."

"Sir, are you under a doctor's care for your heart?"

"No, and neither was Julie."

"How about, Annie?"

"Not that I know of. Go ahead and search the house, the sooner the better. I have nothing to hide. I can't imagine how this could have happened. I'll ask Annie to show you around. She's very upset by Mrs. Stone's death, but I'm sure she'll be glad to help you get to the bottom of this."

Stone pressed the button on the intercom. "Annie, can you come to the library?" Within a few minutes Annie entered the room. "Please show Detective Watson around upstairs and the first floor. Take him anywhere he asks to go. It seems Mrs. Stone died of a drug overdose, and he needs to search the house. We must help in any way we can."

"Oh, Mr. Stone, this is terrible. She was poisoned?" Annie said, pulling a handkerchief from her pocket. Tears spilled down her cheeks.

— •••—

FRED NOTICED WHEN ANNIE answered the door that her eyes were red from crying. Now the puffiness was obvious, especially with this new rush of tears.

"Thank you, Annie," Fred said, following the housekeeper out of the library and up the stairs to the second floor.

Annie showed him the master bedroom, Julie's bathroom and dressing room, Russell's bathroom and dressing room, and finally the two guest suites. Fred checked medicine cabinets and nightstand drawers. A team of officers would come back later to perform a thorough search.

"Annie, do you live here?" Fred asked.

"Yes, sir. Mr. Stone made sure my living quarters were included when he designed the house."

"Sounds as if you've been with the Stones for quite a while."

"Yes, sir. Eleven years. They hired me while the house was being built. They'd only been married a year or two. I hoped there might be some babies, but I guess God planned otherwise."

Detecting a Spanish accent, Fred asked, "Where are you from, Annie?" He noticed an immediate change in Annie's demeanor. She stiffened, her body pulling away.

"Why do you want to know anything about me?" she asked.

"I have to question everyone who saw Mrs. Stone yesterday."

"I'm from Texas," Annie said haltingly.

Fred took out a little notepad from his pants pocket. "Where in Texas?"

"El Paso."

"What's your last name, Annie?"

"I never use a last name."

"Okay, but what is it?" Fred pressed gently. She now commanded his full attention. What she was trying to hide?

"Jackson."

"Thank you, Annie Jackson. I'll finish up in your living quarters and then say goodbye to Mr. Stone."

Fred finished with the obvious places Julie or someone else in the house might have kept a substance if she were going to kill herself and where Mr. Stone might put a prescription drug. He came up empty after a cursory search of the house and returned to the library. The door was open so he rapped on the door frame and went in.

Russell stood on the tiled patio just outside the French doors. Fred joined him. "I'm done for now, Mr. Stone, so I'll be going. Annie was very helpful." Fred started to walk away and then turned back. "Mr. Stone, did Mrs. Stone leave any kind of note?"

"No, but she was not in the habit of writing notes."

"If you do find a note, no matter what the date, please let me know. If you think of anything that might help the investigation, call me. Here's my card."

"Detective, can you give me an idea as to when I can start making funeral arrangements?"

"I'll ask Captain Salinas to call you as soon as the medical examiner knows when your wife's body can be released."

"Thank you. I know she wished to be cremated."

Fred returned to his car. "Cremated! We'd better be sure we gather all the forensics before Sam releases her body to the funeral home," he mumbled, heading back to the department.

Chapter 5

‮ࡇ‬

GEORGE PULLED THE WHITE squad car into a parking spot in front of Stone & Associates. The four-story building screamed *successful business*. At the street level, the building housed a woman's clothing boutique and a travel agency. The three stories above the shops were faced with copper-colored mirrored glass. Administrative offices and design rooms were located on the second floor. A penthouse capped the building which was mainly used for social events. The architectural firm opened from the street into an expansive lobby, the large entrance separating the two street-level shops.

George entered the building and walked along the white marble floor to two elevators. The plaque between the elevators read, "Stone & Associates, 2nd Floor."

He rode the elevator to the second floor and walked out into a spacious reception area. The décor was striking. George stepped onto the sage green carpet and looked around. Light salmon sheers peeked out from beneath green drapes slightly darker than the carpet. Plush couches strategically placed in cozy arrangements were topped with throw pillows—yellow, dark salmon, and various greens—some solid, some pinstripes.

A small wall fountain, the bowl shaped like a seashell, faced the elevator. The musical sound of water splashing as it filled the shell softened the overall silence of the area. He shook his head, feeling a calming ambience settle over him. However, George sensed a pall-like atmosphere—everyone at the company knew of Julie's death.

He approached the receptionist. "Can you tell me where I might find Mr. Stone's assistant? I believe she's expecting me."

"What's your name, and I'll see if she can see you now?"

"Detective George Anderson."

"Detective?" she said, raising her eyebrows.

"Yes."

The receptionist pressed a button on the telephone console. "Detective George Anderson to see you. He says you're expecting him." Looking up at George, she gestured with a manicured hand. "She said to come on down. It's the third door on your right."

Following her directions, George walked through the open door and found an attractive woman sitting behind a desk.

"Hello, Ms. O'Reilly," George said, extending his hand to Russell Stone's assistant. Her name, Maggie O'Reilly, was chiseled into the brass nameplate on her desk.

"Hello, Detective. Russell, ...Mr. Stone called. I've been expectin' you. I can't believe Julie's gone. He said she died of some kind of drug. Is that true?" Tears sprang anew from her eyes, already red from crying.

George guessed her age to be about twenty-nine. She also verified his image of an Irish girl—raven hair, Irish brogue, and deep blue eyes. Her tailored suit told him she was a business professional, but her tears showed the loss of someone close to her.

"Ms. O'Reilly, the medical examiner found a drug, a large amount, in her system. We don't know what happened or how it got there. We're doing a preliminary investigation, questioning anyone who may have seen her yesterday or anyone who is close to the Stones."

"All right, Mr. ...Detective Anderson, but I doubt I know anythin' that can help you."

"Did you know Mrs. Stone well?"

"We were friends, both being from Ireland you know. We didn't spend a lot of time together, but we did have an occasional lunch. A wonderful woman, she was. She helped me acclimate to the area," Maggie said, fresh tears running down her cheeks.

"Julie's from Northern Ireland." Maggie continued. "When her parents were killed in a bombing, she was sixteen, she decided to come to America. She took her small inheritance and flew to New York and then down here to Daytona Beach. She, like I, wanted to be near the ocean, even though a vastly different view from the coast of Ireland you know."

"Sounds like you two had a lot in common. Did she talk much about her husband?"

"A little. She told me when she was twenty she met and fell madly in love with Mr. Stone. They were married in a lovely chapel in Key West. Very romantic."

"How did you and Julie meet?" George asked.

"We met by chance, actually. We were both in the boutique downstairs. She heard me talking to a clerk about some Irish perfume, and, of course, she recognized the brogue."

"Excuse me, but if you don't mind, what is the perfume you're wearing? It's a lovely scent."

"Yes, it's the perfume I asked the clerk about. The name is Inis, the energy of the sea. Julie knew of it. Women ask me for the name occasionally, but you're the first man," she said with a small smile. "Anyway, the next thing I knew we were chatting away at the coffee shop down the street."

"It must have been nice to talk to someone who understood your roots," George said.

"Oh, yes, it was. I mentioned to her that a job had eluded me so far, and she told me her husband needed an assistant. She insisted we go back to his office so she could introduce us. On his wife's recommendation, he hired me. It's been five years since that chance meeting. The Stones have been very good to me."

"Ms. O'Reilly—"

"Please, call me Maggie, Detective," she said, mopping up her tears.

"Maggie, as I said, we are doing a preliminary investigation. Did you see Mrs. Stone yesterday?"

"No, not yesterday." She looked down at her twisted tissue.

Maggie seemed to drift away from him. "Is there something else you'd like to tell me?" he asked.

"No. No."

"Can you fill me in on where you were yesterday, say from nine in the morning until four in the afternoon?" George noted she suddenly seemed nervous.

"I arrived here in the office just before nine and stayed all day. I went to the deli down the street to pick up a sandwich about one o'clock. Mr. Stone scheduled a meeting with the Contract Award

Board regarding his upcoming bid for the Daytona Beach Tower Project, but I guess he never made it to the meeting." Maggie took out her hanky and gently blew her nose.

"Did he tell you why he didn't make it to the meeting?" George asked.

"Yes. When he returned to the office he told me he drove to St. Augustine to look at a piece of property. He said the property showed potential for a new condominium project."

"I see. Did he say what he was going to do about the meeting he missed?"

"Well, yes, after I told him that Bill MacFarlane, he's the head of the Contract Award Board, wanted him to call, Mr. Stone called him immediately. I heard him apologizing profusely. Then he came out of his office and told me he wanted to go home, and he left for the day. I closed the office around five-thirty."

"I see. Can you give me Bill MacFarlane's telephone number? While you're getting that, do you mind if I take your picture for the files?" George asked, snapping a picture with his cell phone before she could answer.

"It's okay," she said, looking up and then back down to scan a computer file. "Here it is, Bill MacFarlane." She wrote the number on a piece of paper and handed it to George.

"Maggie, how did the Stones get along?" George asked, putting MacFarlane's number in his pocket.

"Great. They loved each other very much. Oh, there were a few squabbles here and there but nothing big. A lucky lass, Julie was, to land such a catch as Mr. Stone."

George again sensed unease from Maggie as she answered his question.

Chapter 6

❧

THE EVER-CLANGING BELL announced each classmate returning to the House of Beads. They had agreed to meet the next day after Julie collapsed. The women, accompanied by Tillie, filed into the yellow classroom, which today didn't seem quite so sunny. Even the radio playing Sinatra's "September of my Years" carried a sad note.

Settling into her least favorite chair, Susan snipped, "Did you really think you could save her, Catherine, with your fancy CPR? I don't see why we came back here today. We know she's dead."

"Now, now, hon, we don't know that," Tillie soothed as she pushed the button on the coffeemaker. Soon the aroma of today's blend of vanilla almond began to float in the air.

"She's right. Julie is dead!" Catherine said.

Four heads swiveled to face Catherine. Shocked silence filled the small classroom.

"I phoned Russell, Julie's husband, when I got home yesterday. He had just received a call from the hospital and was on his way out the door. The hospital informed him the EMT crew brought in a deceased female. The wallet in her purse identified the body as Julie Stone. However, Russell thought they were mistaken. He could not accept that Julie had died."

The sound of the bell intruded into the stunned silence as Catherine's revelation hung in the air. A man entered, about six-feet tall wearing a black turtleneck shirt pulled tight over bulging arms and chest. Tillie, pushing strands of her brown hair behind each ear, left the classroom, moving behind the counter at the front of the shop to greet the visitor.

"Good afternoon, ma'am. My name is Captain Salinas," Manny said, showing her his badge. "I'm with the Daytona Beach Police

Department. I'd like to ask you a few questions about an incident I understand happened here yesterday."

"Well, of course, hon," Tillie replied, putting on the best smile her plump red lips could muster. "You're in luck, Captain. The ladies who attended the class yesterday happen to be here now."

Catherine, recognizing the male voice, left the classroom and went over to greet her old friend. "Manny, I thought I heard your voice. It's so good to see you."

As she spoke, the ever gallant Manny raised her hand to his lips and planted a quick kiss on the top of her smooth fingers. "Catherine, what a nice surprise to find you here."

Tillie's eyes grew large at the exchange, a soft moan slipping through her lips.

"What brings a hard-nosed officer like you into this bastion of femininity?" Catherine asked.

"Are you part of this class?" he asked, looking over into the classroom, leaving her question unanswered.

"Yes, I am. There are four of us. Or rather there were four of us. Come, I'll introduce you."

Manny followed Catherine into the classroom, which seemed to shrink as he entered. He was an imposing figure in his uniform complete with a gun on his hip. His short, black, wavy hair, black mustache and olive skin didn't soften his image but seemed to accentuate his size. Before Catherine could say another word, Manny addressed the ladies before him.

"Let me introduce myself. My name is Captain Salinas, Daytona Beach Police Department."

"Captain, I'm Barb Wilson, the instructor," Barb interjected, as they shook hands. "These ladies were all here yesterday. Wendy, Susan, and I guess you already know Catherine."

Manny nodded to each as Barb said their names. "I'd like to ask you what you heard and saw yesterday afternoon when Julie Stone collapsed," he said. "Let me start with you, young lady. What's your full name?"

"Sullivan, Wendy Sullivan. There really isn't much to say. We were ready to start the class when Julie came in. She didn't look well, and the next thing we knew she fainted. Catherine did some CPR, and then the EMTs arrived and took her away."

"I see. Susan, your last name please?"

"Armstrong, Susan Armstrong. I have nothing to add."

"Alright. Barbara, your last name is Wilson?" Manny asked.

"Yes. It pretty much happened the way that Wendy described, except Julie said she felt dizzy when she came into the classroom. It all happened so fast."

"Thank you. One of my detectives will be calling each of you for a statement. In the meantime, if you think of anything I should know, here's my number. Call anytime," Manny said handing each woman his card. "Catherine, can I talk to you a minute?" He led her out of the classroom to a table and a couple of chairs in the corner of the shop.

Much to Susan's consternation, she couldn't hear what Catherine was saying. "Well, I guess we've been dismissed. She doesn't know any more than we do. Goodbye, all. I'm getting out of here." Leaving the shop, she mumbled. "I'm not about to tell him I ate lunch with Julie yesterday."

— • • • —

TILLIE FOLLOWED SUSAN OUT of the classroom, said goodbye to her, and then went over to Manny and Catherine. "Captain, would you like a cup of coffee? I made it fresh for the ladies, and I'd be more than happy to bring it to you."

"Thank you, Tillie. I think I'll pass. Maybe some other time," he said, turning his attention back to Catherine.

"Catherine, do you have anything to add to what's been said about Mrs. Stone?" Manny asked.

"Not really. Julie arrived late by about ten minutes. But then she always came a few minutes late to class. She usually seemed to be in a good mood, but yesterday she appeared ill and said she felt dizzy. She collapsed into her chair and then fell onto the floor. I never detected a breath. Tillie dialed 9-1-1 immediately, and I started CPR. I never got a response from Julie. Manny, what happened to her?"

"We're not sure yet. I know how observant you are, Catherine, so anything you remember, however trivial, may be very helpful. I'd appreciate it if you'd call me if anything pops into your head. Besides, you know I always like to hear from you."

"How's Peaches?"

"Still spoiled, of course. Come on out to the car. She's always a happy dog when she gets a pat on the head from you."

Peaches ecstatically greeted Catherine. Her tail whipped back and forth knocking the rearview mirror askew. She strained to get her head out the window to give Catherine a kiss. Manny opened the car door and she jumped out.

At Manny's command, the dog sat down expectantly in front of Catherine, her tail sweeping the sidewalk. Catherine bent over, scratched the gleeful dog behind her ears, receiving a slurp on her cheek as a reward.

Chapter 7

∽

ON HER WAY TO WORK, Dani stopped at the morgue. Sucking on the rim of her large Dunkin coffee, she walked at a crisp clip down the sterile-gray, cement-block hallway to Sam's lab. She was after the latest information on the Stone case.

"Hi, Sam. I came for Mrs. Stone's purse. I understand you have it." The door swung shut behind her. "Know anything more about the drug?"

"Yes, indeed, Sergeant Trotter," Sam said, massaging his back as he straightened upright from his hunched position over a body. "We're in luck. I found digitoxin in her system, a form of digitalis. The amount prescribed to help people with a heart condition is very close to the amount that can cause serious problems from an accidental overdose. Mrs. Stone's system contained much more than would have been prescribed. I would say she died within a couple hours from when she swallowed it."

"Anything else you want me to tell the captain?" Dani asked. She liked to visit Sam because he addressed her as Sergeant, puffing up her ego.

"I think not. I'll have the complete report to him tomorrow. Here's Mrs. Stone's purse," Sam said, handing Dani a large, tan macramé bag.

"Now that's a purse, huh, Doc?"

"It certainly is. I don't know why women carry so much stuff around. It would kill my back," he replied, again massaging his aching muscles.

Dani picked up the bag. She left the morgue and headed for the department, stopping for a refill at Dunkin.

— • • • —

BACK AT HER DESK, Dani dumped the contents of Julie Stone's bag into a plastic bin and began the inventory. It contained the usual female stuff and a piece of crumpled paper folded in thirds, letter style. Dani quickly inventoried the rest of the bag's contents. Nothing seemed unusual or out of place, except an earring. One earring. Scratching around for the matching piece of jewelry, she came up empty.

Dani picked up the piece of paper, unfolded it, smoothing out the wrinkles with her hand as best she could. As she read the letter, astonishment slowly crept across her face.

> *My Dear Miguel,*
>
> *I know who you are. Better yet, I know who you are not.*
>
> *I'm in need of some cash, $5,000 to be precise, and I think you are in a position to give this cash to me. If you do not, dear Miguel, I will be forced to go to the police with what I know about you and your friends and how you came to work in this country.*
>
> *It would be unfortunate if you and your friends should have to return immediately to Mexico.*
>
> *I will be waiting at the gate at the end of work for your reply. You will know me, dear Miguel, because I will tap you three times on your shoulder after you pass through the gate.*
> *X*

Dani checked her watch. It would be several hours before the team returned for the day's wrap-up session. She finished the inventory and made copies of the blackmail letter. Next she tackled the list of pharmacies, deciding what information she needed to compile in the report. For sure, she wanted the names of anyone who obtained prescriptions for the drug that killed Julie.

Dani worked a couple of hours, then ducked out of the department. She jogged the four blocks to get today's Dunkin special. Foreseeing a hectic day ahead, she needed more than her usual morning jolt. Returning to the bullpen, she leaned back in her chair thoroughly enjoying her large latte. She puzzled over two items in Julie's purse, one earring and a blackmail letter. She didn't know how important the earring was, but the letter stood out like an alligator in a rain puddle.

Chapter 8

かわ

AT FIVE IN THE afternoon Manny and Peaches entered the bullpen. All the team members were back having finished up their day's assignments. They simultaneously swung their chairs to face front and center. Peaches sat on her pillow. The dog seemed to instinctively feel the tension around her.

Dani eagerly piped up before Manny took his seat. "You'll never guess what I found in this little, actually big, bag. First of all, Sam gave it to me. The EMTs transported it to the hospital with Mrs. Stone and then, of course, to the morgue. It contained the normal things a woman carries around—wallet, lipstick, comb, car keys, handkerchief, and aspirin, cell phone, and one earring, not a pair. I found one more item, this letter, crumpled up in the bottom of her bag."

Dani handed each team member a copy of the blackmail letter. Nobody said a word as they read the document.

"Now how in the name of God did she happen to get this letter in her bag?" Manny asked.

"There's no date," George noted.

"No signature either. Just a big *X*," Fred said.

"And, it's handwritten. Very legible," Dani said. "My other news is that a big dose of digitoxin killed Mrs. Stone. Sam's complete report will be on your desk, Manny, in the morning. I started compiling my pharmacy report for prescriptions filled in the last twelve months in Volusia County. A list of names will probably take a few days, but I may have a partial by the end of day tomorrow."

"Whoa, hold on," Manny said. "One thing at a time." He moved to the whiteboard. Under clues he wrote digitoxin drug, and then, blackmail letter.

"Dani, keep the pharmacy information on your desk where we can all get to it. Don't make copies unless you think it's necessary. You know I hate a lot of paper floating around. This blackmail letter is different, thanks. Damn, where did I put that pack of gum?" Manny grumbled, slapping his various pockets. When he slapped the pocket on the right side of his pants, Peaches nuzzled his hand. He withdrew one stick of gum from his left breast pocket, ripped off the wrapping, stuffed the gum in his mouth, and gave Peaches a pat. Angry with himself for having ever smoked, he continued to feel the effects of nicotine withdrawal.

"George, you start the search for the blackmailer," Manny said, chewing rapidly trying to quash the urge for a cigarette. "Get a list of construction sites in the county. Put a notation by the ones you think may be hiring illegals. All we have is the name Miguel. But first, put a call into Homeland Security, Bureau of Immigration and Custom's Enforcement. Tell ICE about the letter and ask to have someone get back to us. Also, I want to keep the existence of the letter quiet until we have more to go on. Fred, did you turn up anything at the Stone house?" Manny asked, chewing hard.

"Nothing. Clean as a whistle. Literally. That Annie is some housekeeper. No bottle, prescription or otherwise, of the drug. I questioned Annie about the Stones' relationship. She said she felt increased tension between them lately. She also volunteered that the morning of the day Mrs. Stone died, they quarreled, *shouting*, and Mrs. Stone left the house very upset."

"Did she say anything specific about their argument?" Manny asked, unwrapping another piece of gum.

"When I asked her why they quarreled, she said what they always fought about—his spending so much time at work and not enough time with her. She also said that Mr. Stone seemed frustrated when his wife left the house, frustrated in a sad way." Reading from his notes, Fred continued. "I'm quoting her now, 'I know they loved each other deeply. I feel they just lost their way because of his trying to build his company.'"

"Anything else?" Manny asked, irritated.

"One other observation," Fred said. "Annie became nervous, almost scared, when I asked her for her last name and where she was from. She finally told me she came from El Paso and that her full name was Annie Jackson. I mention her strange behavior in passing, but, now, the blackmail letter moves her behavior up a notch or two. I bet she's originally from Mexico."

"Okay," Manny said. "Dani, add a search for Annie Jackson to your list. Be sure to try different spelling combinations. See if you can find a social security number for her. Fred, go on with your report."

"Mr. Stone seemed quite upset when I told him about a possible digitalis overdose," Fred said. "He maintains she would not harm herself, but he also didn't think anyone else would want to hurt her. He cooperated fully and gave the go ahead to search the house."

"Did you ask him how they got along other than the friction over his work habits?" George asked.

After taking a swig from his water bottle, Fred answered. "When I asked if there were any marital issues, he said, no. But, he did tell me of the quarrel that morning, the one Annie mentioned to me. He also wanted to know when Mrs. Stone's body would be released so he could begin funeral arrangements. I told him you would call in the morning, Oh, one more thing he volunteered. He said his wife wished to be cremated."

"Do you see a motive for him to kill her?" Manny asked.

"Not with the housekeeper's take that he felt bad about the quarrels, but, of course, we have to bring Stone in for questioning. I suggest a polygraph so we can exclude him or keep him on the list as a person of interest."

"Get him in here tomorrow," Manny directed. "Use the interrogation room. Let the team know what time so we can witness how he answers. You do the questioning first. Be tough. George, what did you find at Stone's office?"

"First of all, Stone's assistant, Maggie O'Reilly, is drop-dead gorgeous. She's a red-haired Irish beauty," George said.

"Sounds like you were smitten with this Irish kitten," Fred said, with a big smile.

"Just take a look at this picture, smart ass. But I digress. I'd put her in her middle to late twenties. She feels indebted to both Stones because of their assistance when she moved to this area from Ireland." George moved to the interview list on the board and added Stone's assistant, Maggie O'Reilly. He then pushed the save button on the electronic whiteboard.

George continued his dissertation. "Maggie said that on the day in question, according to Stone's calendar, he scheduled a meeting with the Contract Award Board. The meeting was regarding his firm's bid for the Daytona Beach Tower Project, but he didn't go. She said that when he returned to the office, he told her he drove to St. Augustine to look at a piece of property with potential for a new condominium project. He was gone about four hours."

George paused and took a sip of his now tepid coffee.

"She told him the board called looking for him, and they would appreciate a response as to why he had missed the meeting."

"Did he call?" Dani asked.

"Yes. She said he called immediately and heard him apologizing to MacFarlane. After the call, he told her he was going home. Of course, shortly after he arrived home, he received the call from the hospital that his wife was dead."

"Stone told me he drove to St. Augustine," Fred said, "but it wasn't to look at property. He said he tried to figure out how to patch things up with his wife, particularly after the quarrel in the morning. He said he found himself driving and happened to head north. He stopped at a bar for a couple of hours and returned to the office. No receipts. He paid cash for everything."

"I hope someone remembers him. Otherwise, he has no alibi," Manny retorted. He returned to his desk, patting Peaches as he sat down. "I guess it's my turn to report. At the House of Beads today, I found all the women who were present when Mrs. Stone collapsed."

Moving to the list of people to be interviewed, Manny wrote each name as he spoke. "Wendy Sullivan, class member, gave the highlights of what happened. Susan Armstrong, class member, didn't have anything to add. Barbara Wilson, instructor, added nothing. Same from Tillie Brown, the shop owner. I spoke with Catherine Hainsworth. She added a little information. She said that, in her opinion, Mrs. Stone never responded to her CPR ministrations."

"How do you want to handle the list?" Fred asked.

"Well, George, you visit the first four, Wendy, Susan, Barbara, and Tillie. I'll keep Hainsworth on my list. Dani, stay on the pharmacy report. Also, let me know what you find on Annie Jackson. Regarding Mrs. Stone's cell phone, get the records—names, numbers, date called, duration. Do you need help with any of this?"

"Nope, I'll have the records for you as soon as I can," Dani replied.

"Okay, and, Fred, you're getting Stone in here for questioning. You have your assignments. That's a wrap for today." Manny returned to his desk, gave his thigh a touch, and immediately felt a nudge from Peaches' wet nose. She wanted to go home.

"Wait a minute," Manny said. He walked back to the board. "Give me your initial thoughts about this blackmail letter." As he spoke, he underlined the entry under clues.

"Her husband hires lots of construction workers. She could have seen it on his desk and picked it up," George said.

"I don't know," Fred said. "If she saw it on Stone's desk, wouldn't she just ask him about it?"

"How about this?" Dani interjected. "Somehow she found out the identity of 'X' and threatened to expose him. So he killed her to keep her quiet."

Chapter 9

◈

MANNY AND PEACHES lived on a houseboat. Like Manny's car, the outside of the boat gave no indication of the state-of-the-art communications center within. He moored the fifty-two foot boat at his dock on Spruce Creek.

The dock survived a fire ten years ago, but the house on the property did not. Manny cleared away the burned out shell, leaving three acres of foliage with two-hundred feet of frontage on the river. The once decimated piece of property had appreciated over the years, but Manny bought it for pennies on the dollar after the fire.

His boat, a Harbor Master beauty, also turned out to be a steal. The owner died and his heirs wanted nothing to do with it. The white interior made a statement—clean and orderly. The stern accommodated a couple of deck chairs, a stool to put his feet up on after a hard day's work, and a table for his scotch on the rocks. He acquired the houseboat a couple of months before he and Peaches found each other at the outdoor market in Daytona Beach.

One end of the dock protruded out over the river, and the other end joined the driveway that led to the house destroyed in the fire. The driveway continued to a rural paved road, but the road rarely carried a car. Manny and Peaches routinely jogged and enjoyed the peace the route offered. Yes, life is good, he thought, turning the car into his driveway. He was looking forward to a quiet evening—time to ponder the events of the day over a glass or two of his favorite drink. He knew he had to be careful not to overdue his nightly libation. However, sometimes his ritual got the better of him.

—•••—

AT 6:36 THE NEXT morning the sun peeked up over the horizon and through the portal over his bunk. The first rays hit Manny in his bloodshot eyes. He liked to call the standard-size bed a bunk, a holdover from his navy days.

"Hey, girl, you lazy bones, not much time for a run this morning," Manny said, swinging his legs over the side of the bed. He reached for his black jogging shorts, black T-shirt, and sneakers. He liked the fact he could reach almost everything in his home without moving much.

After their run, and a shower for Manny, he and Peaches headed to the department. "Come on, girl. Let's see what the team has to report." When the two entered the bullpen Peaches flopped down to rest after her morning's romp, and Manny called Sam.

"Good morning, Sam. I have to call Russell Stone this morning. He wants to know when you'll be ready to release his wife's body."

"Tell him Monday morning. The funeral home needs to call me to make arrangements for the pickup," Sam replied.

"Will do. Have a good day, Sam." Manny ruminated, "I can't imagine a good day, stuck for hours and hours in that windowless vault he calls a lab."

—•••—

FRED AND DANI BURIED their heads in their computer screens, a set of headphones attached to their telephones. They pounded their computer keyboards, mumbled an occasional word into the phone, as well as giving the mouse a workout. The clicking and swinging caused the white arrow to dance erratically on their screens. Neither looked up when Manny and Peaches entered the bullpen.

Manny dialed Russell Stone's number as he fished a breath mint out of his pocket. "Russell, Manny here. How are you?"

"Not great. I've been waiting for your call. Anything on when Julie will be released?"

"I just talked to the medical examiner," Manny replied. "He said to have the funeral home call him anytime to make arrangements. They can pick Julie up at the morgue on Monday."

"Thanks. I guess I might see you this afternoon," Russell said. "Detective Watson asked me to come down to the department to answer a few questions."

Chapter 10

ↄ

THE WAIT STAFF AT the Spicy Mushroom Café, located down the street from Stone & Associates, finished cleaning up after the morning rush of office workers grabbing their stimulus shock.

I've timed this perfectly, George thought entering the café. "Hello, Carol." The counter girl's name embroidered on her pink and white bib apron. "My name is Detective Anderson. Can I ask you a couple of questions?" he said, displaying his badge.

"I guess so," Carol said, glancing over at her supervisor.

The supervisor came over to her side. "What can we do for you, sir?"

"Do you generally work this time of the morning?"

"Yes, we do," the supervisor answered for both of them.

"Do you know this lady?" George asked as he pulled up Maggie's photo on his cell.

"I do," Carol volunteered. "She's in here every morning like clockwork."

"How about this lady?"

"Oh, yes" they both said at the same time.

"That's Mrs. Stone," the supervisor said. "She's always very pleasant."

"The two of them meet often for coffee," Carol said. "They're both from Ireland, you know. You should hear their Irish brogue when they get excited."

"I bet it's something," George said. "By any chance did either of them come in this week, maybe Tuesday?"

"Gosh, yes, they both did, but not the usual time, more around mid-morning," Carol offered. "I know it wasn't Monday because I went to the dentist. I think it was Tuesday. Yes, it was Tuesday because we offered Irish coffee as a special that morning and she made a fuss over Mrs. Stone giving the coffee a try," Carol said, pointing to Maggie's picture again displayed on George's cell.

"Is there anything else you remember about their meeting?"

"They sat at that table over there by the window. I remember now. Mrs. Stone seemed very sad. I think she may have been crying. The other lady kept patting her hand, but I couldn't hear what they were saying."

"Did they come in together or just bumped into each other?"

"More like bumped into each other. But they did that sometimes, so who's to say if they planned to meet or not," Carol said.

"Did they stay long?" George asked.

"No, maybe twenty minutes. I really can't say because I didn't pay much attention to them after they sat down with their coffee."

"Well, thanks for your help," George said to the girl, nodding to the supervisor who left to cash out a customer.

George returned to the department just as Fred began questioning Stone. He joined Manny behind the mirrored window of the interrogation room. Dani entered on his heels.

— ● ● ● —

FRED WENT OVER STONE'S story concerning his whereabouts the day Julie died. Russell Stone recounted the same events he told Fred the day before. When Fred asked him again if he saved any receipts for gas, coffee, or food to verify his story, Stone said he didn't.

"I guess that's it for now, Mr. Stone," Fred said. "I told you yesterday I'd like to schedule a polygraph test."

"Detective, I'd like to wait on that," Stone said.

"Oh? Why is that?"

"I'm making arrangements for Julie's funeral. There are no other relatives. Her parents are dead, and she had no siblings."

"Maybe we can schedule a polygraph after the funeral, later in the week sometime?" Fred asked.

Stone didn't answer. Instead, he stood up to leave. "I have to run along, if it's okay with you?"

"One more thing," Fred said. "If you and I drove north along the same route you took the day Mrs. Stone died, do you think you could find the bar you stopped at?"

"I'm sure I could."

"How about I call you after the funeral to set a date? I'll pick you up around the same time you drove on Tuesday? About nine?"

"I'll try."

Manny opened the interrogation room door just as Stone walked through.

"Good to see you, Russell," Manny said, extending his hand.

"Yes, it's good to see you as well. I wish it were under different circumstances. Unfortunately, I have to go arrange for Julie's burial. I still can't believe she's gone, Manny." With that Russell Stone left the department and Manny's team regrouped in the bullpen.

"Can you beat that," Fred said. "Stone refusing the polygraph test? He's been so cooperative. Why not take it?"

"I've got a strange one as well," George said. "When I talked with Stone's assistant, Maggie, yesterday, I felt she was holding back. She said she didn't see Mrs. Stone that day. She did say she went to the café down the street for coffee, so I went to check."

"What was the name of the coffee shop?" Dani asked.

"The Spicy Mushroom."

"Oh, yes. They always have strong coffee."

George gave a quick grin in Dani's direction and then continued his report. "The counter girl, Carol, knew them both. She said they came to the café a little later than usual Tuesday, and they did have coffee together, Irish coffee. Maggie lied to me. I wonder if she and Stone were getting it on, if you know what I mean."

Chapter 11

❧

"WE INTERRUPT THE weather report for breaking news out of Daytona Beach. An unidentified source confirmed to Channel 13 news that the late Julie Stone, wife of the prominent architect and builder in the area, Russell Stone, died last week of unnatural causes."

"Hey, Manny, get in here," George called from the conference room. "Channel 13 is reporting on Julie Stone's death."

Manny and Peaches did a power walk into the conference room. Sure enough the anchor lady spilled the beans. Working out of the spotlight in anonymity was over.

The Hispanic news anchor continued her report. "It is believed she died of a drug overdose. Our source indicated that her death does not look like suicide. The source went so far as to say murder may be suspected.

"We will keep you informed on this late-breaking story as we receive more information. Now back to the weather."

Chapter 12

A WEEK HAD PASSED since Julie Stone died. Catherine opened the *News Journal* to check again for Julie's obituary. Nothing had appeared so far regarding her death except for last night's unsettling Channel 13 breaking news' report. *Drug overdose suspected!*

Today, however, a two-column article with Julie's picture on the third page of the first section told a little of her personal story.

According to the article, the prominent Mrs. Stone collapsed and died a week ago, Tuesday afternoon. The story included her background that she came from Northern Ireland but had lived in Florida for the past fourteen years. The column listed her involvement in various charities and that she was survived by her husband, Russell Stone, prominent builder and architect. No next of kin and no cause of death was noted.

Friends can pay their respects on Wednesday, April 2nd, from six to seven in the evening, Abbott and Clark Funeral Home, Port Orange. A memorial service will be held the following day, April 3rd, eleven in the morning, at the Church of Christ, Nova Road, Port Orange. A private burial ceremony will follow to lay her ashes to rest.

If you wish to make a donation in her memory, Mr. Stone asks that you call the funeral home for a list of charities Mrs. Stone had supported.

— •••—

THE NEXT DAY Catherine slowly withdrew a black dress from her closet. She last wore the dress at her husband's funeral, three years ago. Peter had showered her with gifts over the years and left her with a small fortune he earned as a real estate broker. Because of his business, they went to many charitable events. Catherine and Julie often worked together on fundraisers for the charities and had become good friends.

Catherine put on the *dress of sad memories* and left for the funeral home. Twenty minutes later she walked through the doorway of the mourning room. Violin music played quietly from speakers embedded in the ceiling. She saw Russell Stone keeping a brave face as he greeted the visitors, giving most of them a hug. He looked very distinguished in his perfectly tailored black suit, always with a white handkerchief in the breast pocket. The suit was striking against his salt and pepper hair and ruddy complexion, a result of the considerable time he spent outside at construction sites. He presented a handsome image.

When Catherine reached his side, he gently took her elbow and guided her to a private spot out in the hall. "Catherine, thank you so much for coming. Julie considered you a good friend." Tears welled in his eyes. "I can't believe she's gone."

"Neither can I," Catherine said.

"The day she died keeps playing over and over in my head. If only I didn't go to work that day. We quarreled, saying things we didn't mean. She slammed out the door in tears, an awful picture left in my mind."

"I'm so sorry, Russell. The last picture I have of her is how excited she was about the gold chain bracelet she created for you at the bead shop."

"The bracelet? God, I never even wore it. It wasn't my style. I wish I'd known how much it meant to her." Russell dropped his head into his hands and shuddered, trying to regain his composure.

"The important thing is that she created the piece of jewelry with her love for you," Catherine said.

"Oh, Catherine, we fought too much. But I remember how happy she was the days she went to her bead class. At least the class kept her happy on Tuesdays and Thursdays." He shook his head, grief in his eyes. "I never thanked you for trying to revive her. If only she had responded to your efforts."

"Russell, you and I both know Manny Salinas. He's the best detective around, and I'm sure he'll get to the bottom of this. Has he said anything about how she died? The newspaper didn't give a cause of death, but the TV reporter said it looked like murder. Where did she get that idea?"

"I don't know who told her that, but by some means, Julie apparently swallowed a drug that killed her. Manny asked me if I knew of anyone who would want to harm her. I know he suspects I caused her death in some way," he said, looking at Catherine through his dark brown eyes.

"Oh, Russell, I can't believe that."

"You hear about the spouse being a suspect, but when you have to live under the cloak of suspicion, it's a whole different matter. The future looks very bleak without Julie. She was the most precious thing in my life."

The door closed softly behind the last visitor but immediately swung back open. Captain Salinas stepped over the threshold.

"Russell, Catherine," he said, nodding to each in turn, popping a Nicorette into his mouth. "Sure hard to kick this dreadful habit. Is the viewing over? Looks like I'm the last one."

"Hello, Manny. Yes, everyone's left," Russell said. "I'll be thankful when tomorrow is over. The finality of Julie being gone hasn't hit me yet, but I'm sure it will when I return to the empty house after I bury her ashes. Is there any more information on what killed her?" Russell noted Manny's raised eyebrows and quickly added, "I told Catherine about the medical examiner's report stating Julie died of some drug that poisoned her system."

"There's nothing more yet, Russell. Right now we're following up with people who saw her that day. Not much to go on. If you'll excuse me, I'd like to pay my respects to your wife."

— • • • —

MANNY ENTERED THE ROOM where Julie lay, peaceful and beautiful. Her red curls looked springy, her eyes open as if she might speak. He wished she could speak, tell him happened to her. With a sigh, he slowly returned to Russell and Catherine to say goodbye.

"I have to be going, Russell, but I'll be at the memorial service tomorrow. Nice seeing you again, Catherine." He headed for the door, but before he reached it he turned back to Catherine. "I'd like to talk to you again as well. I presume you'll be attending the service tomorrow?"

"Of course, but I won't be at the burial. It's private."

Russell quickly cut in. "Catherine, I'd like it if you could be there. You were like family to Julie."

"Well, then yes, of course, Russell. I'll be there. I have to dash now unless there's something I can do for you."

"No. I'm okay. Thanks for your support." Russell gave her a brief hug and then turned back to be at his wife's side one last time.

Manny held the door for Catherine, and with her arm through his, they walked down the stone steps of the old, red-brick funeral home. The elegant eighty-year-old house with white pillars, white shutters, and the ever present black hearse in the portico, wore its age well.

"Cat, are you heading someplace, or do you have time now to chat?" Manny asked, using the nickname he called her in grade school.

"Actually, after seeing Julie, I'd welcome your company," she said, looking back at the funeral home.

"Great. It's almost dinner time and I'm famished. How about you?"

"Dinner sounds wonderful. Where would you like to meet?"

"Peaches is in the car, so I have to take her home. If you can take the sight of an old bachelor's pad, I'm sure I could wrestle up a couple of steaks, excuse me, make that three. Peaches would never forgive us if we didn't include her."

"That sounds perfect. I see you're parked a couple of cars behind me, so you start and I'll follow."

Manny and Catherine headed for their respective vehicles. Manny wasn't surprised at the little lurch in his stomach over seeing Catherine. He'd been fond of her, more than fond if he was being honest since he first saw the pretty blonde at a school dance. He pulled alongside her car and then passed leading the way to his home.

Twenty minutes later, Manny pulled off Spruce Creek Road into his driveway. "Peaches, I should have told her we live on a houseboat." Moving slowly down his driveway, he pulled off onto a grassy strip just before he reached the dock. Catherine pulled in behind him.

The rich land supported oak trees, palmetto bushes, and palms of all sizes. Catherine quickly stepped out of her car and inhaled the cool fresh air from the dense vegetation. "Sorry to keep you waiting. I'm enchanted with the beauty of this setting. I don't see a house. Do you live on that boat?" she asked.

"We do. Come on, and we'll show you around." Peaches was dashing from one spot to another, barking at squirrels and then back to her master, as if to say, "It's good to be home."

Manny and Catherine laughed at the dog's antics as they sauntered arm-in-arm onto the dock. Manny boarded the boat then reached for Catherine's hand to help her aboard. Peaches gave a leap landing behind them. She immediately raced around the boat, checking to be sure no one had trespassed her territory since she left that morning.

"Let me give you the grand tour," Manny said, "which will take all of thirty seconds. It's not very big as houses go, but it is a pretty good size for me and Peaches. Watch your step and your head."

Once again he took her hand and led her down a narrow, short flight of stairs. "As you can see this is the galley. Let me grab the steaks out of the refrigerator while we're here. Would you like a glass of wine for the rest of the tour? Some Pinot Noir, madam?"

"Oh, yes, please," Catherine answered, clearly enjoying herself. "I can't believe the amount of room you have, yet everything is so compact. Very elegant, indeed. Just look at the tufted upholstery on these benches, so comfortable," she said, sliding onto one of the seats at the galley's table. "Did you paint the inside, or did it come this way?"

"What you see is what I bought. The owner died after redecorating it. His heirs didn't have the stomach to maintain the boat so they sold it. I was what you might say at the right place at the right time."

Manny handed a goblet of wine to Catherine. "A toast to you," he said, touching the delicate rim of his glass to hers. "Thank you for accepting my offer for dinner."

"And to you, Captain, for allowing me to come aboard." Her eyes locked on his. Smiling, she said, "Please continue the tour, kind sir."

Walking a few feet to the left, he opened a door. "Here's my bunk."

"Bunk? It looks like a state room to me," she said, entering the room. That must be a king size bed."

"No, just standard. This is the head, or bathroom," he said, opening another door. "My stint in the navy definitely helped with the vocabulary. There's another head back in the stern. Come this way. Watch yourself on the stairs," he cautioned as he led her up a few steps. "Here's the living room area or bridge or wheelhouse. Whatever I'm doing or feeling at the moment is what it is."

Catherine stepped up to the ship's wheel, peered out over the river. The sun had not set, the wisps of clouds beginning to turn crimson. "It's going to be a spectacular sunset," she said.

Manny sat down on the couch sipping his wine. She looks beautiful standing there, he thought. Too beautiful. Maybe this wasn't a good idea to invite her here. Come on, you knucklehead, one dinner does not make a problem. You hope.

Peaches broke into his thoughts with a little bark. Catherine turned to look at the source of the noise. "She seems to want something."

"She wants her dinner. Let's go get those steaks. I have a barbeque out back near where we parked the cars. There's some of that green stuff for a salad in the refrigerator. I usually don't fix one, but for some reason I grabbed a bag the other day. Do you mind tossing one together?"

"Not at all. Where do we eat, the galley?"

"I think not. It's too nice to stay inside. There are a couple of deck chairs and a table out on the aft deck. The evening is warm so I think we'll be okay. While you're putting together the salad, and anything else you see you'd like, Peaches and I will get those steaks ready. How do you like yours cooked?"

"Medium rare would be perfect."

"Done. Come on, girl. Let's go fix dinner for the lady."

— • • • —

CATHERINE MADE HER WAY to the galley, noting the captain certainly had everything he needed—stove, microwave, double sink, all with a view of the river. She found the bag of lettuce and a bottle of dressing, blue cheese. She located the dishes and silverware.

Checking out the aft deck, Catherine opened a compartment with napkins and a candle, a candle for the beautiful setting. She carried everything from the galley, including the bottle of wine, and set them on the table. Looking up at the driveway, she saw Manny returning with their steaks. Peaches ran ahead and again with a leap landed by Catherine's side waiting for a pat.

— • • • —

"Here you are, my lady. Hopefully, one medium-rare steak. Nice job on the table setting," he said, cutting up a piece of meat and putting it in Peaches' bowl. "I'll top off our wine, and then let's dig in."

"How did Peaches get her name?" Catherine asked. "You have to admit it is rather unusual for a black Lab."

"I was at the Daytona Beach outdoor market one Saturday morning buying peaches," Manny said, taking a bite of his steak. "This dog nuzzled my hand holding one of the peaches. I gave her a pat and continued walking. She followed me to my car. No collar. No one was calling a dog to claim her, so I brought her home with every intention of turning her over to the pound."

"But I can see you didn't."

"Monday morning our medical examiner checked her out for a microchip. He said she may have had one at one time, since there was an incision scar, but it must have been removed. Mind you, during the two days she was with me, she never left my side. She adopted me, I guess."

"Is that when you decided to keep her?"

"Sam, the ME, suggested I do just that. I watched the papers to see if anyone advertised for a missing dog and regularly checked the pound's lost dog list. Still nothing."

"So, what then?"

"I kept her," Manny said looking over at Peaches. "Of course, she needed a name, other than girl or dog, so a couple of days later, we came home and on the kitchen counter sat the bowl of peaches from the market. With a carving knife in its shield, I tapped each of her shoulders, and said, 'Dog, I now dub you Peaches. May we long be friends and companions.' Sam guessed her age at about two."

"What a delightful story," Catherine said, petting Peaches who was now lying beside her.

The radio played softly in the background, almost all music. Oldies but goodies, the station called the selections. After they polished off the steak and salad, Manny cleared the table, and the two friends settled back sipping their wine in the candlelight. A slight breeze caused the candle to flicker, and the bullfrogs on the banks of the river started their evening symphony.

"Manny, how long has it been since Marie died?" Catherine asked.

"Over five years. It hardly seems possible. Pete's been gone three, hasn't he?"

"Yes. I know what you mean, it seems like yesterday. I've never seen you at events with anyone. I don't mean to be presumptuous, but are you seeing someone?"

"Nope. Over the years I've dated from time to time. But my work is not very conducive to a relationship, so one by one they dropped from my radar, so to speak."

"Manny, you should be proud with what you've accomplished in our community. You've done so much to keep us safe. You've also created an oasis of sorts for yourself with this lovely home on the water. It certainly is a stark contrast to what you must see on any given day being a law officer."

"That's for sure. How about you, Cat? I know you're dedicated to your charities, but you can't take them home."

"I guess you haven't heard. I'm not sure many people know that I'm an architect."

"By training?" Manny asked.

"Rhode Island School of Design—four years of my life. I never put out my shingle, never needed to. I met Peter. He built a thriving real estate company, and through some of his clients I was able to ply my trade. If someone bought a piece of land but didn't know what they wanted to build on it, I stepped in."

"What a break for the buyer."

"At first, Peter suggested they talk with me for some ideas. The ideas grew to sketches and then to blueprints. I charged a nominal fee. I didn't care about the money, but the work gave me an outlet, something creative to fill my time. Realtors keep long hours. My home designs kept me sane."

Catherine took a sip of her wine and closed her eyes for a second. "About a year after his death, I became very restless," she continued. "I knew I had to do something to move on.

"Is that when you started to design in earnest?"

"Exactly. One day, almost to the day, Russell called. He was inundated with work and desperately needed help. He knew of my avocation and asked if I would be interested in both architectural design as well as interiors. Well, I jumped at the offer, but I had one stipulation. I wanted to work from my studio at home as much as possible."

"Sounds like a perfect fit for you and what a lucky company to get you. Quite a coup," Manny said, pouring the last of the wine into their glasses.

"It was wonderful for me. Peter made sure the studio in our new home was built to my specifications. It's a huge space on the third floor, almost the whole area. There's a kitchen, rather like your galley, also a bathroom, and a setup with comfortable chairs to meet with clients. Now, I can't imagine not working. I'm even thinking about starting my own firm someday."

"How did this secret life of yours escape me?" Manny asked.

"You were moving up the ladder quickly at the department. Cameras were in front of your face one case after another. I looked at the television in awe as you followed the trail and tracked down criminals. It's a wonder you knew what day it was, let alone what home designs were on my easel pads."

"I lost track of you after we graduated from high school," Manny said. "The University of Florida ROTC program afforded me my law enforcement degree and four years in the navy finished my education."

"And the rest, as they say, is history," Catherine said, finishing her wine.

"You and I have seen each other at various events over the years. I'm surprised I didn't read about your designs in the newspaper or in the *Architectural Digest* in my doctor's office," Manny said, smiling. "How about a cup of coffee, Cat? I'd still like to get your thoughts about Julie's death."

"I'd love a cup. Do you want me to help?"

"No. You sit right there and enjoy the evening. Peaches will keep you company, won't you, girl?"

At the sound of her name, Peaches opened her eyes, looked at her master, thumping her tail on the deck of the boat.

Catherine blew out the candle. "It's starting to get a bit chilly," she said, following him into the galley. "I think I'll go up front where the wheel is. It looks very comfortable."

"Not sure how you take your coffee, but I like cream and sugar and a little splash of scotch," he said, handing the sugar bowl and cream pitcher to her. "I'll just be a couple of minutes. Would you care for a shot in your coffee?"

"Not tonight, but thanks anyway."

True to his word, Manny appeared shortly with two mugs of coffee. Peaches had followed them inside and was already fast asleep on her spot in the corner, a cedar-filled pillow like the one beside Manny's desk at the department.

"Manny, Russell said something odd while we were talking earlier at the funeral home. He said Julie enjoyed her Tuesday and Thursday bead classes, but the class only met on Tuesday. I suppose he could have misunderstood her, but his thinking the class met two days instead of one is curious."

"Did he make any other comment about the classes?"

"Yes, he did. Julie made him a piece of jewelry, a gold chain bracelet, the highlight of the second class because of the distinctive link design. I could have sworn she said she gave it to him that evening or within a couple of days at any rate. Yet, when I mentioned the bracelet to him, he said he never wore it. That it wasn't his style. All of us in the class thought it quite special. Julie must not have told him she crafted it herself especially for him."

"I'll make a note of it. I hope you understand that I do need your official statement about the events of that day, or anything else you think might be pertinent, like the discrepancy in the days the class met?"

"It's okay. I understand you have to look at everyone who saw her that day. However, I'm no help. I saw her only in class. As I said before, she was a little late. Russell told me the medical examiner said she died as a result of some kind of drug, and the news report on TV insinuated Julie may have been murdered. I can't imagine anyone trying to harm her. She was well liked in the community, and her friends thought the world of her."

"I know. That's what Russell said, but something happened."

"I'd better be going," Catherine said. "Here you have a big case and I'm taking up your time."

"This has been the best evening I've had in a long while, lady. I'm so glad you joined me for dinner. Maybe we can do it again."

"I'd like that very much, Captain," Catherine said as she gathered up the cream pitcher along with the coffee mugs and headed down to the galley.

Manny helped her off the boat, but he kept hold of her hand as they walked back to her car, a warm, comfortable sign of affection. Peaches leaped off the boat and frolicked in the woods while Manny and Catherine strolled up the dock to her car. Neither said a word, not wanting to end the magic of the evening they had just shared. Manny opened the car door for her. As she turned to thank him, he leaned in and gave her a soft kiss on the cheek. "Thank you, Cat."

Catherine, at a loss for words, or rather for the right words, simply put her hand on his cheek. "See you tomorrow, Captain."

Chapter 13

THE SUN STRUCK THE soaring stain glass windows of the church, casting rainbows over the rows of oak pews. Sympathizers filled the church to capacity. Some people were Julie's friends, but most were business acquaintances as well as friends of her husband.

The urn, placed on the center of the altar, held the last vestiges of Julie Stone. Russell Stone had carried out the wishes of his wife to be cremated. Organ music, playing ever so softly, seemed to shroud the urn as if transporting Julie to a better place.

The music stopped. A hush fell over the mourners and a young girl, Wendy Sullivan, stood up beside the organist. She had left her signature outfit, blue jeans and pink tank top, at home on her closet floor. For this solemn occasion, she chose a black, knee-length dress and black patent heels. With poise beyond her sixteen years, she sang, "Amazing Grace." Seated in the first row, Catherine blinked back tears at the magical transformation of this youthful girl as she listened to the sweetest voice she ever heard drift out over the assemblage.

A man, dressed in a pair of black dress slacks, a yellow golf shirt topped with a black jacket, strolled down the middle aisle to the front of the church. Spotting Catherine, he squeezed in beside her, wriggling his hips to make room.

"Douglas, darling, how nice of you to *squeeze* in," Catherine said, clearly annoyed.

"Now, Catherine, how could I miss the event of the year," Douglas whispered.

Douglas Bradshaw and Russell Stone were bitter adversaries, business competitors. They knew each other in grade school. Both kept their bodies toned, both had dark brown eyes and salt and pepper hair, and both built architectural firms that butted heads for every contract. However, the similarities ended there.

Stone was respected and well liked. Bradshaw, two wives down, and looking for his third, was thought to be somewhat of a shyster. Stone and Bradshaw were barely on speaking terms, appearing cordial only in public.

After the ceremony, the mourners filed out of the church. Each stopped to offer sympathy to Russell and then passed through the door into the sunshine. The few going to the gravesite congregated in the anteroom just off the main area of worship. The Ladies Guild provided a service of coffee, tea, and cookies set on a white tablecloth, complete with silver teaspoons and china cups and saucers. No one said much, still gripped by the finality of the moment.

A cool breeze preceded the white-haired priest when he opened the door and entered the room. His black robe fluttered around his ankles, but the white collar was anchored securely under his ample chin. "It's time to gather for the internment, please follow me," he said.

Much to Catherine's annoyance, for the second time today, Bradshaw stuck to her side, as she walked to the burial site around the back of the church. *I guess he doesn't understand the word private. He has a nerve to show up here.*

— • • • —

RUSSELL WAS ALREADY IN place at the gravesite when they arrived. Douglas cozied up to Russell's right side, in the same fashion he squeezed in beside Catherine in the church pew. Douglas, turning his head slightly to Russell, said, "Russell, so sorry to hear about your wife."

Russell disliked Douglas and wished he hadn't intruded on this very private occasion. Stone, six-foot-four, two-hundred-ten pounds of toned manhood, could easily deck his former schoolmate, and he felt tempted to do just that. Glowering into Douglas's eyes, he whispered, "Why don't you haul your sorry ass out of here?"

"Sorry ass? My, my. I just came to pay my respects, but have it your way," Bradshaw uttered as he backed away and strode to his car.

Trying to shake off the encounter with Douglas, Russell returned to the grim task at hand. He and Catherine laid nosegays of white honeysuckle, violets, and a sprig of lavender around the urn. The hole in the ground accepted the vessel. Julie's presence on earth had ended.

Chapter 14

❦

THE NEXT MORNING Catherine was surprised to receive a phone call from Douglas asking her to meet him for coffee at Angell & Phelps café. He didn't indicate what he wanted to discuss, but she was curious enough to accept his invitation. When she arrived he was sitting at a window table and gave her a wave to get her attention.

As Catherine approached the table he rose to greet her extending his hand. She briefly shook his hand and immediately sat down.

"Catherine, thank you for meeting me." Douglas nodded to the waitress, indicating he would like her to bring over two cups of coffee. The waitress quickly returned setting two mugs on the table and asked if there would be anything else.

"Catherine, would you like a pastry or a muffin with your coffee?" he asked.

"No, thank you," Catherine said, looking up at the waitress with a quick smile. She added a thimble of cream to her coffee and then looked at Douglas wondering what he was going to say next.

"I'm afraid I owe you and Russell an apology for my behavior at Julie's funeral yesterday. I was rude and out of line," he said.

"Yes, you were, Douglas, but I'm not the one who should receive your apology. It would be more appropriate for you to tell Russell."

"Yes, I know and I will, but I particularly wanted to square my actions with you first. I've been meaning to talk to you about a possible design job, and I didn't want yesterday to jeopardize your decision."

"Douglas, you know I'm working for Stone & Associates," she said, taking a sip of coffee.

"I do know you work for them, but I was under the impression it was on a job-by-job basis, not as an actual employee."

"Well, you're right in one sense. I do most of the work at home and I definitely set my own schedule. But still, I don't know about taking on an assignment for you."

"Hear me out, Catherine. I have a new condominium project going up in New Smyrna Beach. The architect I hired suddenly had to leave for Seattle because of a family emergency. The building is sketched out, but the blueprints have not been drawn up."

"Douglas, I don't think I want to get involved with your project," Catherine said shaking her head.

"Could you just drive down and take a look? Here, I brought some sketches," Douglas said, laying a large black leather portfolio case on the next table.

"Douglas, I don't know...I appreciate your asking me, but...these are interesting drawings," Catherine said, flipping the large sheets from one page to another. "Tell you what, I'll run down to see the property this afternoon. I don't want to hold you up, so I'll call you in a few of days with my decision."

"Fair enough, take the portfolio with you. The address for the property is at the bottom of each sketch, and here's my card with my home, work, and cell numbers."

Catherine stood to leave, putting her bag over her shoulder, picking up the portfolio, and then shaking Douglas's hand. "Thanks for the coffee. I'll be back in touch." She flashed him a smile and left the café.

— • • • —

DRIVING TO STONE & ASSOCIATES to drop off some changes to a schematic, Catherine then headed south to New Smyrna Beach.

What do you think you're doing, Catherine Hainsworth, she thought. You know you don't want to work for Douglas Bradshaw. On the other hand, he was most gracious in considering you for his project and his apology for his behavior yesterday seemed genuine.

Glancing in the rearview mirror she mumbled to her image. "Maybe this is the catalyst to go out on my own, build a design firm, accept only projects that are unique." She pulled around a city bus that was slowing down to pick up some passengers.

"I'm not ready yet for my own company. Although I could let it be known I'm available on a contract basis outside of Stone & Associates…I guess."

Chapter 15

THE BULLPEN APPEARED quiet, too quiet for a Monday morning. Manny picked up his messages as Peaches flopped down on her pillow. "Okay, you guys. What's going on? Or should I say, what's not going on?" he snapped.

The team's chairs turned to the center in tandem, a long face on each member. "We're getting nowhere," volunteered Fred. "Russell hired Guy Malone."

"The criminal attorney in Orlando?" Manny asked.

"That's the guy, and Malone advised him not to take the polygraph," Fred said.

"Because of the weekend, I haven't been able to get anywhere with the pharmacies," Dani interjected. "The cell phone stuff is also taking longer than I expected."

"I have an appointment set up with Susan Armstrong in an hour, and Wendy Sullivan later this afternoon," George reported. "Like what Dani experienced, the weekend proved to be a problem. Nobody home. I faxed the blackmail letter to ICE. No response from them as yet. The list of construction sites in the county will be available later today. I'll start site visits as soon as the list arrives."

"What kind of nonsense are you guys dishing me?" Manny said angrily, tearing open the wrapper, popping a piece of a gum in his mouth. "Keep on it. Somebody has to know something." Peaches looked up at her master. "Don't you nag me, too. It's enough trying to quit without your sad eyes," he said to his dog.

George got up to leave for his appointment with Susan Armstrong. With the lack of leads on the case, tension was building in the bullpen. He patted Peaches on the head as he left.

—•••—

SUSAN DIDN'T WANT TO meet at her home. "Nosy neighbors," she said to George when he called. She suggested the Seashell Coffee House on Beach Street. It was a couple of blocks down from the Spicy Mushroom Café where George had learned that Maggie and Julie met for coffee the day of her death.

George entered the coffee house and looked around, but he didn't see anyone fitting the description Susan had given him. He sat down at a table against the wall, his position giving him a good view of anyone coming in. It was mid-morning so the place was almost empty. Mariah Carey was singing softly from the CD player behind the cashier. The aroma of cinnamon coffee permeated the air.

Shortly, a petite woman in her thirties, curly brown hair, entered. She looked around, as George had before, but her gaze stopped abruptly when she saw him. She marched over to George. "Officer Anderson?" she said, hands on her hips.

George stood up, extended his right hand in an effort to be friendly, while displaying his badge with his left. "Yes ma'am. Susan Armstrong?" he asked as they shook hands.

"I don't know why you want to question me," Susan said, sitting down at the small, square marble table. She sat opposite George, as far away as she could get, crossing her arms over her chest.

"We're talking to everyone who saw Mrs. Stone the day she died. You were in the classroom when she collapsed, so we want your statement about what happened." George pulled out a pen and a small notepad from his breast pocket and flipped it open.

"Like I told that Captain Salinas, I don't know anything. I have nothing to add to what Wendy said."

"Okay. Would you tell me, in your own words what happened?" George said, thinking what a snippy woman.

"If I must. We were all waiting for Julie so we could start the class."

"Who is all?"

"Honestly, officer, you know who *all* is."

"I'd like you to tell me anyway, you know, for the record."

"Barb, our instructor. Tillie, the shop owner. Wendy Sullivan, myself, and Catherine Hainsworth."

"Okay. Go on, please. What happened?"

"Julie finally arrived. She said she felt ill and proceeded to collapse on the floor. Catherine thought she could revive her, which was silly the way she pounded her chest. I wouldn't be surprised if she didn't crack some of Julie's ribs. The next thing we knew, the EMTs arrived and took Julie away. That's it. I told you I didn't have anything to add."

"Thank you anyway," George said in a controlled calm voice. "Did you see Mrs. Stone any other time that day?"

"Of course not."

The waitress came over to the table with her order pad, her pen poised to write, "Can I get you two anything?"

"Nothing for me," Susan snapped.

"Yes, please," George said. "I'd like a cup of that coffee you're brewing. It smells good. Make it black, please, and one of those orange-cranberry muffins. You sure you won't join me, Mrs. Armstrong?"

"I said no."

"Okay, one black coffee," the waitress agreed. She hesitated a second and then addressed Susan. "That's something about that lady, Mrs. Stone. She died the same day you and she had lunch here. I'm sorry you lost your friend. You two meeting here for lunch so often, you must have been close."

The waitress turned from the table to get the coffee and muffin and mumbled more to herself than to George and Susan, "You just never know when your time is up. That's for sure."

George looked Susan in the eye. She didn't blink, staring back at him. Challenging him to speak first.

"Mrs. Armstrong, did you have lunch with Mrs. Stone Tuesday?"

"Yes."

"Why did you lie to me?"

"The fact I met Julie for lunch is irrelevant."

"Maybe yes. Maybe no. But I'll have to be the judge of that. Tell me about your lunch."

"Nothing much to tell. We often met for lunch. Julie served on many fundraisers and she'd asked me to help."

"What time did you meet?"

"We both arrived here about noon."

"Did she seem to be okay during your lunch together?" George asked.

"Yes, well not exactly. All right Julie was upset. She had another quarrel with her husband. Her mind seemed to be elsewhere. She was distracted and not paying much attention to me. She said something to the effect that she had better end it now."

"What do you think she was referring to by *end it now*?"

"Her marriage, I guess. Not meeting me for lunch anymore. How am I supposed to know?"

"Why did you lie to me?" George asked.

"I didn't want to get involved," Susan confessed.

The waitress brought George his coffee and muffin and left. He took a sip and then looked at Susan. "Mrs. Armstrong, do you or anyone in your family have a heart problem?" he asked.

"What kind of a question is that? My health is none of your business, neither is my husband's health for that matter. If you're finished with your inquisition, I'll be going," Susan said.

"Yes, that's it," George said, standing up. "I appreciate your information. One thing though, Mrs. Armstrong, I strongly urge you to tell the truth about a matter as serious as Mrs. Stone's death. If you think of anything else that happened that day or anything Mrs. Stone may have said, I'd appreciate your calling me. Here's my card, and thank you again."

George watched Susan as she left the coffee house. He made a few notes in his notepad, put money on the table to cover his order, and walked out into the fresh air. Mulling over his meeting with Susan, he drove over to the Sullivan's home to meet Wendy. Her interview would complete his day's assignment.

— • • • —

SHIRLEY SULLIVAN, Wendy's mother, answered the door. George introduced himself, again displaying his badge.

"Nice to meet you, Detective Anderson. Wendy is expecting you. Do you mind if I sit in on your meeting with my daughter?"

"Not at all. I just want her statement for the record about what happened when Mrs. Stone collapsed at the House of Beads."

"Hi. Are you Detective Anderson?" Wendy asked, joining her mother and the gentleman at the door.

"I am, young lady," George said, shaking her hand.

"Let's go into the living room," Shirley said. "I think you'll be more comfortable." The three went into a sun-filled room, homey but not fussy. George thought it probably befitted Mr. Sullivan, a banker, neat and orderly.

George pulled out his notepad. "I know you told Captain Salinas what you saw when Mrs. Stone collapsed, but I'd like you to tell me, for the record."

Wendy repeated almost word for word what she told Manny. "It was real scary," Wendy said coming to the end of her statement. "I told mom I want to take a CPR class this summer. You never know when you might need it. I felt terrible not being able to help when Catherine asked."

"Wendy, did you and Mrs. Stone meet any other time that day?" George asked.

"No, sir. I only saw her at our class."

"Well, I guess that covers it. If you think of anything else, I'd appreciate your giving me a call," George said, handing her his card. "Thank you both for your time."

George headed back to the department still perplexed over Susan Armstrong's story and the fact she lied. Maybe she was trying to protect Russell Stone.

Chapter 16

✍

AFTER GEORGE LEFT the department for his appointments with Susan Armstrong and Wendy Sullivan, Fred decided to get out as well. He called Russell Stone. It was imperative that Stone verify his alibi. As far as Fred was concerned, Stone had to find the bar where he had a drink the afternoon Julie died. If he couldn't, he would remain high on the suspect list.

Stone said he could get away and agreed to meet Fred. Shortly thereafter Fred picked him up in a squad car. "I'm glad you could make it this morning," Fred said, pulling out onto Interstate 95. The Interstate ran the length of the state of Florida, from Miami north to the Georgia state line.

"You really did me a favor," Russell said. "The office is still in mourning after last week's services. The deathly silence there is very depressing. Everyone stops talking if I pass by. Tell me, Detective, how did you choose a career in law enforcement?"

"I guess you could say I cut my teeth dealing with illegal immigration in Santa Fe before the issue grabbed the spotlight. My size proved an asset in intimidating and apprehending frightened Mexicans crossing the border. However, this cut on my cheek shows clearly that not everyone was intimidated," Fred said, feeling the raised scar tissue on his face.

The two men fell silent escaping into their own thoughts as the squad car continued to eat up the highway.

"You said you drove north to St. Augustine," Fred said, breaking the silence. "The trip would take about an hour from Daytona Beach."

"That's right. I turned off 95 at US 1. Awhile after I turned off, I stopped," Russell replied.

"But you don't remember the name of the bar?"

"No, other than I think the word bar appeared on the front of the building and, of course, the open sign in the window."

The squad car continued north. The two men chatted amiably about the weather and the Jacksonville Jaguars football team. Neither mentioned the case, Fred wanted Stone to relax.

At the first road sign for St. Augustine, indicating they should turn right onto US 1, Fred asked, "Is this where you turned?"

"I believe so. You have to remember I wasn't thinking clearly. My thoughts were on Julie and how to resolve the situation between us."

Fred turned onto US 1 north. He watched Russell out of the corner of his eye to see if he showed any signs of recognition. Fifteen minutes passed.

"Mr. Stone, a couple more miles, and we'll be in the historic part of town. Did you go into the old town?"

"No. Definitely not, but I haven't seen the bar either."

Fred made a U-turn, heading back out of town. "We passed two or three bars coming into St. Augustine. As we pass them again, take another look. There's one on the right and it's open," Fred said. "Should we stop?"

"No. No. It wasn't like that one at all."

Fred drove on pointing out two more bars, but Russell didn't recognize either one. They were approaching the Interstate 95 access ramp. Fred pulled over onto the shoulder of the road and stopped.

"Mr. Stone, did you take another road? Route 207 further up 95? Or is it possible you went south instead of north on US 1? The way the road curves, it's hard to tell at times whether you're going north or south."

"Maybe that's it. Let's keep going. The bar has to be here, but I just can't remember what it looked like."

Fred pulled back onto the road and continued driving south. Two miles down the road he saw a small bar on the left side.

"How about that one, the Lonely Dove Bar and Grill?" Fred asked. A few cars were parked in front and several motorcycles were lined up in the partial shade on the left side of the building.

"It could be. I can't believe this is so hard," Russell said, visibly frustrated.

"Let's go in. I could use a cold soda anyway," Fred said.

With the open sign prominently displayed in the door's window, the two men entered the dimly lit bar. Overgrown bushes in the front two windows blocked the sunlight. Hitching up on the worn, red Naugahyde barstools, Russell ordered a beer and Fred a diet cola.

Fred kept watching Russell for any indication he remembered the bar. There was none. When Russell excused himself to go to the men's room, Fred took the opportunity to talk to the bartender.

"Hey, Jack," Fred said, seeing the name on the bartender's shirt. "Do you work here during the week?"

"Yes, I do, Sunday through Wednesday. I open up at nine and leave around two, depending on how big the lunch crowd is."

"Do you recognize the man with me?"

"No, I don't think so," Jack said, as he dried a glass with a white cotton dish towel.

"He might have been here about this time a couple of weeks ago, a Tuesday."

"Sorry. Most of the guys are regulars and aren't dressed quite the way you two are. They come off construction sites or road crews looking for a cold one. You know what I mean?"

"Yah, I know. When you're hot and sweaty, a cold one is all you want to quench your thirst. Thanks anyway," Fred said, as Russell returned.

The two men returned to the car. "As long as we're this close, let's go up to Route 207, we can run up and down a couple of miles, to see if the bar turns up," Fred said.

Russell agreed. An hour and eight bars later, Fred said, "I guess this is a dead end, Mr. Stone. We might as well head back."

"Yes. I'm sorry I couldn't be more helpful."

It's your alibi we can't corroborate, Fred thought. I guess you stay on the person-of-interest list.

"Mr. Stone, do you or your general contractors hire illegal immigrants?" Fred asked.

"You've got to be kidding, Detective. I have never *hired any illegals,* and I'm positive illegals are not working at any of my construction sites. That's absurd. I'd lose my license to build anything in the future if I was caught doing such a thing."

"Just asking...for the record."

Chapter 17

❧

"THAT GODDAMN, son-of-a-bitch Stone," Douglas Bradshaw snarled, slamming the thick sheaf of papers down on his desk.

"Geez, what did Russell Stone do now?" asked Bradshaw's assistant, Monique, a tall, voluptuous, wannabe model. All her nails, toes and fingers, were painted bright red, matching her lips. She had enormous blue eyes and very bleached blonde hair, fluffed up like a chow.

"I'll tell you what he did now," Douglas said, mimicking Monique. "His bid for the Daytona Beach Tower Project is eighty-five grand lower than mine." His face grew redder and redder. "Stone's always been a thorn in my side—baseball captain in junior high, valedictorian of our class at Florida U, married my pretty Irish redhead."

"Douglas, stop ranting. Your face is turning red. Next thing you know, I'll be rushing you to the hospital, for God's sake. I thought the bids were sealed. How do you know what Stone bid?" Monique asked.

"They are sealed, stupid. I just happened to get a copy of his bid so I could use the format, that's all. The same layout will make it easier for the board to compare bids."

"Well, that makes sense, I guess," Monique said.

"I'll show Stone who the big man is around here. You'll see. This tower project is going to be mine. I have to meet with my guys again to go over their bids."

"What can I do to help?"

"Get me Karl Henderson, that cement contractor on the phone, the one in Port Orange. I bet he can give me a better price than his first estimate."

— • • • —

TWO HOURS LATER Douglas and Karl Henderson met at the Painted Pony Bar. "Kelly, bring over another beer for my friend Karl here. And as long as you're coming over, make it two. Crap, the pretzels are empty," Bradshaw called to Kelly.

An occasional swear word could be heard, but for the most part, it was conspiratorial laughing, more giggling as the beer kept flowing.

Bradshaw swaggered out of the bar around midnight after what he called a good night's work. He knew the tower project was definitely going to be his. He still needed to meet with Tony, the steel guy, and with Willy, the plate glass supplier. Then he had to confer with his Chief Financial Officer to flesh out the bid after getting the numbers from his subcontractors.

The bid deadline loomed ahead in two weeks. He could already see Stone's shocked face when, in front of the town's movers and shakers, he, Douglas Bradshaw III, would be the one called to the podium to receive the project award. Yes, that moment will be sweet. With a smile on his face, his head hit the pillow, and he fell into a deep sleep.

The next day Bradshaw arrived at the office before Monique. He put the evidence of last night's meeting in the top right-hand drawer of his desk. He turned the key in the lock as Monique swirled in.

"Hey, boss," she panted, "you're in early."

"Lots to do today, my girl. Quick as you can, call Tony and Willy. Tell them I'll meet them at the Painted Pony at ten this morning. Let them know I want to discuss our business proposition and not to be late. While you're doing that, I'll call Philip." Grinning to himself, he thought, *that highfalutin financial officer of mine is going to be surprised with the numbers I come up with for the bid.*

At ten o'clock sharp, Douglas pulled into the Painted Pony parking lot. He picked up his yellow pad, along with two sets of blueprints for the project, and entered the dark saloon. He spotted Tony and Willy in the back booth. *Good, nice and private. Nobody will notice us.*

A lone motorcyclist, clad in black leather from head to toe, was perched on a bar stool yakking with Kelly. Johnny Cash was singing "I Walk the Line" from the old jukebox at the end of the bar.

"Hey, guys, good to see you," Douglas said, shaking hands with the men.

"Yep, same here," Tony said, a little disgruntled.

"What can I get you? Beer? Jack Daniels?" Douglas asked.

"You know what I like, and I'd like one right now so I'll be in the proper frame of mind to hear what you have to say that's so urgent."

"Kelly, bring my friend here a Jack Daniels and a Sam Adams for me and Willy, also a bowl of those cheesy pretzels."

Douglas laid out the blueprints on the booth's table covering several initials carved into the wood. "Now, boys, you've given me an estimate for the tower project. The project has grown, but relatively speaking your numbers were too high. You have to come in about twenty-five percent less."

"Shit, Douglas, I'm taking a bath as it is. Where do you expect me to shave anymore?" Tony said.

"Tony, if you can't lower your estimate you'll be out of the biggest project around for many years to come."

"This is very impressive," Willy said, marveling at the details of the design. When do you need my new numbers?"

"Four days, max," Douglas said, rolling up the blueprints. "If you need labor, call Juan, my general contractor. He can always provide extra guys at a very reasonable rate," Douglas said, handing each man a set of prints.

"Okay. Juan was a godsend on the last project I did for you," Willy said. "His boys were strong sons-of-a-bitches and took orders from him, shall we say, *muy pronto*." Willy chuckled at his own joke.

"Gotta run. I'll expect to hear from you both no later than Friday, hopefully before. If you want another drink, just ask Kelly to put it on my tab."

— • • • —

WITH HIS MEETINGS taken care of, Bradshaw drove over to one of his construction sites. His general contractor, Juan Ortega, always came in under budget. Bradshaw turned his head the other way knowing the reason: Ortega hired illegals from Cuba and Mexico. Neither said anything about the origin of the labor force. Bradshaw liked it that way, so, if necessary, he could feign surprise if he was questioned. Hell, he reasoned, all the construction sites did the same thing for workers. Controlling the cost of labor was the key to making a profit.

"Hey, Juan, how's it going?" Douglas asked, walking up to his general contractor and shaking his hand.

"Just fine, Mr. Doug. It won't be long and the building will be finished. Then what will my boys do?"

"Don't worry, I'll have a huge project for them starting in about a month," Douglas said, grinning ear to ear. "You may get a couple of calls for labor from Tony and Willy. You remember them. You helped them out before. I'd appreciate your taking good care of them."

Douglas wandered around the construction site, and then returned to his car. Jumping into his black Mercedes, he headed back to his office. It had been a good day for the architect. *A good day indeed,* he thought, a smile crossing his face.

Chapter 18

THREE WEEKS HAD PASSED since Miguel received the blackmail letter. Always nervous that he would be arrested, he now slept fitfully with a new nightmare. Someone was going to squeal on him or worse yet, beat him up so he couldn't work.

Miguel, a quiet, stocky Mexican, never gave anyone his last name. He had crossed the Mexican-U.S. border a year ago with his brother, Roberto. The two brothers were scared to death the night they crossed into Texas.

Over the next couple of months, they made their way to Daytona Beach, Florida. Miguel quickly found others who were also in the country illegally. Word had it that Señor Juan Ortega was hiring. No questions asked. He paid in cash at the end of the day on Friday. The only stipulations—work your ass off and keep your mouth shut.

Miguel still vividly remembered the day he found the letter in his lunch pail when he and three of his friends gathered in the shade near the building where they were working. His boss had told him if he needed any help to come see him. I definitely need help, he thought.

—•••—

THE DAY MIGUEL RECEIVED the letter he went to the trailer, poked his head into the construction site office. Juan, surprised to see him, almost dropped the phone. "I have to go now," he said and hung up.

"Miguel, what the hell are you doing here? I pay you to work."

"Señor Juan, I am so afraid. I found this letter," he said, withdrawing the now wrinkled piece of paper from his pants pocket. "See this, please."

Juan took the letter from Miguel. *This is the last thing I need to deal with right now. My labor force is crucial to my builders,* he thought. Finished reading, he looked up. "Miguel, calm down. It's probably a prank. You did the right thing bringing it to me. Let me know if anything happens. Now go back to work."

Chapter 19

MIGUEL ONCE AGAIN made his way to the office trailer. "Excuse me por favor, Señor Juan."

"What is it, Miguel? Can't you see I'm busy?" Juan snapped.

"Si, señor, but you asked me to let you know if anything more happened with that letter I gave you."

Juan's head jerked up. "Well, did anyone *tap* you on the shoulder?" Juan asked sarcastically.

"Si. Señor Raul. Twice he contacted me."

"Did he have anyone with him?" Juan asked.

"No. The first time, the day I gave you the letter, he got into his truck and drove away, but Raul found me again. He said he wanted the money tomorrow night."

"What did he tell you to do, Miguel?"

"He said to put the money in a plastic bag and tape it shut. I'm supposed to walk under the Route 92 causeway of the Halifax River, west end, and look for a green trash barrel. I'm to do this between nine and nine-fifteen."

"Okay, Miguel, I will prepare the package. I want you to follow his instructions and leave the bag where he says. Find a place to hide, and if Raul doesn't pick it up, or the barrel isn't where he said it would be, bring the package back to me in the morning. Now get back to work."

— • • • —

JUAN PICKED UP THE phone and dialed, the same action he had taken when Miguel first brought him the letter. At that time, his contact asked him to bring over the blackmail note. The two were going to wait to see if the blackmailer made another overture for money.

"Looks like this man was real. He goes by the name, Raul," Juan mumbled, disconnecting the call.

Chapter 20

"WELCOME to the eleven o'clock morning news update.

"We have breaking news on the story we reported to you yesterday. Russell Stone, the husband of Julie Stone who was allegedly murdered last week, has been listed as a person-of-interest in her death. He has retained the renowned criminal attorney, Guy Malone of Orlando. Neither Mr. Stone nor Mr. Malone was available for comment.

"Another story just in to our desk. Two unidentified male bodies were found in Daytona Beach on the shore of the Halifax River. Both appeared to have died of gunshot wounds. Stay tuned to Channel 13 for updates on both of these stories."

Chapter 21

❧

AT THE SOUND of the telephone, Catherine stood up from the pansy bed she was tending. She wiped the dirt off her hands onto the towel tucked into her jeans and hurried into the kitchen. The screen door slammed behind her as she picked up on the fourth ring.

"Hi, Cat, it's me, Manny."

"Manny, I know it's you. Like after all these years, I wouldn't recognize your voice. What's up, Captain?"

"Hey, knock off that captain stuff. It's just me, plain old Manny. Can I buy you a cup of coffee, in say, an hour?"

"Of course, but you sound so mysterious."

"I want to go over a few things you said the other evening when we were having dinner on my houseboat. At least I'll use that as an excuse to see you. How about meeting at Aunt Catfish on the river?"

"Aunt Catfish it is. See you there." Catherine hurried up the spiral staircase to her bedroom. With a quick shower, a dab of makeup, and a fresh pair of tan Capris topped by a white silk blouse, she was ready. Twenty-five minutes after Manny called, she was behind the wheel of her BMW on her way to meet him. "I'm acting like a school girl. He's only asked me to have a cup of coffee. Maybe seeing him will take my mind off how I'm going to reply to Douglas' job offer. I can't put him off much longer. Honestly, Catherine, I don't know why you're even considering working for him," she said, chastising herself.

Catherine parked her car and walked inside Aunt Catfish. She followed the waiter to a corner table overlooking the river, visible over a stand of palmetto bushes. "Thank you, Kendall. This is lovely."

"Nice to see you, Ms. Hainsworth. Can I get you some coffee?"

"Yes, please. Two cups of coffee with cream and sugar on the side. I'm meeting a friend."

Three minutes later, Manny strolled in. As he looked around to find her, she caught his eye and he headed her way. Because it was late morning, only a few patrons were lingering over a second cup of coffee, but those who were there appeared to take note of the handsome captain.

"Cat, lovely as ever," he said, as he kissed her delicate hand.

"I ordered your coffee, cream and sugar on the side," she said, bathing him in the glow of her smile. "Now tell me, without another moment's delay, what's up?"

"You knew Julie personally, as a good friend, and through Russell as your employer. Is that fair to say?"

"Yes. I work with Russell's design team. Julie and I saw each other frequently, either having a chatty lunch or working on committees for charitable organizations."

"You were with Julie when she died and during the weeks before. Do you remember seeing or hearing anything else since we talked?" Manny asked.

"Well, the only thing that seemed odd, which I've already mentioned to you, was the fact Russell thought Julie attended the bead class two times a week. The class only met once a week, but that tells me he just didn't know what she was doing."

Kendall returned placing a cup of coffee, cream, and sugar in front of his two guests. "Is there anything else I can get for you?" he asked.

"No. This will be all for now, Kendall. Thank you," Catherine replied.

"Cat, do you think there is any chance she committed suicide?"

"Oh, dear me, no. Never. Other than wishing Russell didn't work so much, she had a wonderful life. Speaking of Russell, what's this I heard on the news that he hired a lawyer?"

"That's right," Manny said, adding a healthy splash of cream and a not too healthy spoon of sugar to his coffee. "And not just any lawyer. Malone is a high-powered defense attorney," he said, stirring his syrupy concoction.

"I can't believe Russell had anything to do with Julie's death," Catherine said, returning her cup to the saucer. "He adored her. I will say Julie was not quite herself the last few weeks, rather melancholy during our bead classes."

"Do you think she was worried about something?"

"Yes, looking back, something was definitely bothering her, but she never said anything about Russell. Whatever bothered her couldn't have been bad enough for her to end her life. Of that I'm sure."

"Do you know Russell's assistant, Maggie O'Reilly?" Manny asked.

"Yes. She's a lovely woman, quite pretty. Men's heads turn in her direction when she walks by, I can tell you that. I've seen it when she comes into the design room of Russell's company. I believe she and Julie were quite friendly with both of them being from Ireland."

"Do you think anything illicit was going on between Miss O'Reilly and Russell?" Manny asked.

"Not that I ever noticed. As I've told you, Russell loved Julie. I can't imagine him even thinking of a dalliance with Maggie."

"Okay. What about Susan Armstrong? What do you know about her?"

"The Susan Armstrong in my bead class?"

"Yes," he said, taking a sip of coffee.

"She's very hard to get along with, if that's what you're asking. It's a shame too because she's a pretty woman and very bright. But she has a way of souring milk when she speaks, a very negative person.

"How did Susan and Julie get along?"

"Maybe Susan and I just rubbed each other the wrong way, because I know she and Julie got along well. Julie often called on her to help on this or that committee. Julie liked how she took charge of an assignment. She often said Susan did a bang-up job."

"Well, as you and Russell have said, it seems everyone liked Julie. I'm missing something somewhere. In my experience, the biggest clue is always in plain sight, but I can't see it."

The two friends sipped their coffee in silence. Kendall came by and topped off their cups with more steaming liquid.

"Cat, I presume you're attending the upcoming Chamber of Commerce Charity Ball?"

"Of course, I am. In fact, because of Julie's death, Russell asked if I would help with the arrangements. They were co-chairmen, you know. That reminds me of something that might help you."

"Well, I sure could use some help."

"The day before Julie died, we met for lunch. I was helping her with some of the arrangements for the ball. We were so excited. We giggled like school girls getting ready for the big dance.

"That would have been something to see—two grown women giggling over a dance," Manny said with a chuckle.

"We were both fashioning earrings to match our gowns. That's one reason we took the class at the House of Beads. Using our cell phones while we were eating lunch, we both made hair appointments for the day before the ball at the same salon. She also said something to the effect that she was going to make it up to Russell."

"Do you know what she meant by that? Make what up?"

"No, and I didn't press her. It seemed like a personal matter. She said it to herself more than to me."

"I wasn't aware of her involvement with the ball," Manny said. "Can you give me the name of the beauty shop?"

"Yes, of course. It's the White Gardenia hair salon, in Port Orange. Ask for Heather. Manny, are you going to the ball?"

"Yes, I'll be there, in a semi-official capacity."

"Oh, how exciting. Will you share a dance with me?" she asked, with a lilt in her voice.

"Stop teasing, Cat. You know I hate that celebrity stuff."

"Will you be in uniform or undercover?"

Manny rolled his eyes.

Chapter 22

WITH THE DEADLINE for bids on the multi-million-dollar tower project fast approaching, the tension at Bradshaw & Associates was palpable.

"Monique," Douglas yelled from his office, "get Willy, Tony, and Karl on the phone. There's only a week until the bid cutoff, and I haven't heard from the bastards."

"Okay. Okay. Who first?"

"Who first?" he mimicked. "Shit, I don't care. Whoever answers first. If you have to leave a message, say it's urgent or they can forget about bidding."

One by one Douglas put the muscle on his cement, steel, and glass subcontractors. All replied they would have the numbers to him by the end of the day. Feeling pretty good about his subs' responses, he called Philip Longwood, his chief financial officer.

"Hey, Prince Philip, can you meet me for lunch about two o'clock today? We need to discuss how we're going to position the bid on the tower project. I have to stop by the New Smyrna Airport to arrange a tune-up for the plane I rented, so I suggest we rendezvous at the River View Restaurant. It's near the airport."

"Knock off the Prince Philip moniker, and yes, I'll meet you for lunch. Why don't you just buy that plane? You treat it with such tender loving care."

"Yah, well maybe I will."

At 2:20 that afternoon, Douglas parked his Mercedes and sauntered to the door of the River View. It was a warm sunny day, and the Halifax River sparkled brightly. A sailboat docked alongside the deck of the restaurant, unloading a couple of kids with their mom and dad. Douglas found Philip on the patio sitting under an umbrella, enjoying a martini.

"Hi there, my man," Douglas said, putting down his briefcase. He waved at the waiter and signaled he wanted a drink like Philips. "Look what I have, a copy of Stone's preliminary tower bid."

"That's sealed," Philips said in astonishment.

"I know it's supposed to be sealed, but a copy slithered under the door nonetheless."

"That's terrific. How'd you do it?"

"Never you mind how I did it. It's now your job to make sure our bid is less. Our preliminary estimate is eighty-five thousand dollars more than Stone's, so you're going to have to sharpen your pencil. You'll have to take into account that my design has expanded. I met with the subs last week and followed up with them this morning. They all promised that their part of the bid will be in our hands by late this afternoon."

Bradshaw speared the olive in the bottom of his martini glass, popping it into his mouth. "Juan will be rounding up the labor," he said, "so you shouldn't have any trouble beating Stone's numbers.

"Sounds good. When do you want to get together?"

"Let's meet in the conference room at nine tomorrow morning. We'll take a look at the boys' figures and see how they match up with Stone's. Then I'll leave you to do your magic. The final bids are due next Wednesday, but I want to submit ours as soon as we can, Monday if possible. The board already has the proposed designs. All they need are the final numbers. At any rate, I want to submit the bid no later than Tuesday morning."

"That shouldn't be a problem," Philip said. "I'm looking forward to seeing what the subs come up with."

"Me, too. The board will award the contract the Friday before the charity ball, just two days after the annual Chamber of Commerce dinner.

"Are you going to the dinner?" Philip asked.

"Yes. It'll give me a good opportunity to publicly wish Stone good luck on his bid. I can't wait for the award ceremony. It's going to make Bradshaw Architects and Building Corporation the biggest on Florida's east coast. Hell, it may even become the biggest on the entire U.S. east coast. My calling you Prince Philip may not be far off the mark."

Philip raised his glass to Douglas as the waiter served his drink. "Here's a toast to the tower project. May it be on time, under budget, and the crown jewel of the Florida coastline."

The two men clinked glasses, eagerly anticipating their next meeting. Tomorrow they would complete their plans to become royalty.

— • • • —

DOUGLAS LEFT THE restaurant confident that Philip would bring the bid in where he asked. He took his Mercedes north on the Dixie Freeway. Four miles up the road he swung into New Smyrna Beach Airport. Skirting the runways, he drove along the access road and headed for his Cessna.

It's such a beautiful day, he thought. *A shame to waste it.* Pulling into the open hangar, he parked next to his plane. Leaning his head back on the car's headrest, he could feel the tension beginning to flow out of his body. *Yup, it's too nice to sit around.*

Douglas got out of the car and walked over to the plane. *She's so sleek. A real beauty.* Unlocking the plane's door, he climbed aboard. A few minutes later he taxied the plane out to the runway.

"This is CS548 to Control Tower asking for clearance to take off," Douglas said.

"This is NSB Tower to CS548. You are cleared for takeoff."

"Roger that, I won't be long. It's just too nice a day to let the bird sit on the ground."

Gaining speed, Douglas sat back as she rose clearing the trees that lined the highway. He headed north, flying over the beaches. Looking down he saw the property he had asked Catherine to look at. *I wonder if she's going to accept my offer. I'd better give her a call, or maybe not. Let her come to me.*

He flew over the property earmarked for the tower project. "Oh, Russell, too bad you're not going to win the bid. My design is going to bring a lot of business to this area. Everyone will view me as a hero."

Douglas darted in and out of the cotton puffs dotting the sky, then dropped down close to the ocean. Then up again, clearly enjoying the freedom of the air. An hour later, he grew tired of the cloud game and returned to the airport. After landing, he checked the fuel gauge. The tank was three-quarters full, but he didn't want to take any chances on running out the next time he went up. He taxied to the gas pumps and filled the tank. Returning the plane to its parking spot, stepping out, he locked her up.

"I leave you now, my little bird, but I'll be back. Then maybe we'll take a longer ride," he said.

Chapter 23

❧

MANNY ENTERED the bullpen, irritated with the lack of progress in the Stone case.

"Dani, what's the status of the pharmacy report?" he barked.

"I contacted all the pharmacies—Walgreens, and drug outlets, like supermarkets such as Publix, Wal-Mart, and Winn Dixie—for any prescriptions filled for digitoxin in the past year. I came up with a list of potential names. In crosschecking, over half were snowbirds and have left town. The rest I checked for a possible connection with the Stones."

"From what you found so far, there's no indication that Julie Stone had personal access to the substance that killed her. Is that what you're telling me? Did you check with her doctor?" Hearing the agitation in her master's voice, Peaches looked up from her pillow.

"I guess that's what I'm saying," Dani said. "She *personally* did not have a prescription for digitoxin. Yes, I did check with her doctor. No, she didn't have a heart problem. No, he did not prescribe digitoxin for her."

"Given the way she died, anywhere from one to three hours after she ingested the substance, I figure she probably knew her killer," Manny said. "Sam thinks the drug was mixed with alcohol, plus there were trace amounts found in her stomach." Growing more agitated, he popped a piece of gum into his mouth. *God, I wish I had a cigarette.*

"And it was probably someone she was not afraid of," Manny said. "No marks on her body. No indication she was forced to drink or eat the stuff."

"Wait. I have more, and it gets interesting," Dani said, interrupting her boss's tirade. "Because the Stones are definitely movers and shakers in the community, I checked the pharmacy list for prominent people in the area. There were several big mucky mucks, a.k.a. company presidents, VIPs, and charity donors who might know the Stones."

"Like who? Give me names," Manny said.

"There were four who were particularly interesting because they form a tight circle. First on the list is Bert Sullivan, a VP at Florida Bank and Trust and husband to Douglas Bradshaw's first wife, Shirley. Also, Wendy Sullivan, their daughter, was at the House of Beads when Mrs. Stone collapsed."

"Okay, and who else?"

"Second on the list is Douglas Bradshaw. It seems he has a heart condition and takes the stuff. But get this," Dani paused for dramatic effect. "A prescription was filled on the same day at CVS for Mr. Douglas Bradshaw and another one filled for Mrs. Helen Bradshaw, same address. Turns out, Helen Bradshaw is Douglas Bradshaw's mother. The prescriptions were filled three months ago. But wonder of wonders, Helen Bradshaw's been dead for a year and a half."

"Good work, Dani," Manny said, walking over to the board. He added Bert Sullivan and Douglas Bradshaw to the persons-of-interest list.

"Hey, wait a minute. I said there were four. The fourth person on the list was none other than Mr. Russell Stone," Dani said, loving the astonished look on her teammates' faces.

"He said he didn't have a heart condition," Fred said. "Never took digitoxin, let alone leaving the drug around in the house."

"Fred, I suggest you pay Russell another visit. Check with his doctor first. It's not looking good for our friend Stone. No alibi and now a lie about the drug."

Manny stepped back to the case board, underlined Russell Stone on the persons-of-interest list. "Now let me tell you about an interesting conversation I had with Catherine Hainsworth yesterday."

Dani gave a quick look to Fred and George. Fred raised an eyebrow. "Catherine Hainsworth, sweet," he mumbled, loud enough for all to hear.

Manny ignored Fred's comment "We can't totally rule out suicide," he said. "But, it's looking more and more likely she did not take her own life." He filled the team in on the purchase of a gown for the ball, the hair appointment, and Julie's puzzling remark to Catherine about making it up to Russell.

"Dani, call the White Gardenia hair salon," Manny said. "Verify the appointment for Julie Stone with Heather the day before the charity event. It certainly doesn't sound like she was depressed enough to commit suicide if she made an appointment to have her hair done for a ball. Maybe we're finally getting somewhere." Manny paced back and forth a couple of times.

"George, pay a visit to Mr. Sullivan at the bank. Find out where he was the day Mrs. Stone died. Fred, you drop in on Bradshaw at his office as well as check Stone's prescription for digitoxin." Manny continued to chew his gum vigorously as he looked at the list of people on the board. *We're going to find you, whoever you are,* he thought, his eyes narrowing to small slits.

Suddenly Peaches stood up and gave a throaty growl, signaling an intruder. The team looked at Peaches and then followed the direction her nose was pointing.

"Excuse me. I guess I've been discovered," said a tall, well-dressed man looking at the dog. "The sergeant at the front desk told me I could find Captain Salinas here."

"I'm Captain Salinas. Who are you?" Manny asked. As he stood up he gave Peaches a pat on the head and the signal to sit. Peaches sat, but she kept her eyes on the stranger.

"My name is Stephen Hutchinson, Bureau of Immigration and Customs Enforcement. You faxed us a letter a few days ago," he said, displaying his Homeland Security, ICE badge.

"Well, it's about time," George said, standing up and shaking the agent's hand. "I was beginning to think you guys didn't exist."

"We exist all right. Just a little tight on manpower," the agent said with a grin. "We've received several reports about a possible group of illegals working in this area. I'm here to follow up personally. By the way, call me Hutch."

Manny guessed the agent was in his late thirties and a little taller than his own six feet. *He's dressed like a typical undercover guy,* he thought. *Gray suit, white shirt, black tie—nothing memorable.*

The agent took a swipe at his unruly shock of dark brown hair. Manny's team could only guess about the muscles underneath Hutch's jacket.

"Okay, Hutch. We're glad to see you. Let me introduce you to the team," Manny said. "Dani Trotter. Fred Watson. George Anderson." Hutch shook hands with each in turn.

"George, let's bring Hutch up to speed. Give him a list of the construction sites you have. George has visited a few of the sites," Manny said to Hutch. "We look forward to your expertise in this area. We aren't sure as yet how the letter fits into our case. It was found in the purse of our victim, Julie Stone. With your help, maybe we can piece it together."

Manny's phone rang. "Let me get this. George you start filling Hutch in. I'll be with you in a minute," he said.

"Salinas here," Manny barked into the receiver. "Sam, you want me to come to the morgue now? I'm in an important meeting. Can it wait?" Manny asked. "...Okay. I'll be there in ten minutes." He hung up the phone. "I have to run over to the morgue. I'll catch you later, Hutch, unless you're still here when I get back."

—•••—

THE FIRST THING Manny saw when he opened the door to Sam's lab was a medium-build man, probably Mexican.

"Captain Salinas," Sam said, "I'd like you to meet Roberto. He doesn't seem to have a last name. Roberto, tell the captain why you're here."

"Si, señor." Looking at Manny, Roberto said, "I am very worried. My brother, Miguel, has not been home for two nights. He never no come home before. I hear on the television that two men were found last night. Shot dead. Please, señor, do you know who they are?"

"Sam, is he talking about the two bodies we pulled out of the Halifax River last night?" Manny asked.

"Could be," Sam said.

"Show him the two men, Sam. Let's see if one of them is his brother, Miguel."

With Manny close on his heels, Sam took Roberto into the refrigerated vault. He pulled out two drawers and lifted the white sheet from the first body.

"No. He's not my brother," Roberto said, sighing in relief.

Sam replaced the sheet and then lifted the covering off the second body.

"Oh. No. No. Miguel," Roberto cried out. "I knew we should go back home." The man sobbed, laying his head on his dead brother's chest, his arms circling the ice cold form. "Now you are dead. How I tell Mama?" Roberto's body shook with grief as he held his brother.

"Sam, take Roberto back to the lab. I have someone in my office I'd like him to meet."

Manny flipped open his cell and punched the code for George. "George, I believe we've just found Miguel, as in blackmail. I'm on my way back. Tell Hutch to stay put."

"What did Miguel say?" George asked.

"Nothing. He's dead."

Chapter 24

BRADSHAW ARCHITECTS and Building Corporation headquarters was as big as, if not bigger than, the Stone Corporation two blocks away. Fred looked at the three-story edifice. Quite impressive, he thought as he sauntered across the street and entered the marble lobby. He asked Miss America at the Information Desk how to locate Mr. Bradshaw's office. Following her instructions, he headed for the elevator and rode to the second floor. Exiting the elevator, he found Bradshaw's office two doors to his right.

"Hi," Fred said, entering the office. "Is Mr. Bradshaw in?"

"Not today," Monique said. "He's out of the office. If you tell me your name, I can give him a message."

Fred's immediate conjecture was that he could get more information from Monique if he wasn't a police officer, so he didn't divulge his identity.

"My name is Fred Watson. I've heard a lot about Mr. Bradshaw, and I wanted to discuss a potential business opportunity. I tried to see him a couple of weeks ago, March twenty-fifth, to be exact, but there was no answer on your phone. I guess he was away."

"Because of all his construction sites, he's in and out a lot," Monique said, scanning the calendar. "Anyway, mister, I see on the twenty-fifth, he was out all day. Do you want to leave a message?"

"No, not this time. I'll be back in town in a few days and will try again. Thanks for your help, Monique," Fred said, catching her name from the silver plate on her desk.

—•••—

THAT WAS QUICK. I have time to swing by where Bradshaw lives, Fred thought, pulling out into traffic. In a few minutes he arrived at his destination. He parked his unmarked car in front of Bradshaw's condo building where he owned a penthouse. Fred pulled out Julie Stone's picture from the file Dani had given him, putting it in his jacket pocket. He knew this building had a doorman and just maybe he would recognize her photo.

The name badge pinned to the shirt of the portly little Hispanic man behind the desk identified him as Orly Sanchez.

"Hello, Mr. Sanchez. How are you today?" Fred said, extending his hand.

"Hola, señor."

"I wonder if you could help me, Mr. Sanchez. Have you ever seen this lady?"

Orly took the photo in his pudgy hand and examined it carefully. "No, I never see her before," he said.

"Are you sure? Take a good look."

"No. I don't know her."

"Okay, thanks anyway, Mr. Sanchez," Fred said as he turned and left the building. "Bastard. He recognized her."

Pulling out his list of names to be contacted from the file, Fred found the name of the doctor who had prescribed digitoxin for both Douglas Bradshaw and his mother. He decided to pay a visit to the doctor. His office was only a few blocks away so Fred hoofed it.

—•••—

ENTERING DR. HICKEN'S waiting room, Fred inhaled sweet-perfumed air from an air freshener. He went up to the patient check-in window where a gray-haired, matronly woman with a telephone to her ear was writing a note. She finished the call and looked out at Fred. "Can I help you?" she asked.

"Yes, Detective Watson here," Fred said, showing his badge. "I wonder if I might have a brief word with the doctor?"

"I'll see what I can do, Detective Watson." The woman disappeared from behind the window and reappeared a couple of minutes later. "You're in luck. Dr. Hicken was just going to step out for lunch. He asked me to show you to his office." She disappeared again but immediately opened a door a few feet from the window, beckoning Fred to follow. She led him to an office with a sign on the door: Dr. Charles Hicken, Cardiologist.

Fred entered the office. The desktop held several file folders and the doctor seemed to be searching for something on his computer screen. Hearing Fred come through the door, he looked up.

"Thank you, Dr. Hicken, for seeing me. I'm Detective Watson," Fred said, again displaying his badge. "I have a couple of questions. Some facts I'd like you to verify if you can. I have information that Douglas Bradshaw III is one of your patients. Is that correct?"

"You know, Detective, you may be getting into doctor-patient confidentiality."

"I understand, Doctor. I just want to know if he is a patient of yours. His name came up on a list from a pharmacy indicating you prescribed a drug for him. I need to verify information I already have."

"Well, let's see where this goes," the doctor said. "Yes, he's been a patient of mine for several years."

"The same information I have for Mr. Bradshaw I also have for a Mrs. Helen Bradshaw, his mother. Did you also treat his mother, Helen Bradshaw?"

"Yes, yes. Very nice lady."

"Mr. Bradshaw and his mother came up on a list we obtained from a pharmacy that recently filled a prescription, written up by you, for digitoxin."

"I'd have to check the files, but it is quite possible. Both, Mr. Bradshaw and his mother had the same heart condition. But his mother died of pneumonia a year ago, I believe. So she wouldn't have filled a prescription recently, but Mr. Bradshaw could well have."

"Dr. Hicken, when you write a prescription, do you typically include refills?"

"Yes, that is a general practice. Makes it much easier on the patient and my office staff," the doctor said chuckling.

"Could you tell me when you last prescribed digitoxin for Mr. Bradshaw and his mother, and how many refills were noted?"

"I guess I can do that being you already have the information from the pharmacy. Let me ask Peggy to get it for you. Do you have any other questions? I have a lunch date with my wife and I certainly don't want to keep her waiting, if you know what I mean," Dr. Hicken said with a wink.

"I know what you mean. You've been very helpful and by all means, don't keep your wife waiting. If I have any more questions, I'll get back in touch with you."

Fred picked up the information from Peggy and left. As he headed for his car, he glanced at the copies of the scripts. Douglas Bradshaw's was written three months ago with six refills. His mother's was written nineteen months ago with six refills.

— • • • —

ACROSS TOWN, George entered the marble sanctuary of Florida City Bank. He spotted Sullivan's glassed-in office with his name in gold letters on the window. The room was at the end of a string of identical offices. Only the names changed. He sauntered over to the open door, rapping lightly with his knuckles.

"Can I help you?" Sullivan asked, looking up with a practiced smile.

"Yes, sir," George said, pulling out his badge. "Detective Anderson, DBPD. I'm working a case and your name came up on a pharmacy report."

"Well, officer, whatever I can do to help," Bert answered.

"Did you fill a prescription for digitoxin a month ago?"

"Yes. Yes, I did. I have a heart condition, and my doctor thought it might give me some relief. I'm happy to say, the medication has helped greatly."

"I'm glad to hear that, Mr. Sullivan. Oh, by the way, I read where your daughter had quite an experience at the House of Beads a couple of weeks ago. I saw in the paper that she was attending a class when Julie Stone collapsed," George said.

"Oh my, yes. Her mother called me here at the bank and asked me to come home. She said nothing was wrong really but that Wendy was upset by what happened. It was closing time, so I hurried right home. So sad. My wife, Shirley, and I know the Stones. Shirley worked with Mrs. Stone quite often on various fund raising events."

"I see. Mr. Sullivan, we're compiling a report on people who knew the Stones. You know, tying up loose ends in an investigation. We have your daughter's statement. Can you tell me where you were on Tuesday, the twenty-fifth?"

"Oh my, Officer. I only knew Mrs. Stone socially. Am I under suspicion?" Bert asked, taking a handkerchief out of his breast pocket, dabbing his brow.

"It's all preliminary, sir, nothing to worry about."

"Yes. Well," he said, flipping his calendar back to the day in question, "I see it was Tuesday. I always arrive at nine in the morning. You can set your clock by me. I had two appointments in the morning, lunch with the bank president and two of my associates from noon to two o'clock, and one appointment in the afternoon at three o'clock. Nothing else until my wife called about Wendy. I've already told you about that."

"Okay. That's all for now. Thanks for your help, Mr. Sullivan," George said, shaking Bert's hand. He retreated from the office and the bank. *Looks like a dead end,* George thought. He started the car and turned in the direction of the department.

Chapter 25

⁍

MANNY LEFT the morgue returning to the department with Roberto in tow. While driving, he called Hutch on his cell to confirm he was still there. "I have someone I want you to meet," Manny said. "We'll be back in ten minutes. Ask Dani to take you to interrogation room A."

—•••—

HUTCH MET MANNY and Roberto at the door to the interrogation room where Manny introduced the two. Hutch extended his hand in a sign of friendship and trust. Roberto hesitantly took the hand in his.

"Roberto, please go in and have a seat. I'll be back in a minute," Hutch said. Hutch and Manny stepped out of the room closing the door behind them.

"Hutch, you may be our lucky charm," Manny said. "You arrive and a link to the mysterious Miguel shows up at the same moment."

"You know what they say," Hutch offered, "timing is everything."

"I'm not naive enough to stamp the case closed, but it sure is a good start."

"Tell me about this link you found," Hutch said.

"I didn't find it. It walked right into the morgue. Seems Miguel had a brother, Roberto, the man you just met. Roberto was worried because his brother didn't come home a couple of nights ago. Then he sees on the news about two bodies found in the Halifax River. He puts two and two together and goes to the morgue to see if one of the bodies was his brother. Now he's in there waiting to talk to you."

"Interesting indeed."

The two lawmen went back into the interrogation room.

"Roberto, I asked Agent Hutchinson to meet with you. We're glad you came to find your brother. We didn't know who he was. There was no identification on his body. We hope you can help us find out who did this to him. Will you help us, Roberto?"

Roberto put his head in his hands and replied, "Si, señor."

"Agent Hutchinson is going to ask you some questions."

"What will happen to me?" Roberto asked, looking up, eyes filled with fear.

"We don't know yet. That's why Agent Hutchinson is going to talk to you."

Manny left the room and Hutch took a seat across the table from Roberto. *He has all the signs of being here illegally. Nervous. Fidgety.* Hutch thought.

"Would you like a cup of coffee, water, cold drink?" Hutch asked.

"Si. Coffee."

"Cream? Sugar?"

"No, señor."

"I'll be right back. Try to relax, Roberto. We're not going to hurt you." Hutch left to get the coffee and ran right into Manny. "Good thing I didn't have his coffee in my hand or you'd be wearing it," Hutch said, chuckling.

"What do you think? Does he know anything?" Manny asked.

"Whoa, I'm just getting the man some coffee. I'll tell you one thing. It can take months or longer to get a lead like this. I'll catch you later after he and I have time to become friends." Hutch winked, poured two cups of coffee, and headed back to Roberto.

"Here you go, Roberto." Hutch gave him the coffee and took a sip from his own cup. He pulled out a tape recorder and set it, a notepad, and pen, in the middle of the table. Still in his suit and tie garb, he decided a more casual approach would be best. The jacket and tie were discarded to a chair, and the top two buttons of his white shirt unbuttoned.

Hutch sat down and asked, "What's your last name, Roberto?"

"I don't have a last name. I go by Roberto, only Roberto."

Hutch leaned back in his chair. "Roberto, you say you're Miguel's brother. We have reason to believe Miguel was here illegally. Do you have papers, a green card, or visa to show you are here legally?"

"No, señor."

"Well then, Roberto, you are in a lot of trouble. Not only is your brother dead, but I'm going to have to send you back to your home country. Mexico?"

"No. No. My family will have no money. Please don't send me back."

"Roberto, did you and your brother live together here?"

"Si. We rented a small room. We walked to work."

"Did you work in the same place?"

"No. Miguel worked at a big site. I wasn't so lucky. I work at a small site—a new gas station three blocks from Miguel. It is very bad, señor. I was let go yesterday. Miguel did not come home, and now he is dead. And you say you send me back to Mexico. This is a very bad day."

"Well, let's keep talking and see what we can do, Roberto. But if I'm going to be able to help you, you have to talk to me. You have to give me some answers. Above all, Roberto, you have to tell me the truth. Do you understand?"

"I think so."

"Good. Now, let's try again. What's your last name?" Hutch asked.

"Marquez."

"Where does your family live?"

"Juárez." Roberto seemed resigned to his fate. "When Miguel and I crossed the border several months ago, we were full of hope and excitement, a grand adventure. It no seem exciting now. Now, all seems very bad," he moaned.

Roberto took a sip of coffee, blinking to hold back tears. "My family is very poor. They have no money, only what Miguel and I send. My father is dead, and my mother must care for my three little brothers and my little sister."

"Who was the oldest, you?" Hutch asked.

"No. Miguel was my big brother. He was very smart and knew how to make plans."

"What did you do for work in Mexico?"

"Oh, Miguel and I dreamed one day to bring the family here to become landscapers. We sent money home to our mother and she saved some each time so we could start our own business. Now that dream is dead. It died with Miguel. I cannot do it alone."

Roberto couldn't hold back the tears any longer. Trickling slowly down his cheeks, he quickly wiped them away with the sleeve of his orange shirt. He straightened up in his chair showing he still had some pride. "I'm now the head of the family," he said.

"Roberto, did Miguel show you a letter asking for money? Please tell me the truth," Hutch said, leaning forward, placing his hand gently on Roberto's hand.

Fear suddenly filled Roberto's eyes. "Si," he said.

"Did he discuss the letter with you?"

"Si, señor. We didn't know what to do. One thing Miguel did know. If he tried to pay the money, the man would ask for more. Miguel was smart that way."

"Did the man contact, Miguel?"

"Si. Miguel was very scared. The man was big and drove a big truck. Miguel decided to take the letter to Señor Juan, his boss. Señor Juan always said if Miguel needed help to come to him. Señor Juan no want any trouble either."

"And did Miguel give the letter to Señor Juan?"

"Si. When Miguel gave him the letter, Señor Juan was glad he brought it to him. He told him to play along with the man. If the man contacted him again to let Señor Juan know right away."

"Did the man contact Miguel again?"

"Si. He told Miguel where to put the money and when. When Miguel told Señor Juan, Señor Juan told him to do as the big man instructed. But Miguel no come home. I was scared and didn't think through what I was doing. I came here and now you send me back to Mexico."

"One more question, Roberto. To your knowledge, did Miguel show the letter or talk about the letter to anyone besides you and Señor Juan?"

"Oh, no. Of that I'm sure. He was too scared. Señor Juan was going to help him, and Señor Juan asked him not to tell anyone. Miguel asked some friends to loan him money, but they laughed at him."

"Did Miguel tell Señor Juan he had shown the letter to you?"

"He told Señor Juan he show it to *no one*."

"Very good, Roberto. I have to go make a phone call. Do you want another cup of coffee? Use the men's room?"

"Si, señor."

"An officer will come in to take care of you. I'll be back shortly."

Hutch left Roberto and headed for the bullpen. Manny had already gone, but Dani gave Hutch his cell number, which he punched in immediately.

"Manny," Hutch cut in as soon as he heard Manny pick up, "Roberto is talking. Unless you see some reason not to, I'm going to offer him a deal for his testimony as soon as ICE clears my plan," Hutch said.

"What kind of a deal?"

"Papers for him and his family to work here legally, as well as protective custody until the case goes through the courts. We may even give him a new identity. Right now, he's on the lowest rung of society. Hell, he isn't even on a rung. He and his brother were under the ladder and the legs were skewering them into the dirt. I think he'll grab the opportunity to change all that, to someday become a real citizen. He wants to be a landscaper, even dreamed of owning his own business."

"If you can pull that off, it sounds good to me."

"I'm also going to put a wire on Roberto and set up a sting. I want him to apply for a job with Juan Ortega, the boss at the construction site on Beach Street where Miguel worked. I may ask you for some officers if this works out. I'm hoping we can get the guy at the top and the trigger man."

"Anything you need, Hutch, just ask. Our cases seem to be intertwined. Did Dani tell you her idea that maybe our victim was killed by the blackmailer?"

"Yes. Both she and your detectives talked about the possibility."

"Get a copy of Julie Stone's picture. See if Roberto recognizes her."

The two lawmen ended their conversation. Hutch asked Dani for Mrs. Stone's picture and then he called his Washington office for the go ahead to set his plan in motion. Because his boss, the director of the illegal immigration department, had witnessed him solve some tough cases many times, he hoped he could count on the director to authorize the operation. Ten minutes later he received the go ahead and Hutch returned to Roberto.

Entering the interrogation room, Hutch said, "I see you got your coffee. Anything else you want right now?"

"No, señor. Your nice officer even give me a doughnut."

"Roberto, do you recognize this lady?" Hutch asked, placing Julie's picture on the table in front of him.

"No. I never see this person before."

"You're sure. Take another look."

"No. I am sure."

"All right. Now, Roberto, do you want to get your brother's killer?" Hutch asked.

"Oh, si. Until the day I die, I will search for this person."

"And, Roberto, do you want to help your family?"

"Señor, I am so worried about my mama and my brothers and sister. Now Miguel is dead, they cannot survive on what I send."

"Roberto, I have a deal to offer you. It must remain a secret between you, me, and Captain Salinas. You must never talk about it to anyone unless I or the captain say it's okay."

"What kind of deal, señor?"

"We want to get your brother's killer as much as you do. Perhaps even more because we fear he will kill again. We are going to set a trap for this very bad person, but we need your help."

"What kind of help?" Roberto asked, fear once again returning to his eyes.

"You will have to be very brave, Roberto. If you are brave and help us, I believe you and your family will live a better life. Roberto, I want you to apply for a job at the Beach Street construction site where your brother worked."

Hutch leaned back in his chair, sipping the fresh coffee. He waited before saying more to let the idea sink into Roberto's head.

"You will ask Señor Juan for a job," Hutch said. "If the guard at the gate tells you to wait, tell him you want to go with him instead. In other words, try very hard to see Señor Juan in his office. It is most important you get into his office.

"I will try, but I don't know if they will believe me," Roberto said.

"It is very important that they do. I will give you a listening device about the size of a bottle cap, like a beer bottle cap. It's very powerful, so powerful we'll be able to hear back in this building everything that's said within many feet of where it's placed."

"Do I just sit and talk?"

"Not quite," Hutch replied. "Once you are in Señor Juan's office, grip his desk or a table with the device in your fingers to stick it in place. We will show you how. Listen to what Señor Juan is telling you and follow his instructions. If it helps, answer the way you think your brother Miguel would have answered."

"Señor, what if I don't know the answer?"

"He isn't going to ask you anything hard. In fact, I want you to be truthful. The important thing is to get the job, no matter what you have to do. Got that?"

"Si."

"Remember, above all else, do not talk to anyone about our conversation. The only exception is Captain Salinas. If you have to get in touch with us, call the department and ask for Agent Hutchinson or Captain Salinas. If we're not here, leave a message that Roberto is calling. You will be transferred to one of us. Do you have any questions?"

The interrogation room door opened after a sharp knock announcing the arrival of another officer. Dani came in carrying the listening devices.

"Roberto, I'd like you to meet Sergeant Dani Trotter. She is your friend, and you can also talk to her. Sergeant Trotter is going to give you the electronic tool to put in your pants pocket. Whenever you leave the room you are renting, it doesn't matter what time of day or night, you must put this device in your pocket."

"Hi, Roberto," Dani said. "When you put this little thing in your pocket, be sure you push it down as far as your pocket goes so it won't fall out. Are you right handed?"

"Si, señorita."

"Señorita. I like that," Dani said, smiling. "Relax, Roberto. This little disc won't hurt you. I want you to keep the device in your left-hand pocket. That way you won't accidentally put something on top of it, like a handkerchief, or a wallet, or money. If you change to another pair of pants, be sure to transfer the round disc to the new pair. Okay?"

"Si."

"Good. The second device feels a little different. The one we just put in your pocket is smooth, very thin, and round. This one is a little thicker and square. Here, feel it."

"Si, señorita. I feel the difference."

"Good. When you are ready to stick this second one to the bottom of a table, a chair, or whatever you find, reach into your pocket for the feel of the square. When you have it, be sure the smooth side is next to your fingers. Remove your hand from your pocket. Grab the edge of the tabletop with your thumb on top and your fingers underneath. Push up very hard on the device and remove your hand. Let's try it. I want you to look straight into my eyes as you do it. Okay, now stick the device to the table in front of you."

Roberto put his hand into his pocket. Smiling, he said, "I feel them." He carefully withdrew his hand holding the little square piece, all the time looking at Dani. He grabbed the edge of the table, but the device fell out of his hand onto the floor. Roberto was horrified at his clumsiness.

"Señorita, I cannot do this," he said, casting his eyes down to the floor.

"Of course you can, Roberto. This is your first time. Let's try it again." Dani retrieved the small object and gave it to Roberto to put it back into his pocket. Again Roberto felt for the square piece, but this time he kept his thumb on it so the gadget wouldn't fall until he pressed it under the table top. He withdrew his hand and sat back in his seat.

"Si, Roberto, Si. I knew you could do it," Dani squealed, a big smile on her face. She removed the square wafer and placed it on top of the table.

"Hutch, give me a few minutes to test my equipment. It would be best if you keep talking. I want to be sure I'm receiving the signal from both of the devices and that your voices are coming through loud and clear." Dani left the room to the two men.

"Roberto, once you stick the device to the desk, you just do whatever Señor Juan tells you," Hutch said. "If he says you can start immediately, all the better. Follow your normal routine. If you usually stop for a beer on the way home, stop for a beer. But make it just one. Whatever you do, do not tell anyone about the devices. Don't mention your brother or that you know he's dead. Keep to yourself. Got that?"

"Si, señor."

Dani rapped on the door and entered. "Okay, Roberto. You're hot."

"Excuse me, señorita. Hot?"

"You're on the air, live, prime time," Dani said, giggling.

Roberto said, smiling, "Prime time."

Hutch got up signaling the plan was ready for action. Roberto stood, put the square object in his pocket with the disc, and shook Hutch's hand, sealing the deal. "I pray I can keep my end of the bargain," he said.

Roberto walked out of the department into the heat of the day.

Chapter 26

&

IT WAS ABOUT noon when Roberto arrived at the construction site. The shirts of the men working behind the fence were soaked with sweat.

"Whatta you want?" the man asked, standing guard at the gate.

"I'm looking for a job," Roberto said. He hoped the man didn't notice he was shaking. His left hand touched the two objects in his pocket.

The guard flipped open a cell phone and punched the keypad. "I have a guy here looking for work. Need any more?" the gatekeeper asked.

Roberto couldn't hear what was being said on the other end. He stood fidgeting, fingering the devices. The man flipped the phone closed. "Boss said to come over. He'll see what he's got available. See that white trailer over there?"

Roberto nodded. He didn't trust himself to speak.

"Go in that door with the sign, 'Office.' Can you read?"

"Si, señor." *Does he think I'm stupid? I may not be as smart as Miguel, but I'm not dumb.* The shaking stopped as his anger took over. *I'll show them who's stupid.*

Roberto walked over to the trailer, opened the door, and stepped inside. A blast of cold air from the air conditioner hit him in the face. No one was in the small room. There was a counter, a couple of rickety folding chairs, a water cooler, a telephone, and a hallway.

"Halo," Roberto called out.

"Keep your pants on, I'll be out in a minute," a voice bellowed from somewhere down the hall.

Don't worry, I'll keep my pants on, Roberto thought, fingering the small wafers to be sure they were still there.

Juan Ortega emerged from the hallway. He was rather short and his stomach hung out over his belt. His jeans were clean as was his light blue shirt. No sweat under his armpits indicated he spent most of his time in the trailer. "So you're looking for a job, are you?" he said.

"Si, señor."

"Come on back in my office so I can sit down."

Roberto followed the man down the hall and into another small room. It was very messy. Papers were everywhere, and a couple of empty coffee cups had been tossed on the floor near the wastebasket. A full cup of coffee sat on the desk with vapors circling above it. The nameplate on the edge of desk indicated that Juan Ortega was the man sitting before him.

"I expect my employees to be on time, work hard, and no fooling around with the other men. Understand?"

"Si."

"Do you have papers?" Juan inquired, slurping some coffee.

"No. I hope to soon."

"Sure, that's what you all say."

The phone rang, and Juan grabbed it on the first ring. He turned away from Roberto indicating the conversation was private. Roberto reached into his pants pocket, feeling for the square piece. With Juan's back to him, Roberto withdrew his hand and took a peek to be sure the rough side was up. He grabbed the edge of the desk, just as Dani had directed. He pressed the piece very hard and then withdrew his hand. It stuck. A small smile crossed Roberto's face.

Juan swung around, slamming the phone back in its cradle. "Damn contractors," he mumbled. "Okay, you got a job. What's your name?"

"Roberto."

"Roberto what?"

He hesitated and then remembered that Miguel told him never to give his last name because they might trace him back to mama. "Only Roberto," he replied.

"Right," Juan said, nodding his head in agreement. "You can start after the noon lunch break today. I pay cash every Friday at the end of the shift. Not a minute before, so don't quit early thinking you'll get first in line. You'll be paid today for the hours you work. Go see the man you spoke with at the gate. He'll tell you what to do. Now get out of here. I have better things to do than to talk to you all day."

"Thank you, señor. I work very hard, you will see."

— ••• —

DANI SMILED. "Hot dog, our man is in."

Chapter 27

✍

FRIDAY DAWNED SUNNY and humid. By nine in the morning the light blue sky gave way to dark gray clouds promising a downpour. Trumpeted by thunder and lightning, the storm moved in, but Bradshaw didn't notice as he concentrated on the sheets of paper in front of him filled with columns of numbers. His subcontractors didn't let him down. The emails containing their estimated costs to do the job had arrived one after the other in his email account.

Bradshaw pranced into his CFO's office, looking as if he'd already been awarded the contract. "Philip, wait until you see the numbers the guys came up with. After a quick perusal, I think we have Stone beaten by a mile," Douglas said, laying the email printouts on Philip's desk.

"Calm down, Douglas. You're too emotionally involved in this contract," Philip said. "I hate to think what you'll do if you don't get the project."

"Ever since Stone and I were in grade school together we've been competitors. I won a few things, but Stone always managed to come up with the big prizes. He even took away my pretty Irish redhead for his wife," Douglas ranted.

"You dated Julie Stone?"

"We went out a few times until Stone stole her from me. He was the only son of Russell Walker Stone, Sr., a self-made millionaire. He didn't have to work for what he got. It was handed to him on a silver platter. The old man's firm was the biggest in central Florida."

"I heard his father was wealthy," Philip said.

"I, on the other hand, had the misfortune of being born into poverty. My old man couldn't care less if I was an architect. He said architectural design was for the artsy type, and I wouldn't make a dime."

"Come on, Douglas, your father was a respected contractor here in Daytona Beach. He paid your tuition for college didn't he?"

"So what if he did? I've been living for this day, the day I can rub Russell's face into defeat. So, Philip, you'd better be darn sure I get that tower project. Let's put it this way, if Bradshaw Architects and Building Corporation isn't offered that contract next week, you won't have a job here anymore."

"What a shitty thing to say after the years I've slaved for you. Covered your ass is what I've done."

"Don't get huffy, Philip. All will be the same as long I get that contract. Now start cranking the numbers. I alerted Monique to be on standby this weekend. When you think it looks right, give me a call at home. We'll go over the bid forms at my place on Sunday. That way I can take a final look and make any refinements. Then you take it to the board on Monday. We'll beat Stone to the punch," Douglas said, as he sauntered out of Philip's office.

—•••—

PHILIP SAT FOR A moment, steam coming out of his ears. "That SOB. Threatening me after all I've done for him," he muttered, staring at the closed door. "Calm down. He's just a hothead. Working for him so long, you know he can be cruel better than anyone else."

Philip picked up the emails and started to *crank* the numbers.

Chapter 28

∂

THE NOW FAMILIAR silver bell at the House of Beads heralded Catherine's arrival. "Hi, Tillie. How's business?"

"Business has been off-the-wall, so to speak. I guess what they say is true—there's no such thing as bad publicity. Ever since the article ran in the *News Journal* about Julie dying here in the shop, lots of curious people have stopped by. Then when they see my beautiful beads, they usually end up buying some, taking classes, and more," Tillie said, with a smile. "In fact, your young friend Wendy is at the table in the corner picking out some beads to match her dress for the charity ball."

"Wonderful, I'll go say hello. I brought a swatch of my ball gown as well. It's such a pretty shade of pale-lime green but I couldn't find any earrings to match it at the mall. I felt so stupid because, of course, that's why I took the class, to make matching jewelry for my dress. I'll go say hi to Wendy and then have a look around."

"If you can't find what you're looking for, let me know. A new shipment just arrived, still in their velvet pouches."

Catherine headed for the corner, at the same time taking a quick gaze at the many crystal and pearl strands hanging in the green area of the wall of beads.

"Wendy, how nice to see you. Under happier circumstances, I might add," Catherine said, as she wrapped the young girl in her arms. "Tillie said you're creating a piece to match your ball dress. I'm so happy to hear you're going."

"Yep. I was invited to sing a couple of songs, so mom bought a ticket for me at her table. She took me to a bridal store to pick out a dress. Catherine, I think she's corrupting me. We found the most beautiful wine-colored strapless gown. Then she insisted on a pair of gold strappy heels."

"My, my, I agree you have been corrupted. Now what are you going to wear for jewelry?"

"She wanted to take me to the mall, but I told her I was sure I could find matching beads here and make some spectacular dangle earrings. What do you think of these?" Wendy held a strand of garnet-colored crystals up to the light.

"They are beautiful, and that's exactly why I'm here as well. Not too many more days until the big event and there's so much to do. Russell Stone asked me to help him. He's a bit lost without Julie. They were co-chairs, you know."

"Mom told me she heard you were stepping in to help."

"I must try to match this swatch of my gown. I hope I'm as successful as you," Catherine said, holding the piece of fabric out for Wendy to see.

"Catherine, what a beautiful, soft green," Wendy said, touching the silky material. "I noticed some crystal strands and pearls, too, almost the same color. They were coated with something to make them iridescent. Tillie can tell you about the special stones. With your blonde hair, and your gown set off with sparkly crystal beads, you'll be the belle of the ball."

Chapter 29

THE HAMPTON INN on International Speedway Boulevard was buzzing. All of the major architects and contractors in Florida, and several from around the world, had gathered to learn their fate—did they get the prized contract worth millions for the Daytona Beach Tower Project?

The development was one of the largest ever awarded in the state. It included a marina, a boardwalk with shops, and several arcades. The plan also called for a conference center and two multi-floor condominium buildings, featuring three penthouses. The top of the other condominium building was to be designed with a large garden complete with swimming pool, snack bar, flower beds, and private benches and tables tucked between flowering bushes, all overlooking the Atlantic Ocean. The condominium towers would be the tallest buildings on the east coast of Florida.

The firm winning this contract would no doubt become known worldwide; however, the Contract Award Board stipulated that the major building materials for the project be purchased locally. Specialty items were left to the discretion of the winning bidder. A decorating firm for the interior rooms and a landscaper were also left up to the winner.

"Hey, Russell," Bill MacFarlane, head of the award board, called out. "It's good to see you. Is there any more news on the case?"

"Hi, Bill," Russell said, shaking MacFarlane's hand. "No, nothing yet. To be honest, I'm glad I had to prepare my bid for this contract. It helped to keep my mind occupied."

"Well, grab your seat. The bidder's table is up front. Just look for your name tag."

MacFarlane hustled off to the podium. Stone found his seat and was pleased to see that Bradshaw was at the opposite end of the table.

In back of the podium, high on the wall, were three sixty-inch, flat screen, television monitors. The screens were black for now, but soon they would come alive to display the plans and designs of the winning bidder.

There were over two-hundred people gathered for the event, including several from the media: newspaper, magazine, and television. Individual subcontractors were also present to see if their fortunes might change if the firm they supported won the contract. Of course, many Chamber of Commerce members were present. The awarding of this contract was a big deal for the community, as well as the architects.

MacFarlane banged the walnut gavel on a marble block, signaling for silence.

"I welcome you here this afternoon to witness the beginning of a truly remarkable event for our community," MacFarlane said. "Volusia County is becoming one of the most sought after areas in Florida, not only as a vacation destination and retirement paradise but also for business expansion. The tower project enhances the growth of all three." He paused to take a sip of water.

"The process to determine the winning designer and whose firm will bring the dream to life has been long and hard fought. Initially, we received over two hundred designs from around the country and internationally. This group was narrowed to five. Two of the finalists are from Volusia County. The three others are headquartered in Los Angeles, California, Rio de Janeiro, Brazil, and Tokyo, Japan. The five firms are represented here today by the presidents of their respective companies and are seated at the table in front of me."

MacFarlane paused a moment to take another sip of water. Looking back at the assembled audience, he continued with his speech.

"The board took into account not only the projected cost for such a development but also the scope and design. Cost was a significant issue, but it was not the overriding factor. I can tell you the final decision was very difficult. However, that said, we are confident the selected firm will capture all aspects of our vision for the enterprise. We believe the winning design will have a positive impact on our area and will bring a boom to our commerce. Without further ado, the winning firm is right here in our own backyard."

MacFarlane paused as he looked over the assembled crowd staring expectantly back at him. "It is my pleasure to award the contract to Stone & Associates. Congratulations, Mr. Stone."

The television screens behind the podium sprang to life with pictures, drawings, and descriptions of Stone's submission for the tower project.

The room erupted into rounds of applause, cameras flashed, and reporters ran outside with cell phones to their ears. A crush of people surrounded Russell. As the pictures on the flat screens dissolved one into another, "oohs" and "aahs" could be heard around the room, intermingled with "beautiful, clever, look at that, spectacular."

—•••—

DOUGLAS BRADSHAW COULD not believe his ears. His face turned red. He couldn't breathe. Once again, he had lost the prize to none other than his arch rival, Russell Stone.

Chapter 30

❦

CATHERINE, ELEGANT in her form-fitting gown, walked briskly down the hotel's carpeted hallway to the ballroom. A slit up the side of the dress to her knee allowed her to move gracefully. Catching her reflection in the mirror opposite the doorway, she turned slightly to see the effect of the plunging neckline. The bodice was held in place by thin straps that crisscrossed her back.

Her only jewelry was a pair of inch-long peridot earrings which sparkled when she moved her head. The earrings she fashioned of pale green crystals on threads of gold were a perfect complement to her gown. A bracelet sparkled on her wrist. Two combs holding her blonde hair in a tight twist were studded with crystals matching the earrings and bracelet.

Everything looks in place, she thought, as she turned to enter the elegant hall.

"Catherine, you look ravishing," Russell exclaimed, as he caught her coming in the main entrance of the ballroom.

"Thank you, Russell. Congratulations on winning the bid for the tower project. You are the toast of the town. Everyone is talking about you. What a nice way to celebrate, at a ball, and you look like a winner in that dashing tuxedo."

"Thank you, Catherine. I wish Julie could be at my side to enjoy this moment with me."

"I'm sure she is in spirit, Russell," she said, touching his sleeve. She knew there was nothing she could say to ease his pain. "I see we're the first to arrive. If you'll excuse me, I want to go over my checklist with Judy, the event coordinator. I'll join you at our table a little later."

"Thank you again for helping me out. I know Julie would be pleased."

— • • • —

CATHERINE STEPPED TO the large dining room. The room's layout facilitated the guests spilling out through the double-wide doors into the ballroom.

The dining room was beautiful with large bouquets of lilies at the base of huge palm trees brought in for the occasion. The flowers' delicate scent perfumed the air. The tables were set with votives at each guest's place. In the center stood a large cream-colored candle circled with a tall, slender, glass hurricane shade.

She took note of the wait staff scurrying around, checking that each place setting was correct. A few of the waiters were setting crystal flutes on the tables for the champagne toast. Catherine found Judy in a corner, pencil in hand, checking off items on a sheet of paper.

"Hi, Judy. Any hitches I should be aware of?" Catherine asked.

"No, Mrs. Hainsworth, everything is a go. The two volunteers you arranged to help the guests find their tables are at the door with the master-seating chart. The table numbers are at the base of each flower arrangement. The chef and sous chefs are busy preparing the canapés."

"Thank you, Judy. Please tell the waiters to begin serving the champagne."

"Mrs. Hainsworth, there is an additional guest. Mr. Stone called. He asked me to set a place at his table for a Mr. Hutchinson. He arrived a few minutes ago, a very handsome man I might add," Judy said.

Catherine looked over at the table she was sharing with Russell and thought Judy was right. He is a handsome man. "Thank you, Judy. I'll go over and introduce myself."

— • • • —

CATHERINE MADE HER WAY across the parquet floor to meet this stranger. "Welcome. I'm Catherine Hainsworth. I understand you're joining us tonight," she said, extending her hand in greeting.

Hutch stood up. "Delighted to meet you, Catherine. My name is Stephen Hutchinson, but please call me Hutch," he said, receiving her hand.

"Hutch." She nodded to him as she gently pulled her hand from his. "What brings you to our fair city?"

"I'm here to help out with the Stone case," he said. "Captain Salinas suggested it might be a good idea to attend this charity event. Let me be so bold as to say that Manny's been holding out on me."

"And how is that, Hutch?"

"He told me you are a witness in the case, but he left out you are a most beautiful woman."

"Thank you. I'm so glad you took him up on his suggestion to attend the ball. Many of the people involved in the case will be here this evening. I'm sure Manny will take care of the introductions, but I'll be happy to introduce you as well. Please excuse me. There are a few more details I have to check on. I'm also sitting at this table, so I'm sure we'll have time to chat during dinner."

"I look forward to that, Catherine. I hope you'll save me a spot on your dance card."

"I certainly will, Hutch."

My, my, I bet there's some physique under that suit, she thought, as she left him to check on the champagne service.

— • • • —

THE NEXT TWO HOURS were a blur for Catherine as she greeted guests, made sure all found their tables, and that dinner appeared on time. It was a beautiful setting. As soon as dinner was finished, she and Russell led the way to the ballroom, which was truly spectacular. Crystal chandeliers hung from the sculpted-plaster ceiling, and little bistro tables topped with candles were placed in the outlaying patio areas.

The musicians were playing the "Blue Danube" waltz as they entered. Catherine and Russell started the event off dancing to the music. Soon some couples joined them while others went to find a table on the patio or to order an after-dinner drink. Scrumptious looking pastries and silver tea and coffee services were ready at the far end of the ballroom.

The musical ensemble outdid themselves with violins, flute, drums, piano, and a harp to entertain the guests.

— • • • —

CATHERINE SPOTTED MANNY approaching her. *My, what an impressive figure of a man he is. His tuxedo fits him perfectly, and how dashing he is with the high-neck Nehru shirt.* Her face lit up in a smile.

"Cat, you are a vision. I'll arrest anyone who comes near you. I believe you mentioned something about sharing a dance?"

"I did and now seems like a perfect time."

Manny took her hand and led her to the center of the ballroom floor. "You must realize I'm not much good at this," he said. As he spoke, the musicians started a rendition of "What Lola Wants Lola Gets," a tango. Taking her in his arms, he asked, "Do you tango?"

"Why, yes I have been known to Tango."

"Well, let's start easy and see where it leads us," he said flashing her a smile.

Before she knew it, Manny had his right hand in the center of her back, his hand at a slight angle. With his left arm, bent only slightly, and his palm up, she put her small hand into his. Holding her close but their bodies not quite touching, he took two slow steps forward, two more quick steps, and then a slow one. Another two slow steps. Quick. Quick. A sharp pivot to his left. She followed his lead precisely.

"Manny, you've been holding out on me."

Slow slow...quick quick...long slow...slow slow...crisp pivot...dip, "You are lovely tonight," Manny said, as he held her, looking down into her soft brown eyes. Then he sharply brought her up straight into the tango hold and continued around the floor.

At each pivot, Catherine's floor-length gown flipped, following her body's movement. The slit up the side revealed her lovely leg at each quick turn. Other than the dips, they never looked at each other, keeping perfect rhythm to the music. Each sequence of steps became more and more intricate. Catherine held her head high, her back straight, her head giving a sharp twist in perfect alignment with the pivot of her body.

Slowly the other dancers drifted back forming a large circle to watch the handsome pair perform a most magnificent tango. Their dance ended with Manny holding her in a deep dip. The music stopped. From the dip position, Catherine looked up at Manny who was gazing down at her with an adoring look. Carefully, he brought her to her feet. She was rather flushed from the pace of the dance routine, or was it the strength of Manny's arm around her? The spectators gave a round of applause as she graciously curtsied to Manny.

The music resumed. Couples returned to the floor but the pair who performed the tango was lost in the moment together.

— ●●● —

DOUGLAS BRADSHAW came up behind Manny and tapped his shoulder. "Well, man, that was quite a show. I wonder if I might cut in?" he asked.

"Catherine?" Manny asked.

"Why, yes, of course," she said, not wanting to leave Manny. She especially did not want to dance with Douglas.

Manny let go of her hand and backed away. "Douglas," he said.

As Manny left Catherine with Douglas, Russell Stone stepped onto the stage and took the microphone in front of the musicians. "Ladies and gentlemen, we have a special treat tonight. It seems a budding star is in our midst. Wendy Sullivan is going to favor us with a couple of songs. Wendy, the stage is yours."

Catherine clapped with the others in welcoming Wendy. The musicians started, and Wendy began to sing "Memories," the popular song from the Broadway show *Cats*. She was beautiful in her wine-colored strapless gown. The dangling earrings she crafted for the occasion were a perfect complement to the dress. Again, as at the funeral, Catherine marveled at how poised she was and how magical her voice sounded. After the first few bars of the melody, couples began to slow dance as Wendy's voice floated over them.

Catherine and Douglas joined the other couples on the floor. "It's nice to see you, Douglas. I hope you're enjoying the ball. I'm sorry I haven't called about your offer."

"Did you see the property?" Douglas asked.

"Yes, I did. It's a great location and a perfect setting for what you're planning. However, now that Russell has the tower project, and, by the way, I'm sorry you weren't selected, I feel I must say no. It's a shame you both couldn't head up the development."

"I'm sorry to hear that, Catherine," Douglas said, keeping his composure. "Maybe another time. If you change your mind, the job is yours until I find another architect."

"That is most generous, Douglas. Did you bring a date to the ball?"

"No, but I am sharing a table with friends."

"I saw you talking with Shirley and her husband," Catherine said. She knew Shirley was his first wife. The marriage ended in a nasty divorce. They seemed to be cordial to one another now, seventeen years later. "I'm glad to see you two getting along."

"Shirley is a good woman. We were both much too young for the responsibilities that come with marriage," Douglas replied.

Catherine was surprised at his openness. Sometimes that's the benefit of social occasions and a little stress-relieving champagne. He held Catherine's hand as they danced, and she noticed his gold bracelet. "Douglas, that's a lovely bracelet you're wearing. Most men don't wear bracelets well, but it looks very nice on you."

"Thank you. I like it. Tracy gave it to me for my birthday. You remember Tracy, don't you? My second wife? She moved to Atlanta several years ago."

"Yes. Well, it's beautiful. Douglas, I'd like to return to my table if you don't mind. That tango with Manny has left me a little depleted."

"Certainly, but I'm glad we had a chance to talk. Maybe we can share another dance later."

— ••• —

DOUGLAS STEERED HER through the dancers, but he stiffened as they approached her table. "Well, if it isn't the big architect. I suppose you're feeling particularly happy today, the day after you were wrongly awarded the big contract," Douglas said, addressing Stone.

Russell rose from his chair. "Douglas, I know you're disappointed, but the board awarded the contract to Stone & Associates because they felt we would do the best job."

"Oh, yah? Well, I happen to know my bid was lower than yours. I have a half a mind to raise a protest and ask for an inquiry as to why it wasn't awarded to Bradshaw Architects and Building Corporation."

"How do you know your bid was lower? The bids were sealed, and the contract was awarded on merit as well as price," Stone retorted, raising his voice. "It's illegal for you or any member of the board to discuss the contents of any of the bids outside of the board members. Maybe I'm the one who should launch an inquiry."

Douglas, helped along by three martinis, clenched his hands into fists and moved into Russell's face. "I wouldn't accuse me of breaking the law, you shithead," he growled, poking Russell in the chest with his finger.

"Don't touch me again, Douglas, or—"

"Or what, shithead? You gonna punch me?" Douglas replied, again shoving Russell backward.

"You wise ass," Russell said, as he clocked Douglas in the nose. Douglas went down screaming in pain. "You broke my nose, you SOB." Lying on the floor, blood squirting out of his nose, Douglas squealed, "I'll get you for this. I'm not done with you."

At the sound of Douglas' raised voice, the music abruptly stopped. Guests asked each other what the commotion was about. Judy, seeing what happened, called 9-1-1. At the same time, Manny, who had witnessed the punch, rushed up. "Go sit down, Russell," he ordered. Then he bent over Douglas. "What the hell do you think you're doing? This is supposed to be a ball, not a brawl."

—•••—

DOUGLAS WAS STILL ON the floor bleeding when the EMTs arrived. He did not appear in any physical danger other than having a very sore nose. "Mr. Bradshaw, let's have a look at that nose and see if we can stop the bleeding," one EMT said, opening his first-aid case.

"Russell broke my nose. He hit me for no reason," Douglas said.

"You'll have time to resolve that, but right now let's get that bleeding stopped. We can take you to the emergency room at the hospital to see if your nose is broken."

Douglas got to his feet with the help of the two EMTs. "No, I don't want to go to any hospital. Just stop the bleeding and I'll take care of the rest myself. You'll be hearing from me, Stone. You can bet on that."

— • • • —

SHIRLEY SULLIVAN, Wendy's mother, walked over to Douglas. She had spoken to him only a few times over the years. She never wanted to be too friendly because of the secret she carried in her heart. "Doug, are you okay?" she asked, handing him a glass of water.

"Yah, Shirl. Nice to see you still care," he replied sarcastically.

"I see your temper still gets the better of you, but, really, Douglas, fighting in front of everyone...and Wendy..."

— • • • —

LEAVING THE MUSICIANS, Wendy saw her mother talking to Douglas and went over to them. Wendy knew her mother was once married to Douglas Bradshaw many years ago.

As Wendy approached her mother, Shirley quickly turned away from Douglas to intercept her. "Come on, dear, the excitement is over," she said.

"But, Mom, Mr. Bradshaw is bleeding. Blood is spattered all over his shirt. Maybe I can help."

"It's not your problem. The EMTs are taking care of him."

Walking by her mother, Wendy plucked a napkin off a nearby table and walked over to Douglas as the EMTs were closing their first-aid cases. "Here, Mr. Bradshaw, use this to wipe the blood off your face," she said.

As Douglas wiped his face, Wendy noticed a small red birthmark on his cheek, very close to his right ear. It was barely visible. Wendy put her hand up to her cheek and touched a spot close to her right ear.

Taking her daughter's arm, Shirley quickly turned her away from Douglas and guided her back to their table.

"Mom, did you see Mr. Bradshaw's face? He has a birthmark just like mine, in the same place even."

"Nonsense, dear. It's not like yours at all."

Chapter 31

THE SULLIVANS LEFT the ball after Wendy's last song, turning into their driveway about eleven-thirty. They wanted to escape because of all the commotion between Douglas and Russell. Wendy went straight up to her bedroom, still puzzling over Douglas' birthmark identical to her own.

"Hon, would you like a nightcap?" Bert asked. Bertram Sullivan, a forty-five-year-old banker, still couldn't believe how lucky he was to have Shirley for his wife. It didn't matter to him that she was carrying Douglas' child at the time of their marriage. He would have married her no matter the circumstances. Their marriage had turned out well.

He loved Wendy as much as if she had been his own blood. Shirley's delivery had been hard and as a result, she was unable to have more children. Again, Bert didn't complain. If truth be told, he liked a calm atmosphere. He doted on his wife and child and thrived as Vice President of the Florida City Bank.

"No, thank you dear, but you know what I would like is a cup of chamomile tea, something soothing before turning in," Shirley said.

They both headed to the kitchen. Like married couples familiar with their routines, she put on the kettle to heat the water. He put out the cups and saucers placing a tea bag in each cup.

"Bert, something happened tonight that I feared might happen one day."

"What's that, hon?" Bert questioned, turning to look at his wife. He noted the worry in Shirley's eyes.

"Did you see the fight between Douglas and Russell this evening?" Shirley asked.

"Yes, I did. You'd think grown men could keep their temper under control, especially at a social event."

"I agree. Well, just as the EMTs helped Douglas to his feet after the fight, Wendy walked over. I steered her away immediately. Not only because it was Douglas, but it was not a pretty scene with the blood he lost. But she insisted on giving him a napkin to wipe the blood off his face. Wendy told me she noticed Douglas had a birthmark just like hers."

"Does he have a mark like hers?"

"Yes, a perfect match—same size, same color, same location."

"What did you say?"

"I told her she was mistaken. That it was nothing like hers."

"Did she press you any further?"

"No, but knowing Wendy, the wheels are definitely turning. Bert, you and I decided when we married that we would never tell Wendy about her father. I believed it be the right thing to do at the time, but what if she continues to question me?"

"Now, now, don't go borrowing trouble," Bert said, trying to allay her fears.

"Worse yet, what if she really looks at him sometime and sees the same eyes, same color hair, same smile, and same birthmark! She is the spitting image of him," Shirley said.

"Yes, I suppose there is a close resemblance."

"Then there's the date of her birth, a little earlier than nine months after you and I were married. And one more thing, she has the same habit of twisting her hair around her right index finger, something Douglas' mother used to do."

"Well, his mother is dead. I think you're being overly concerned. Let's see if she brings it up again. In the meantime, drink up your tea so we can get some sleep."

"Okay, dear. I'll be up in a minute."

Shirley put the cups and saucers in the dishwasher. "I'm afraid this is not going to be the end of it," Shirley mumbled as she started the rinse cycle. "Wendy was preoccupied when we got home. If I know my daughter, she's going to go see Douglas."

Chapter 32

&

WENDY DIDN'T SLEEP well the night after the ball or Sunday night. She kept thinking about the birthmark she saw on Bradshaw's face. She wasn't sure why the mirror seemed to beckon to her. Obeying the call, she got up several times, turning on the light each time, staring at her reflection. As far as she could tell, their marks were identical and positioned in exactly the same spot. She also noticed they had the same dark brown eyes.

Turning a strand of hair with her right hand, Wendy also thought their hair color was the same—brown, almost black. Her mother had none of these characteristics, neither did her father.

Her mind was reeling. Her mother had told her that she was conceived on a cruise she and Bert had taken a month before they were married. That and the fact she was premature, accounted for her birth just seven-and-a-half months after they were married. She was six pounds at birth in spite of being premature. Her mother and Bert were married the day after Shirley's divorce was final.

Wendy never questioned her mother about when she had separated from Douglas. She knew her mother had flown to Mexico for a quickie divorce, down and back in two days, she was told.

On Sunday, Wendy decided she had to see Douglas again. She came up with a reason to go to his office, which actually was legitimate. She was looking for a summer job after school let out.

—•••—

THERE WAS NO SCHOOL on Monday because of a teacher's conference. Taking advantage of classes being canceled, after breakfast Wendy drove to Bradshaw's corporate headquarters. At this time of morning, she had no trouble parking. Getting out of the car, she looked up at the impressive building and saw Bradshaw Architects and Building Corporation chiseled into the granite over the large front entrance.

Inhaling deeply, she walked through the revolving plate-glass door. In the lobby, the receptionist gave her directions to the president's office. Following the directions, she entered his office.

"Hi," Wendy said. "The receptionist told me I might find Mr. Bradshaw here. Is he in?"

"Sorry, hon. He's out on an appointment. If you'll give me your name and what you'd like to see him about, maybe I can help you," Monique offered.

"My name is Wendy Sullivan. I saw Mr. Bradshaw at the charity ball Saturday night. I was in the store down the street," she lied. "I dropped by to see how his nose is. He thought it might be broken. It was bleeding awfully."

"Well, Wendy, I actually haven't seen Doug, er Mr. Bradshaw, yet today, so I can't say. He went straight to his appointment this morning. What I can do is tell him you inquired about his health," Monique said, fluffing her big set of blonde curls.

"Oh, no, that's okay. It's really not important. As I said, I was in the area. Thanks anyway." Wendy turned to go and walked right into Douglas. "Oh. Excuse me, Mr. Bradshaw."

"Wendy, how nice to bump into you," Douglas said, laughing. "What brings you here?"

"She was inquiring about your nose, Doug, which I can see is *very* bruised. Did you really break it?" Monique asked.

"I didn't break anything, Monique. Russell Stone hauled off and hit me at the charity ball. It was all very unpleasant. Wendy, come on in. I'd be glad to visit with you," Douglas said, escorting her into his office. "I must say you have a beautiful voice. I was very impressed at Julie Stone's funeral and then the songs you favored us with at the ball were very nice. Very nice, indeed. Now tell me how you happened to come to see me."

"Well, actually, I wanted to inquire about the possibility of a summer job, you know after school lets out in a couple of weeks." As she looked at Douglas' face she nervously twisted her hair around her finger. She hadn't been mistaken. His birthmark was identical to hers. In fact, looking at his face was like looking in the mirror, except, of course, he was a man.

"I suggest you go down and see Ann Bell. She's our Human Resources Manager. We do try to hire a few students in the summer, and I'll put in a good word for you." Douglas got up from behind his desk and came around to shake Wendy's hand, signaling the meeting was over.

"Thank you, Mr. Bradshaw. I'll go down and make an appointment now." Wendy took Douglas' extended hand. "What a handsome bracelet," she said admiringly.

"Thank you, Wendy. It was a gift from my late mother. Speaking of mothers, please give my regards to Shirley."

"I will, and thanks again for your time." Wendy left his office, saying goodbye to Monique as she passed her desk. As long as she was here, she might as well stop to make an appointment with Mrs. Bell.

Ann Bell was very helpful. "We do hire a few students for part-time summer jobs," she said, handing Wendy some forms to fill out. "The program helps you and it's good public relations for the company. I'll give you a call as soon as I see an available spot."

"Thank you, Mrs. Bell."

Wendy left the building and got into her car. Lost in thought, she headed home but found herself in front of the House of Beads. She spotted Catherine's Beemer parked nearby. "I'll run in and tell her what a great job she did with the charity ball," she mumbled.

— •••—

THE SHOP BELL ANNOUNCED Wendy's arrival. "Hi, Tillie, is Catherine Hainsworth here? I saw her car out front."

"She sure is, hon. She's in the classroom looking at some beads in the light from the window."

"Thanks." Wendy went into the classroom, admiring the beads displayed as she passed. "Hi, Catherine," she said.

"Wendy, how nice. This gives me a chance to tell you again how beautifully you sang on Saturday and also how lovely you looked." Catherine was holding several strands of beads and a few gold chains in the air.

"What a pretty chain," Wendy said, touching the links with her finger. "I don't' believe I've seen that before. Oh, wait a minute, yes I have. I just came from Douglas Bradshaw's office, and I swear he had a bracelet just like that. He said his late mother gave it to him. The links really are handsome. Are you going to create something with it?"

"I'm not sure. Perhaps. Are you starting something new?"

"No, I spotted your car and thought I'd tell you what a good job you did with the ball."

"Why, thank you, dear."

"I just put in my application for summer employment at Mr. Bradshaw's company. Lucky for me they have a summer program for students."

"What a nice idea and it will give you good experience, I'm sure."

"Hope they call me. Well, I'd better get going. See you later."

— ●●● —

CATHERINE FOLLOWED WENDY out of the classroom and called to Tillie, "I'd like this gold chain, Tillie. It really is lovely."

"It is pretty, isn't it, Catherine. I've only had this chain a few months. It's one of the supplier's new designs. Quite unique don't you think?"

"Yes, it is, but I believe I've seen it before."

"Sure you have. Julie Stone used this piece for the bracelet she made her husband during your classes. She bought two lengths. I'm not sure if she made anything with the second one."

"Of course, now I remember. I'll take a strand and see what I can come up with. Nice to see you again, Tillie."

"Now that's odd," Catherine mused. Leaving the shop, she kept mulling over what Wendy had said. "Douglas told Wendy his late mother gave him the bracelet, yet it's a new chain. She must have been mistaken about the design. It probably just looked a little like it."

Chapter 33

THE MORNING SUN rose bright over the east coast of Florida, but Russell's mood was dark. It had been four weeks since Julie died, and the police seemed no closer to solving her case than they were the first week.

Russell stopped shaving. Leaning on the sink with both hands for support, he stared at his image in the mirror. Maybe I should go ahead with the polygraph, he thought. "I have to do something, but what?" he said to the man in the mirror. "Call your lawyer, Russell. Maybe he'll have some ideas on how to bust the case open." Toweling off his face, he walked to the telephone and placed the call to Guy Malone.

"Guy, Russell Stone here. I'm so frustrated with the lack of progress on my wife's case. Do you have any suggestions on how we might help it along?"

"Salinas called again today wanting you to take a polygraph," Malone answered. "I told him I didn't think they were reliable and some crazy question could give a false positive and implicate you. He did say they were making some progress, but he wouldn't elaborate. I do have one suggestion, Russell."

"Let's have it."

"Somebody must have seen Julie that day who hasn't come forward. How about we give her picture to that Channel 13 news' reporter? She could show Julie's photo in her update. If anyone saw her on the day she died, they'd be asked to call a tip line."

"Sounds as good as anything right now, Guy."

"I'll give Captain Salinas a call and see if he can run with it. His people would man the tip line."

— • • • —

MANNY WASN'T TOO thrilled to receive Guy Malone's phone call, but he agreed that the idea might bring in some new information. He said he would set up the tip line at the department. If any calls came in on that number, they would go directly to his team.

Channel 13 news was delighted to receive the request. They would be on the inside of the story and agreed immediately to run Julie's picture in several time slots. The tip-line number would stay on the screen fifteen seconds. If nothing happened the first day, they would repeat the story the following day and again after that if needed.

Manny set up the tip line with his team. They drew up a schedule so the line was manned at all times, but especially during the evening hours. The rationale was that someone might recognize Julie's picture while watching television after work.

The team settled into the department's conference room the next day. The TV tuned into Channel 13 and four telephones were on the conference table. If a call came in and the first line was busy, it would roll over to line two and so on. All calls would be recorded.

Breaking News flashed on the television screen.

"We have breaking news regarding a story we've been reporting for the last four weeks. The Daytona Beach Police Department is asking for your help in the murder of Julie Stone on March twenty-fifth.

"Take a good look at this woman's picture, Julie Stone. If you saw her on March twenty-fifth, or if you have any information regarding this case, please call the number at the bottom of your screen."

The story aired several times over the next two days. George took some of the calls writing down the tips to be followed up. Fred did the same, but none sounded promising.

—●●●—

TUESDAY AFTERNOON, Dani was not having much luck retrieving some Egg Fu Yung with her chopsticks when her tip-line phone rang.

"Hello. I seen you are looking for information about a lady who died. I seen her that day at Pelican Bay Tower." The line went dead.

"Interesting," Dani said to herself. "Hey, George. Listen to this." She played the recording of the message she had just received.

"Could be something, or someone just playing games," George said.

"Right." Dani called Fred to come into the conference room and asked him to switch duties with her while she got a list of tenants at the Pelican Bay Tower building. She suggested he listen to the message she just recorded.

She reached the management's answering service which gave her an emergency number. Within thirty minutes, the bullpen fax machine came to life, spitting out a list of twenty-eight tenants who either owned or rented a condo in the building. One name popped off the sheet at her: Douglas Bradshaw.

Dani got in touch with Manny and filled him in on the tip message. He told her to ask George to give him a call. He wanted him to canvass the building to see if anyone recognized Julie's picture.

Dani joined George and asked him to call Manny regarding a new assignment. She gave him the tenant list with Douglas Bradshaw's name circled. "The names with an SB next to them are snowbirds who leave before summer starts," Dani reported. "Three condos are empty. The owners rent them, but right now there are no takers. The owners of two other condos are traveling in Europe. That leaves ten units occupied on March twenty-fifth."

"Hey, comrades," Fred said. "I stopped into that building a few days ago. I was in Bradshaw's neighborhood before visiting his doctor about the prescription Dani found. I showed the doorman Julie's picture, but he said he didn't recognize her. I gotta tell you, I had the feeling he was lying."

"What was his name?" George asked.

"Orly, Orly Sanchez."

"Dani, can you make a flier with Julie's picture and the same text the reporter used?" George asked. "I'll check out Mr. Sanchez if he's on duty. If someone in an occupied unit isn't home, I'll slip a flier under the door."

"Give me fifteen minutes," Dani said as she hightailed it back to her desk in the bullpen. She was back in less than thirteen with a folder full of fliers. "I'll take your tip-line shift."

"You are a woman after my heart," George said.

— ●●● —

GEORGE TOOK THE FOLDER and left the department. He drove to Pelican Bay Towers and parked in the section for visitors. Entering the building, he was greeted by the doorman.

"May I help you, sir?" the man asked.

"Yes. Have you seen this woman in this building?" George asked, giving the picture to the man, flashing his badge at the same time.

"No, sir."

"You're sure? Look again, please." George took note of the doorman's name tag: Orly Sanchez.

"I tell you, I never seen this woman."

"Okay. Thanks anyway. Do you mind if I take your picture?" George asked as he snapped a picture of the doorman with his cell phone.

"I guess it's okay," the doorman answered flashing a big say-cheese smile.

"Thanks again. I'm going to check with the people who live here, in case they've seen her. I'll see you on my way out."

George went to the ten units that Dani had indicated were currently occupied. They might be occupied on paper, but nobody answered his knock, not even Bradshaw. George slid a flier under each door and returned to the department. Another dead end, or was it? His gut told him to keep digging. Like Fred, he felt the doorman was lying.

Chapter 34

෨

ROBERTO RETRIEVED his lunch pail, along with the other workers, from the tool shed and went over to the shade of his favorite tree at the construction site to eat his lunch. It afforded a little protection from the stifling heat. He had been on the job almost three weeks and nothing had happened to lead him to Miguel's killer. *Señor Hutch said to be patient. But patient for what?*

He opened his pail eagerly. He had packed his favorite food for lunch, a tortilla with black beans and tomatoes. He took his tortilla out of the pail and froze at the sight of a folded piece of paper. He knew this paper. It was exactly like the one Miguel brought home before he died.

"Miguel's letter," he whispered to himself. "How can it be?" Roberto had forgotten that whatever he said was heard back at the police department.

— • • • —

DANI DRAGGED THE bottom of her frosted hazelnut latte with a squashed, lipstick-smeared straw. The construction sounds usually emanating from Roberto's device now transmitted his whisper.

"Hey, Hutch, come here. Listen to this," Dani said.

Hutch walked over to listen through Dani's headset but heard nothing more than cement trucks churning their cargo. He gave the earphones back to Dani with a shrug.

— • • • —

ROBERTO READ THE LETTER, but no sound came from his lips. His eyes darted back and forth over the words.

Dear Roberto,

I want to enter into a business deal with you. In order to satisfy my end of the business, I need $8000. Raising this money for me will be a good deal for you and your friends. You will receive protection from those who would send you back to Mexico. You see, Roberto, I know you are here illegally. In fact, I know many you work with are also here without, shall we say, papers.

Now, Roberto, don't do anything foolish or I will go to the police. They would send you and your buddies back to Mexico immediately.

When you leave work today, come out of the gate and look down the street for a red truck. Get in the truck, the door will be open. You will then receive further instructions. Do not be stupid like Miguel. He talked to someone other than your friends, who are like your brothers. If you do, you will end up dead like him.
X

— ● ● ● —

ROBERTO LAID CEMENT block the rest of the day. Sweat poured off of him, some from the humidity and the heat, but more from his jangled nerves as he struggled with what to do. In his mind he kept hearing Hutch's words, "Do what Miguel would do."

The man at the gate blew the horn signaling the day's work was done. Men chatted as they put their tools away and headed for the gate. Roberto clutched his lunch pail and stood in line. Leaving the construction site took a little longer today. Juan was handing out fliers with an upcoming holiday schedule. It was finally his turn. "Good work, Roberto. You ever need help, come see me," he said.

Roberto passed through the gate and looked for a red truck as he scuffled along. He saw the truck to his right. The door was ajar. As he was instructed, he opened the door and got in.

"Roberto, my friend," a rather heavy, dark-haired man said. "You received my note, I see."

"Si, señor. But there is no way I can get so much money."

"Roberto, Roberto, all your brothers here are like you. They will be glad to donate to such a cause—*protection*. A cause that will keep them working. If not, I'm afraid I will have to tell what I know about all your brothers to the police. Then you will all be sent back to Mexico. So you see, my friend, I think they will help you."

"Who do I tell them is going to protect them?"

"Say Red Dog will help them, but only those who pay for it."

"I don't think this is possible, señor. What am I to do?" he said, wringing his hands.

"Tell your friends if they pay they will be safe. The cops will not know they are in the country illegally. Those who do not give to the fund, their names will be given to the police."

"I don't think they will believe me."

"Nonsense. You must convince them. My time is short. I need money, and I need it now. Here's a suitcase for the money," Red Dog said. He reached behind his seat and pulled out a small suitcase. "Take it. I will contact you tomorrow after work to see what success you have and give you further instructions. Now leave."

Roberto scrambled out of the truck with the suitcase. He was left standing on the hot pavement all alone when the truck turned the corner out of sight. With a deep sigh, Roberto walked down the street in the opposite direction. I will go home and call Señor Hutch, he thought.

— • • • —

NO ONE WAS IN THE bullpen except Dani. As she listened to Roberto's conversation with Red Dog, she also captured the whole exchange on the recorder. All Dani could hear now were street sounds—cars honking, large trucks passing, occasional chatter as people passed Roberto. It was five-thirty, almost dinner time. She punched in Hutch's cell number.

"Hey, Dani, what's up?"

"Roberto was contacted by a blackmailer who calls himself Red Dog. Sounds like the same MO as Miguel's so-called buddy. I'll play back the tape for you, but I bet Roberto will be giving you a call soon."

Dani played the tape. "What do you think, Hutch?"

"I think we finally have some action."

— • • • —

ROBERTO CLIMBED THE two flights of stairs to his room. The air was hot and dripping with humidity, but he hardly noticed as he flopped down on his bed. "Miguel, I am scared. I am not strong like you," he said, looking over at Miguel's empty bed. He struggled to sit up on the edge of his mattress. He reached for the cell phone Hutch had given him. From the bedside table, he retrieved the piece of paper on which Hutch had written his number and carefully punched them in.

"Agent Hutchinson," Hutch said into the mouthpiece.

"Señor Hutch, I found a letter just like Miguel's in my lunch pail today," Roberto said, in a weary voice.

"What did it say?"

Roberto read the note to the agent. "Señor Hutch, I do what it said. I look for the red truck. It was down the street. I got in the truck and this man, he said to call him Red Dog, gave me a suitcase and said to get the money or I will end up dead like Miguel."

"You are very brave, Roberto. What did you say to Red Dog?" Hutch didn't tell Roberto he had already heard the conversation.

"I told him I would try. He said he would contact me tomorrow with instructions. Is he going to kill me?"

"No, Roberto. He will not kill you. He needs you. I will be with you."

"What do I do?"

"Follow our plan, Roberto. You will continue just as Miguel did."

"But then I end up dead."

"No, you won't. I will protect you. You go to work tomorrow as usual. When you get a chance, after the men are busy laying the cement block, go to the trailer and give the letter to Ortego, just like you and Miguel planned to do. Whatever Ortega says to do, you follow his instructions. Don't forget that we can hear you. We'll be with you every step of the way."

Chapter 35

CATHERINE HAINSWORTH you're driving me nuts, Hutch thought. "So, Mr. Hutchinson, what are you going to do about it? Well, Mr. Hutchinson, I'm going to ask her out." Hutch retrieved Catherine's number he saved on his cell phone.

"Hello," Catherine answered with a lilt to her voice.

"Do you always sound so cheerful, or did I catch you at a particularly good time?" Hutch asked.

"Well, sir, I do like to think of myself as cheerful most of the time. I was arranging a bouquet of roses and daisies from my garden, a favorite ritual of mine when the garden bursts into bloom. I was using the peace of my garden to help me puzzle through a new house design and some other issues. Be that as it may, it's nice to hear from you."

"I'm faced with another lonely meal in an unfamiliar town. I was hoping you might take pity on a stranger and join me for dinner this evening. There's only one stipulation," Hutch said.

"And what is that, pitiful stranger?"

"You have to pick the spot."

"I see. Well, I would be happy to join you for dinner tonight, and I think I can satisfy your stipulation. What time would you like to dine, o'pitiful one?"

"Is seven good for you?"

"Perfect. Do you know where I live?" Catherine asked.

"Hey, lady, finding the address of the woman you're taking to dinner is covered in the first day of training to be a Homeland Security agent. See you at seven."

"I didn't ask her what I should wear," Hutch mumbled. "That wasn't too bright. I'm sure she would have said if the spot is dressy.

On the other hand, everything beachside in Florida is casual. I'll throw a jacket in the backseat, just in case."

His cell phone gave a soft beep indicating an incoming call. The display showed it was Sherry. He hadn't seen her for a few weeks so he decided she could wait until tomorrow. He found himself whistling as he headed for the shower—the call from Sherry forgotten.

— • • • —

AT SEVEN O'CLOCK on the dot Catherine's doorbell rang. "My, you are punctual, Agent Hutchinson. Come on in," Catherine said.

Hutch was caught off guard by how beautiful she looked. He saw her dressed to the nines at the ball, but this little black dress was a whole new twist. "Do you always answer the door looking like that?" he asked.

"Only when I dine with pitiful, lonely, Washington agents. Would you care for a martini before we head out?"

"Now that's the best offer I've had all day."

"Come along then. I put the fixings out in the kitchen. It is such a beautiful evening I thought we could have our drinks outside on the patio."

Hutch felt at home right away in Catherine's kitchen. He fixed the cocktails as she mixed a small bowl of salted cashews with raisins and dried cranberries. He followed her out to the patio, drinks in hand.

"Your home is beautiful, Catherine, and this garden is something else. It must be a full-time job keeping up with it," Hutch said.

"I enjoy puttering around, no time to do much more, but I do have a gardener to cut the lawn and do some of the heavy lifting. Hutch, I'm glad you called. After I met you at the ball, I was hoping we would have a chance to get better acquainted. I'm sure Manny is happy to have you around."

The two new friends chatted amiably on the patio surrounded by a small half circle of lawn edged with robust flowerbeds in brilliant colors of pink, purple, and gold. The air had a slight scent of jasmine coming into bloom. Andrea Bocelli's CD could be heard through the windows, track two, "Besame Mucho."

"I hate to break this up. Actually, I think I could sit here forever, but I'm starving," Hutch said. "Where have you decided to take me tonight?"

"One of my favorite spots, very Florida, very beachie, and they usually have a lively band."

"Sounds like my kind of place. I bet they have great fish too."

"And gator bites," she laughed.

Hutch enjoyed the drive. Catherine acted as co-pilot, directing him to the restaurant. "We're going over the Port Orange causeway to the ocean side. I always get a thrill going over this span of road seeing the Halifax River with sailboats as well as yachts. It's like an appetizer for the eyes," she said, smiling, glancing over at him. "Another few minutes and you'll be able to stifle those hunger pangs."

The Inlet Harbor was busy but not crowded. Because the evening was so balmy, Catherine suggested they eat outside at a high table protected with an umbrella. Their table stood against a weathered railing overlooking the inlet's water. A power boat had just docked and a couple disembarked walking hand-in-hand up the plank, ready for dinner. The sun was low in the sky, gold slowly turning to burnt orange as it sank behind the far shore of the river.

The outdoor dining area ringed a small dance floor in front of a platform for the musicians. The mariachi band was returning from their break and soon their music swelled out over the water. A couple of children jumped up to dance, and several couples joined them.

"Just to let you know, Catherine, I no longer feel pitiful. This is wonderful."

They ordered dinner, both selecting shrimp scampi. Catherine ordered an appetizer of gator bites to be served before their meal. Hutch completed the order with a bottle of Pinot Grigio to complement their fish.

"How do you like living in DC?" Catherine asked.

"It's terrific. I was born in Boston but grew up in Europe. Once in law enforcement, I had some rather special *streets* of LA training."

"Sounds a bit dangerous."

"You have to stay alert, that's for sure. When I was recruited by Homeland Security, I wasn't certain if I'd like what I thought would be a confining, bureaucratic nightmare. The job hasn't turned out that way because most of my work with the Department of Immigration is out in the field."

Their dinner arrived hot and spicy. The waiter poured each a glass of wine, after Hutch accepted a taste, and left the bottle in an ice-filled terracotta wine cooler.

Hutch raised his glass to Catherine's. "Here's to a special lady who has rewarded me with a beautiful evening."

Catherine took a sip of her wine. "It's been a while since I've been able to enjoy this restaurant. Peter, my late husband, and I used to come here quite often." Catherine turned to the water, her mind wandering.

"Hey, where are you? I lost you for a minute."

"I'm just enjoying the evening air, and the company, I might add."

The band started to play a Latin number, and couples scrambled to the floor. "Come on, Miss Cat, I do a mean Merengue."

"I don't know how, Hutch," she said as he pulled her off the high chair.

He took her into his arms. "It's easy. Everything is a count of eight. Just follow me."

Follow him she did. She wasn't sure how because he was swinging her wide every eight counts with one arm extended, then back again, dips, and circles. Finally the music stopped, and he helped her back up on her high chair.

"Agent Hutchinson, it's a good thing the music stopped because I don't think I could take another set of eight steps. You are a real Latin swinger. Wherever did you learn to dance like that?"

"I told you, I do a lot of field work," he said, with a wink. "I will tell *you*, however, I never enjoyed it as much. You're a natural."

The sun set leaving a starry night and the sound of the river lapping softly against the deck. The band continued to play, but their music now seemed distant. The two friends were held in their own world, a new world, at least for tonight.

"I hate like the devil to end this evening," Hutch said. "But duty calls, or something like that. If we stay one more minute, I'll probably have to kiss you."

"Well, Agent Hutchinson," Catherine said, leaning forward and giving him a peck on the cheek, "I guess we'd better get you back to work."

"You're quite a woman, Catherine Hainsworth." Watch out, Agent Hutchinson, he thought. You could get in over your head...very easily!

Chapter 36

❧

THE SULLIVANS' HOME was in an upscale, gated community, a development where everything was provided—the grass cut every week; resident bingo held every Tuesday night in the clubhouse, dancing and parties, two pools, one heated, one not, and a gym outfitted with the latest equipment. Bert liked it that way. He didn't have to feel guilty about not doing chores when he arrived home every night at exactly 5:15 to drink his scotch on the rocks.

"Mom, where are you?" Wendy called out, entering the kitchen through the garage.

"I'm in the study, dear."

"Hi," Wendy said, plopping down on the red-leather recliner. She pulled the lever and stretched out.

"Tell me about your day," Shirley said. "Anything interesting happen you want to share?"

"Actually, yes. I went to see Douglas Bradshaw at his office about a possible summer job."

"Really." Shirley turned to face her daughter, her heart beating a little faster. "Whatever made you think of asking him?"

"Well, he's been on mind ever since that scene at the charity ball last Saturday. He has a big company, and I found myself in town near his building, so I stopped in."

"Did you see Douglas?"

"Yes. When I arrived he wasn't there, out on some appointment, but he came in before I left so I got the opportunity to ask him in person. He was very nice and suggested I go to Human Resources and fill out an application. He said he'd put in a good word for me."

"I see. And is that what you did?"

"'Yep."

"Well, that's nice dear." The thought of Wendy working anywhere near Douglas for the summer threatened to send Shirley into a panic.

"Actually, Mom, that wasn't the real reason I stopped in to see Mr. Bradshaw. I wanted to get a good look at that birthmark I noticed at the ball. You know, I told you about it. I thought it looked just like mine and in the same place."

Shirley felt her heart stop.

"Mom, I really got a good look at him. We have the same eyes, hair, nose, and mouth." Wendy paused, leaning forward and looking straight into her mother's eyes. "Is he my father?" Wendy continued to stare at her mother, holding her breath, waiting for her answer.

"Yes...he's your father, Wendy," Shirley whispered. "I guess the time has come to tell you the truth. Bert and I had decided not to reveal this information to you unless it became impossible to keep secret."

Shirley looked down at her hands, clutching a hanky she had pulled out of her skirt pocket.

"I didn't know I was pregnant until a couple of weeks after Douglas and I separated. I had moved out of the house and within a week went to Mexico for the divorce. It was final immediately."

"When did you meet daddy?"

"I had known Bert for several years because he was our banker. He asked me out to dinner to go over my financial affairs before I went to Mexico. We hit it off. We went out a couple of times when I returned from Juarez. My period was late, but it never occurred to me I could be pregnant. I thought it was just stress."

"Sounds like you two hit it off right away," Wendy said.

"Yes. Bert and I were seeing a lot of each other. I think in some respects, I fell for him on the rebound, but he said that he had loved me from afar for years. I was in trouble, and I told him about the pregnancy. He didn't even hesitate. He asked me to marry him and said he would be delighted to start with a complete family. He loves you, Wendy, as his own. He always has."

"I know he does, Mom. He's a wonderful father." Wendy walked over to her mother, knelt down in front of her, and grasped her hands.

Shirley wrapped her daughter in her arms as she had so many times when Wendy was a little girl. Tears trickled down her face, dropped onto Wendy's face, mingling with Wendy's tears falling on her skirt. "I was afraid to tell you, Wendy," Shirley sobbed, no longer able to keep her emotions bottled up. "As I said, Bert and I decided not to tell you unless it became necessary. Douglas is a very prominent person in the community, and he can be ruthless. I was afraid he might take you away from me if he knew."

"I'm guessing Mr. Bradshaw has no idea I'm his daughter?" Wendy asked, lifting her head and again looking into her mother's tear-stained eyes.

"No, he doesn't."

"Mom, I love Dad, and nothing will ever change that, but I may tell Mr. Bradshaw the truth at some point. Do you have a problem with that?"

"I would rather keep it between us, but you are almost a grown woman, and as such, you are free to follow your heart. Please remember, Wendy, Bert and I love you very much. We did what we thought best under the circumstances."

"I know, Mom."

— ••• —

WENDY STOOD UP, knowing she was going to work for Douglas Bradshaw somehow. She also knew that before the summer was over she would disclose to him that she was his daughter.

Chapter 37

ROBERTO WENT to bed knowing he had to be extra brave the next day, or he would end up dead like Miguel. He slept fitfully. The next morning he stuffed the letter into his right-hand pocket, the listening device in his left pocket. "I'm leaving now," he said. "I hope you can hear me."

About mid-morning, Roberto decided it was time to go to the office trailer. The men around him were busy so he headed for the lavatory. He would have smiled to himself if he had known it was the exact route Miguel had taken, but he wasn't smiling. Fear again took over his body as he approached the back of the trailer. He found the door and entered the small storage room. He opened the room's door and found himself in the hallway leading to Señor Juan's office. He walked to the closed office door and knocked.

"What the heck?" Ortego yanked open the door and looked at Roberto. "What do you think you're doing here? Get your ass back to work."

"I will, señor, but you say to come to you if I need help. I need your help." Roberto pulled out the crumpled letter and handed it to Juan.

The blood drained from Juan's face as he read the letter. He looked up at Roberto through squinting eyes, a hateful look on his face. "Who gave you this?" he asked.

"I found it in my lunch pail yesterday. I don't know what to do, so I finished work and then looked for the red truck. It was there, down the street. The man inside, I never see before. He gave me a suitcase. He said to put money in it from my brothers and that he would contact me today with further instructions. Señor, I never talk to no one. I no have brothers who would give me money. I'm scared."

"Roberto, you did the right thing. Did you ask him for his name?"

"Si, señor. He said to call him Red Dog."

"If this Red Dog contacts you again, let me know. Talk to no one. Is that clear? No one."

"Si. No one."

"Now get your ass back to work. Shut the door on your way out."

—•••—

THE SECOND JUAN heard the trailer door close, he was on the phone.

"We have another problem," Juan said, pacing around his cramped office. Juan heard a snarl from the other end.

"Now what?"

"Another blackmail note. This time a fellow named Roberto found it. This blackmailer wants $8,000. He told Roberto to call him Red Dog. How do you want to handle it?"

"We'll handle it the same way. If this Roberto person comes back to you with the suitcase, fill it with phony bills. Tell him to follow the instructions he was given and scram. Scram like in get away as fast as he can. The last time that stupid guy hung around and he got caught when we took out the blackmailer. This time we'll *really* make an example of the extortionist—not only will he be dead but his body will not be a pretty sight. No one will try this shit again, I guarantee you."

Juan hung up the phone—he did not divulge the fact that he had told Miguel to *hang around*.

—•••—

BACK AT THE DEPARTMENT, Dani's equipment translated the clicks of the number Juan dialed. She entered the information into her computer searching for the name linked to the telephone number. Seconds later the answer displayed on her screen.

—•••—

AT THE END OF WORK, Roberto again walked through the gate. He didn't see the red truck so he started back to his room. He advanced only a block when a man came up beside him and told him to keep walking. He recognized the voice. It was Red Dog.

"When will you have the money for me, Roberto?"

"Señor, it is such a large amount. It will take some time."

"I told you I don't have time because of your stupid brother Miguel. I will give you until Friday. Payday. Put the money in the suitcase I gave you. Take the bus to the Port Orange beach access road at the end of Dunlawton Avenue. At exactly nine o'clock walk along the beach to the pier. It will be dark by then. Go up under the pier. You will see a green barrel with two yellow stripes. Put the suitcase in the barrel. Then walk back to the beach access road and go home. Do you understand, Roberto?"

"Si."

Red Dog left Roberto's side. When Roberto turned to look for him, there was no one. He had evaporated.

Chapter 38

⁀

MANNY WAS IRRITATED. He couldn't stop thinking about Catherine. He wanted to see her again. He did have some questions for her regarding the relationship between Stone and Bradshaw. "What the heck. I'll give her a call."

"Hi, Cat. I'm glad I caught you at home," Manny said, cradling the phone as his heart did a little flutter dance at the sound of her voice.

"Manny, how nice to hear from you. Does this call mean we can have another coffee?"

"It sure does. I have to stop at the VA hospital to pick up a report so I'll be in your neck of the woods in about an hour. Mind if I stop by? Couple of things I'd like to fly by you regarding the Stone case."

"How exciting. Of course, come on over. I'll start a batch of chocolate-chip cookies."

"Now, Cat, I'm watching my waistline so be careful with this old man."

"I've told you before, stop calling yourself that," she chided. "See you soon."

The captain closed the top on his cell phone catching himself smiling.

— • • • —

MANNY ARRIVED AT Catherine's house and rang the doorbell. He had been to the house before when her husband died. *You can't call this a house,* he thought. *It's more like a mansion.* Peaches stood patiently by his side, her tail wagging slowly.

"Manny, come in," Catherine said, opening the door. "You too, Peaches."

In his usual fashion, Manny lifted her hand and gave it a quick kiss. Peaches nudged Manny out of the way so she could get in on the action. Catherine bent down and gave the dog a warm welcome, receiving a slurp on the ear in return. The aroma of chocolate-chip cookies lured Manny to follow her into the kitchen. "Hope you don't mind my barging in like this," he said.

"Heavens, no. I needed a break from the house schematics I'm working on. They're not due for another week, but I always like to submit them early. Baking seems to release my creative juices."

"You push yourself too hard, slow down a little."

"With Russell ramping up to start the tower project, I want to make sure everything is perfect. The coffee just finished perking and your cream and sugar are on the table." A china plate full of cookies was also on the counter.

"Catherine Hainsworth, how did you bake these magnificent cookies so quickly?" Manny groaned taking a bite. *She looks cute in those jeans and white shirt,* Manny thought. *I'm glad I called.*

"Here's your coffee, Captain," Catherine said, handing Manny a mug of strong, piping hot liquid. "Just like you like it." Catherine poured herself a cup, added a thimble of cream, and sat down opposite Manny. "Now, for heaven's sake, give. What's happening?"

"Well, first let me tell you what an interesting piece of information I received when I stopped at the VA hospital on my way here. After I parked my car, Peaches and I got out and started up the long walkway to the entrance."

"I know the building. The grounds are beautiful."

"There were several vets out in the side yard, some in wheelchairs, others chatting at a table. All of a sudden Peaches started barking and took off like a shot across the lawn. She puts on the brakes in front of this guy on crutches." Manny paused, taking a bite of a cookie. "The man leaned over and gave her a couple of pats. Next thing you know he falls down and the two of them are rolling on the ground, hugging and kissing."

"Good heavens, what was going on?" Catherine asked.

"Well, you can imagine my surprise, and at first I thought the guy probably hurt himself. So I hustled over to help him up and tell him I was sorry Peaches caused him to fall. You'll never guess what he told me."

"What? Go on," Catherine said, scratching Peaches behind her ear.

"This guy said he was in Baghdad on a search and rescue mission with his dog, Patty, when he was seriously wounded. Both he and Patty were transported back to the States where he had to go through a series of operations."

"But how did she end up as a stray?"

"Well, he couldn't take care of a dog so she was assigned to a new handler. A military liaison called him over three months later to let him know that Patty was lost. They surmised she went looking for him, her original handler. We discussed when she was lost and narrowed it down to within a few weeks of when Peaches and I found each other at the Farmers' Market. So Peaches is really Patty. Can you beat that?"

Peaches came over to Manny when she heard her name. She put her muzzle on his lap and looked up adoringly at her master. He gently stroked the fur on her nose.

"Now, military dogs always have a microchip implanted," Manny said. "When Sam, our ME, examined her, he couldn't find one. He did see a small scar. We think someone had it removed so they could keep her without being detected."

"But, Manny, does this mean the veteran wants her back?"

"No, no. He made it clear he couldn't be happier that she found a good home and a new career with a police department. He did ask if she could visit him from time to time."

"What an errand you had, my friend. I wonder what clever actions she has stored in that head of hers. I guess you two will have to visit her former handler again for a debriefing."

"Good idea," Manny said, pouring more coffee into their cups. "He did give me the command to attack in case I need it. Speaking of debriefing, I called earlier to ask what you know of the relationship between Stone and Bradshaw."

"I know they don't like each other very much, and they're fierce competitors. Then they had that fight at the ball. Usually they're civil so it was probably the liquor talking."

"Anything else you can think of? Anything you've seen or heard?"

"No." Catherine pondered. "There is one thing, but it probably isn't relevant."

"You never know, Cat. What is it?"

"Well, I saw Wendy the other day at the bead shop. She had just been over at Douglas' company and spoke to him about a possible summer job.

"I've heard of their program to hire kids during the summer," Manny said. "It's a great idea."

"While she was with Douglas, she commented to him about the bracelet he was wearing. How handsome it was, I believe were her words. He told her it was one of his prized possessions because his late mother had given it to him."

"What's strange about a gift from his mother?"

"I'll tell you. At the ball, when Douglas asked to dance with me, I, too, remarked on the bracelet he was wearing that night. He told me Tracy, his second wife, gave it to him. Well, Wendy told me that she noticed the bracelet because it looked like one Julie had fashioned for Russell. She was sure one of the chains I was holding was of the same design."

"Go on," Manny said, taking a sip of coffee and helping himself to another cookie.

"Well, after Wendy left, I remarked about the chain to Tillie. She said it was a new design from her distributor. She'd only carried it for a few months and was thrilled because it had turned out to be a popular item. In fact, Julie was one of the first to buy it and bought two lengths.

"What are you getting at, Cat?" Manny asked, putting his cup down on the table.

"This is the same bracelet I mentioned to Russell, but he said he wasn't sure, maybe she had given him one but it wasn't something he would wear. Manny, do you suppose Julie made a bracelet for Douglas? I mean, why would he tell Wendy and me a different story. On the other hand, under what circumstances would Julie give Douglas a bracelet?"

"Well, it could tie her to Douglas. There could also be some innocent explanation and for some reason Douglas wanted to hide it. For that matter, maybe Julie was also hiding something. I hate to eat and run, so to speak, but I have a meeting with my team, so I'd better get going."

"Oh, how disappointing. I was hoping you would have another cup of coffee. Tell you what, I'll package up the rest of these cookies for your officers so I won't be tempted to eat them myself. I'm the one with a waistline problem."

"Cat, believe me, there is nothing wrong with your figure. The team is going to think I've gone soft when I show up with cookies, but I'll risk it." Manny gave her a peck on the cheek and then he and Peaches were gone.

— •••—

MANNY AND PEACHES entered the bullpen with the bag of cookies from Catherine. He opened the bag a little and passed it under the team's noses.

"Hey, boss, have you gone soft on us?" George said, as he helped himself to a cookie.

Peaches sat at attention on her pillow hoping Manny would drop a piece her way. No one in the bullpen was allowed to give Peaches a treat. A pat on the head, yes. Treats, no.

"I had a few things to ask Cat, smart ass, and she very nicely offered to give me the cookies for you guys. Any more remarks and I'll take them back," Manny said, dropping a large bite into the very patient dog's drooling mouth.

"Okay, you knuckleheads, let's get to work," Manny said, moving to the case board. "I think we're getting a convergence of information pointing to Bradshaw and Stone."

"Did you get some new information from Catherine?" George asked.

"Yes, but I'm not sure how it fits together. We have a gold bracelet on Bradshaw's wrist that is identical to one Julie made for Russell. Stone remembers it, but says he never wore it. How a bracelet got into Bradshaw's possession we don't know, and we don't know if Julie made two. Also, the chain of the bracelets is an exclusive item at the House of Beads for only the last couple of months. Bradshaw evidently told Wendy Sullivan that his mother gave it to him. He told Catherine his second wife gave it to him. Now, let's suppose Julie did give Bradshaw the bracelet, and he lied about how he got it. Why would she give him such a personal gift? Could it be a neglected wife getting back at her husband? If so, were they having an affair?"

"But, if they were having an affair, something that Douglas would surely relish, why would he kill her?" Fred said. "Hell, maybe he was hoping she would divorce Stone and marry him."

"Good question," Manny said. "Bradshaw and Stone were on the list for the drug digitoxin."

"By the way, I did ask Stone about his prescription. He then remembered it, but he said he never took it. Said he forgot about it," Fred added.

"How convenient," Manny said. "Julie was seen by our anonymous caller going into Bradshaw's building. Stone can't find the bar in St. Augustine to corroborate his alibi. The blackmail letter tied to construction sites with illegal labor could, I say could, also lead to both of them."

"Also, we don't know where the three of them — Julie, Russell, and Bradshaw — were from noon to four o'clock on the day she died," Fred said. "Stone or Bradshaw could have met her for a drink. The doorman at Bradshaw's condo said he didn't recognize her picture, but he could have been lying. Plus the tipster didn't give us a time of day she was there. She also could have been visiting someone else about some charity work."

Manny walked back to his desk, popping the last cookie in his, then reached for his pack of Nicorette gum.

"Don't forget the possibility," Dani said, "that if Julie learned who wrote the blackmail letter, that knowledge could have led to her death."

Chapter 39

❧

TWO MONTHS had passed since Julie's death. Russell still could not bring himself to clean out her things. Her clothes and jewelry were bitter-sweet reminders of his wife. Annie, his housekeeper, kept urging him to remove Julie's clothes. "It will help you to heal," she told him.

"I don't want to heal," he muttered. "I want to feel her with me, but I know Annie's right."

The only person he trusted with such a task was Catherine Hainsworth. She would know what to do with all of Julie's beautiful clothes. Russell reluctantly picked up the phone and dialed the code Julie had stored for her friend.

The phone rang several times, and Russell was about to hang up.

"Hello," Catherine said breathlessly.

"Hi, Catherine. Russell, here. I'm calling to ask a favor of you."

"Name it. You know I'll only be too glad to help."

"It has to do with Julie's things, her clothes, mainly. Annie thinks I should start sorting through her closet, but I can't bring myself to enter her dressing room. Catherine, I know it's a lot to ask, but could you go through them for me?"

"I'd be glad to. When would you like me to start?"

"Anytime, at your convenience, even today. If I'm not here, Annie will show you Julie's dressing room and closets."

A couple of hours later, Catherine parked her car in Stone's driveway and rang the front doorbell. Annie quickly answered the chime.

"Hello, Mrs. Hainsworth. Mr. Stone said you would be by. Come with me, and I'll show you where Mrs. Stone kept her things. I've put some plastic bins out for you," Annie said, as she went up the stairs ahead of Catherine. "Mr. Stone said you might want to give some of her designer clothes to the Chamber of Commerce charity auction next month."

"Yes, that's right, Annie, and thank you for the bins. I'll sort through everything, and we'll see what I end up with."

Catherine entered Julie's dressing room and was taken aback for a few seconds with the fragrance of Julie's perfume still in the air. The room was typical of Julie, very organized.

"This shouldn't take me long," Catherine said to herself. She saw that Julie had her designer dresses, evening clothes, shoes and bags grouped on one side.

It took less than an hour to separate the items out for the upcoming auction. Catherine folded the gowns and carefully placed them in the bins marking the containers "Auction" with a chunky black pen. The built-in shelves and drawers held scarves, more handbags, and lingerie. Three hours later, Catherine was glad she was almost finished. It had been more of an emotional roller coaster than she had anticipated.

She sat down on the floor and pulled open the bottom and last drawer in the dressing room. She lifted out two silky nightgowns, shaking them out so she could fold them on the carpet. When she shook the second gown, a lavender envelope fell into her lap. It was not sealed and had no writing on the outside. Catherine opened the envelope and found a letter, four pages long. Her hands began to shake as she read the contents, written in Julie's hand on her lavender scented stationery.

March 25
My dearest Russell,

I don't have the courage to tell you in person what I've done. I'm not even sure I have the courage to give you this letter. But I must. I have betrayed your trust and your love. I only hope you can find it in your heart to forgive me.

What I have to confess started about three months ago, but long before that, actually about four years ago—you spent more and more time at the office. You were working late into the night and most weekends. I tried to keep busy, taking courses at the university and doing charity work, but I wanted to spend this time with you. I even thought maybe a baby would be the answer. But then we just never seemed to be able to conceive.

One day after a charity meeting, I stopped at the country club dining room to get a bite to eat. You weren't going to be home for dinner. Douglas Bradshaw was having a drink at the bar. He saw me and came over to my table. He asked if he could buy me a drink, as it appeared we were both alone. I told him, yes.

We must have chatted for two hours. I have to say I enjoyed his attention. He told me it was a shame such a beautiful woman was having dinner alone. He asked me if I'd stay and have dinner with him. I did. He said he'd enjoy having coffee with me sometime because he'd like my advice about a woman he was dating. We met for coffee a couple of times. One day he asked me to meet this woman he was talking about, and could I come to his home. I said I'd be glad to.

Well, my dearest Russell, I went and it was a mistake. I don't think there ever was a woman. Looking back, I think he used it as a ruse to get me there. He said she had called and was not coming; that she didn't want to see him again. So, he was very sad. I was lonely, and I did a really terrible thing. I must tell you what happened because if I don't tell you all, then I can't really ask you for forgiveness.

We had a couple of drinks. The next thing I knew he was kissing me. Russell, it had been so long since we had really kissed, since we had made love passionately, that I was lost in the heat. I know now, it wasn't Douglas I was making love with. It was you. Oh, how can I make you understand this?

Meeting him at his home became a regular thing every Tuesday and Thursday afternoon. We'd talk, have a couple of drinks, and make love. It seemed so idyllic, so dreamlike. I made excuses that you didn't care what I was doing so I could live with myself. I created a gold chain bracelet and gave it to him so he could feel I was close to him wherever he was. He wore it every day after, professing his love for me. He asked me to divorce you so we could be together always.

That was when I realized that it was you I love, my dear. I knew you two were bitter competitors and realized how much my being with Douglas would hurt you.

Last week while I was at his home, I happened to see a note to a local steel company. I wouldn't have read it, except I caught the words: "enclosed is the $10,000 I promised you to bring your bid for the tower project under Stone's." I was horrified because I had given Douglas a copy of your draft proposal. I don't know what I was thinking. He asked me one day if I had seen anything like an old draft so he could use the same format. He said that the board was going to give him the guidelines but hadn't as yet. Oh, Russell, above all else, this was the worst of my betrayals.

Then I became frightened because last week I saw a letter on his desk blackmailing an illegal immigrant. I didn't tell Douglas I saw the letter but if it is still somewhere on his desk today I'm going to take it. I believe what he is doing is bad. I'll bring the letter to you, because you will know what to do with it.

I'm going to try to make it right between us, Russell. I'm going to see Douglas this afternoon and ask him to return your draft proposal to me. He's probably already used it, but I'll ask anyway. I'm also going to tell him I can't see him anymore, that I truly love my husband, and our affair was a horrible mistake.

When I see you this evening, I hope I have the courage to give you this letter. If you throw me out of the house, I will understand. You are everything good in my life. I hope you have it in your heart to forgive me. I know I have damaged our marriage and your trust in me. I pray I haven't destroyed your love completely. I beg you for a chance to help heal the wounds somehow.

With all my love,
Your wife, Julie

Catherine put the letter down. Her whole body shook with the import of her finding. The date on Julie's letter was the day she died. Douglas must have been the last to see her.

With quivering fingers, Catherine called Russell at work.

"Russell, this is Catherine. I'm at your house. Please come home as soon as possible."

"Catherine, what's the matter? You sound frightened."

"I am frightened, Russell. Please hurry. I'll wait for you in Julie's dressing room."

"I'll be there in ten minutes."

In a daze, Catherine sat down on the small velvet vanity chair, the note still in her hand, waiting for Russell. She thought about calling Manny but decided not to. Russell should be the one to notify the captain.

Catherine went over what she had just read. She couldn't even imagine how Russell would take it. There were so many things to absorb—Julie's infidelity, Julie's death apparently at the hand of Douglas, the fact that she had given Douglas a draft of Russell's bid for the tower project. "Thank God Stone & Associates was awarded the contract," she whispered.

Catherine heard the front door close and Russell running up the stairs. She heard him enter the bedroom, and then he was kneeling in front of her. "Catherine, what is it? You look ill."

"I found this letter in Julie's drawer. It wasn't sealed. There was no writing on the envelope, so I opened it. Forgive me, Russell, I read it." Catherine handed the scented lavender pages to Russell.

He began to read the letter. After reading the first few lines, he glanced up at Catherine and then walked into the bedroom and sat down on the lavender satin bedspread. Catherine followed and sat on a dainty bedroom chair facing the bed. Russell finished reading the letter, his arms dropping to his side. His right hand gripped the lavender paper as if it was the last piece of Julie and he couldn't let go. Tears started to stream down his face as Annie entered the room.

"Mr. Stone, what are you doing home so early—"

"Annie, please get Captain Salinas on the phone for me. His number is in my address book on my desk."

"Yes, Mr. Stone. Right away." Annie, frightened at seeing her boss in tears, hurried down to his desk to get the telephone number. It was the second time she had seen Mr. Stone in such a state and crying. The last time was a couple of months ago when his wife died and now. She found the phone number just as Mr. Stone had indicated and put the call through to the captain.

"Captain Salinas here."

"Hello, Captain. This is Annie, Mr. Stone's housekeeper. He asked me to call you. Can you hold for a minute while I give him the phone?"

"Of course, Annie."

"Hello, Manny. Catherine Hainsworth just found a letter Julie wrote. I think you'd better come over right away to read it for yourself."

— • • • —

MANNY, ALARMED BY the sound of Russell's distraught voice, left the department immediately. Peaches barely got in the car in time before her master squealed away from the curb.

Manny arrived at Stone's home, snapped the leash onto Peaches' collar and hustled to the front door.

"Hello, I'm Captain Salinas," Manny said, identifying himself to the lady who opened the door. "You must be Annie."

"Oh, yes, Captain," Annie said, wiping her hands on her apron. "Come with me. I'll show you to the library. I know Mr. Stone is anxious to speak with you. Everything has been topsy-turvy since Mrs. Stone died." She looked at Peaches but did not touch her.

"I'm sure you're a big help to him, Annie."

"I try, sir. Mrs. Hainsworth is here as well. She's been here all day going through Mrs. Stone's things."

"Were you helping her, Annie?"

"A little, but mainly showing her which closets were Mrs. Stone's. Her death is just so terrible," Annie said, breaking into tears. "Excuse me, sir. I miss her so much. She was wonderful to me." Annie dried her eyes and motioned the officer to enter the library. Manny signaled Peaches to lie down by the door. He found Russell sitting on the couch, his head in his hands.

When Manny entered, both Russell and Catherine stood up. "Manny, thank you for coming over," Russell said, extending his hand.

"Catherine," Manny nodded. "I came as quick as the traffic would allow. Now, what's this about a letter, Russell?"

"I asked Catherine to come over to help me select which of Julie's clothing should go to the charity auction and wherever else she might suggest. Catherine, please tell him how you found the letter."

"I was going through the drawers in Julie's dressing room," Catherine said. "I had almost finished with only one bottom drawer left. The drawer contained some lingerie. I picked up a nightgown and a lavender envelope fell out. It was not addressed. The flap was not even tucked in, so I opened it."

"Here's the letter that was inside," Russell said.

Manny took the letter, transferring the scent of lavender to his fingers. After reading the first few words, he sat down on the couch. He closed his eyes a second and then continued to read.

"I'm sorry, Russell. Did this come as a surprise to you? Did you know your wife was having an affair with Douglas Bradshaw?" Manny asked.

"No, I had no idea. I told you she wanted me to spend more time with her. I knew she was lonely. I didn't realize how bad it was for her."

"Well, this letter gives real teeth to the investigation," Manny said. "I have to ask you both not to speak of the letter to anyone. That goes for Mr. Malone, your lawyer, too. If he has a problem with that, I'll explain it to him personally. I have to take the letter with me as evidence. You'll get it back after the case is closed. Did you find anything else, Catherine?"

"No. That was it. The drawer was the last place I was sorting through."

"Good. I'm heading back to the department. Russell, and you too, Catherine, let me say again, do not speak of this to anyone. If Bradshaw happens to contact either of you, let me know immediately."

"I doubt he will," Russell said. "We really have nothing to do with each other, especially after I won the contract. He has always held some kind of grudge against me, ever since we were kids. He accused me of feeling superior. *Holier than thou* was a familiar phrase. No matter what happened over the years, we seemed to be at loggerheads, in competition for the same thing."

"Well, Russell looks like he tried to win your wife away from you. When she said no, he killed her."

Chapter 40

&

MANNY LEFT RUSSELL'S house, his brain trying to piece together the information in Julie's letter and all its implications. The letter was the keystone of the puzzle, of that he was sure. His car somehow arrived at the department. He pulled into his parking spot and slammed on the brakes. Peaches fell to the floor, landing with all four paws in the air.

"Sorry, girl," Manny said, pulling the keys from the ignition. Peaches righted herself, and they both jumped out the driver's side door.

Manny burst into the bullpen and immediately went to the copy machine. He made a copy of Julie's letter for each team member plus one for Hutch. Peaches seemed to understand that something big was happening so she hunkered down on her pillow immediately. She didn't close her eyes, however, but shifted her gaze from one to another as all seemed to speak at once.

"Where's Hutch?" Manny asked as he handed out the copies.

"He's right here," Hutch said, entering the bullpen. He walked quickly to the desk assigned to him while he was working the case.

Manny handed him a copy of the letter. "Read this, everyone, and then we'll set up our sting." Manny dialed Sam. "Sam, can you join us right away? ...Thanks."

"How do you like that? Julie fingered her killer from the grave," Fred said.

"It looks that way, but I want to find the drug in Bradshaw's possession. And we still haven't placed Julie *in* his penthouse on the day she died." Manny strode over to the case board. "First, I want a tail on Bradshaw immediately. George, go set that up and get back here."

"Second, Fred, get search warrants for Bradshaw's office building, his penthouse, and the construction site where Miguel worked. Go get the paperwork started now and then come back here."

"Wait a minute, Manny," Hutch interrupted. "I have an operation going at the Beach Street construction site. Let me take care of the information there so we don't compromise each other's mission. My case, as you well know, also points to Bradshaw. It's going down Friday, tomorrow night. I suggest we coordinate searching Bradshaw's penthouse Saturday morning. I already have a warrant on the construction site from ICE."

"Okay, but let's not get in each other's way. I don't want you stepping on my team's toes," Manny said, in a gruff voice.

"Hey, illegal immigration and murder of illegals is a federal offense, don't forget," Hutch countered.

It looked like a tennis match as the team glanced from Manny to Hutch and back. Something was bothering the two officers, causing them to spar with each other.

Hearing raised voices, George re-entered the bullpen. "Manny, the Bradshaw tail is on her way."

"Who'd you put on him?" Manny asked.

"Lorna. She's a crackerjack when it comes to surveillance. She also said it was personal. She liked Julie Stone's history—her coming to the U.S. as a young girl, making a life for herself. She evidently followed Julie's charity efforts in the community after she married Stone."

It was now close to five o'clock. The warrants would not be ready until mid-morning tomorrow because the Judge is down on the Florida Keys. He was alerted to the urgency of the situation and is on his way back.

"The best thing we can do now is gear up for a raid Saturday morning." Manny glanced at Hutch then turned his attention to his team. "George, you prep a couple of men for Bradshaw's office in case he decides to go there. Fred, you and I will take the penthouse. Hutch, I would appreciate it if you keep us posted every step of the way on your operation."

"Okay, and if I wrap up the construction site in time, I'll join you at the penthouse," Hutch said.

"We'll convene late tomorrow night," Manny said, "to go over our strategy and any last minute changes, ready to suit up Saturday morning. George, let us know if Lorna suspects Bradshaw is getting ready to bolt. If he looks suspicious, we'll have to move on him immediately."

Next, Hutch took center stage and briefed the bullpen on Roberto's instructions. Hutch then notified his team at the Holiday Inn that the operation was going down tomorrow tonight. Two men, Navy SEALs, had driven to Daytona Beach from Homeland Security's Miami field office the day before. Plans for the takedown were in place.

Chapter 41

WITH THE MISSION SET, Hutch saw a perfect opening to spend some time with Catherine. Hopefully, she will understand a last minute invitation. He dialed her number feeling relieved and excited when she answered the phone.

"Hi, Catherine, it's Hutch. I'm sorry this is at the last minute, but we wrapped things up at the department earlier than I thought. I would very much like to take you to dinner."

"I'd love to have dinner with you."

"I can be at your house within the hour, say six-thirty. Is that too soon?"

"You just come along. I'll be ready."

Hutch was euphoric. "Calm down, mister," he told himself as he raced to the shower. While dressing, he broke into song, "Come fly with me, let's fly, let's fly away." When he couldn't come up with the words, he just hummed the tune.

Forty-five minutes later, he was on her doorstep ringing the bell. The door opened and there she stood, framed in the doorway wearing a white halter-dress made of some sort of soft drapey material revealing the lovely curves of her body. "Catherine, you take my breath away."

As she moved back from the door, he stepped into the house, closing the door with his foot. Looking down into her soft accepting eyes, he lowered his lips to hers tenderly tasting the sweetness he had been dreaming of. Catherine gently leaned forward into him, receiving his kiss, returning the warmth of his embrace.

Still holding her in his arms, he pulled back enough to speak. "I've missed you, Catherine Hainsworth. It's only been a few days since I saw you, but it feels like weeks." Releasing her, but only so far, he slid his hands down her arms and took her hands in his. "Forgive me for being so bold, but seeing you in the doorway—"

"Sometimes you talk too much, Agent Hutchinson. I couldn't be happier with your greeting. Now, come along and fix us a martini. I think we could both use a cold drink."

"Sounds good," he said, slowly regaining his composer. "Where would you like to have dinner?"

"Have you been to the River View in New Smyrna?" Catherine asked, as she put out the glasses.

"No, I haven't." Hutch mixed the drinks, getting the ice from the refrigerator's ice maker. He pulled out the martini pitcher, remembering where it was from the first time he fixed their cocktails in her kitchen.

"I really don't have anything to nibble on except these pepper strips and some tomato-basil hummus. I hope you like hummus."

"Lady, anything you serve me will be happily received. Do you want to sit out on the patio?"

"No. I have another place to show you. If you'll please bring my drink, I'll carry the peppers and dip. Come along. Let's see what kind of shape you're in. Do you think you can climb two flights of stairs?"

"Hey, you're talking to someone who almost, I say almost, finished the Boston Marathon a few years ago."

They walked side-by-side up the first flight of a wide spiral staircase and then up another flight. When they came to the top of the stairs, he was surprised to see a huge open space. The walls were a soft cream with matching Berber carpet. One wall was all windows, about thirty feet long. Palladium windows highlighted the two end walls, each reaching to the peak of the vaulted ceiling. The long inside wall was filled with framed pictures of room interiors, office buildings, and homes.

There were four large easels grouped to his left. Each had a drawing pinned in the center with swatches of fabric tacked around the edges. Across from the easels was a huge rectangular counter with drawers making up the base. Some drawers were only a few inches high but long enough to hold architect's blue-line schematics.

Hutch handed Catherine her drink and walked to look out the wall of windows. He looked down on a panoramic view of her garden. The focal point was a shapely Grecian lady holding an urn.

From the urn flowed water into two cascading bowls. Shaking his head a little, he turned from the beauty of the garden to see what was on the countertop.

"These are architect's blueprints for a very large house," Hutch said, puzzled. "Did you do these designs?"

"Yes. There are more on the two drafting tables behind you," Catherine said, smiling.

He turned to follow her gaze. Seeing drawings for another big home on one and what appeared to be the beginning of a restaurant dining room on the other. "Who are you, Frank Lloyd Wright's protégé?"

"I wish," she said, laughing. "I work for Stone & Associates. When my husband died, I was doing some freelance work for Russell. Then he became inundated with jobs and asked if I could work more hours. I agreed but only if I could do the majority of the designing from home, in my studio."

"I have new respect for Mr. Stone," Hutch said. "He saw brilliance and knew to grab it before someone else did. Catherine, your designs are wonderful, and this space is perfect."

"Thank you, but I'm afraid it's taking over my very existence. Of course, I love designing and especially the challenges of bringing the architectural plans to life. However, it doesn't leave much time for anything else."

Catherine led him over to the client-meeting corner. The area was delineated with a large oriental rug, predominately red in color. Four small, but comfortable, upholstered chairs sat around a glass-top coffee table. Carefully placed in the center of the glass sat a vase filled with fresh flowers—lilies, roses, and spikes of blue delphiniums. The fragrance of the flowers permeated the air.

Hutch sat down and took a sip of his drink. He was not a man known for his lack of words, but looking at Catherine, her work, and her studio, he didn't know what to say. He finally found his voice. "You are quite a woman, Ms. Hainsworth."

They sat quietly, sipping their drinks, talking about local and world events. He suddenly realized the radio was playing the song he had been singing earlier, *Come Fly with Me*. *Hutch, my friend, you are definitely in trouble.*

"Now, Agent Hutchinson, just because I dragged you up two flights of stairs, don't think you aren't going to march right back down and take me to dinner. All we did was work up an appetite."

"Then I suggest we take those stairs and get some nourishment, Miss Catherine." She had suggested the last time they had dinner that he could call her by her nickname, Cat. Somehow, seeing this sophisticated woman in her professional workspace, Hutch felt he must call her Catherine. He picked up her empty glass as she retrieved the now empty pepper dish. Standing at the top of the stairs, he took another look at her studio. He didn't want to forget any of it.

— ••• —

THE REST OF THE EVENING flew by much too fast for both of them. They walked arm-in-arm to the car. From the car to the restaurant, they held hands. Waiting for their dinner, he held her hand across the table. Hutch wasn't aware of the beautiful river outside the window. Catherine was all he could see. The sun sank below the shoreline on the far side of the river. As darkness fell, candlelight enveloped the two, cloaking them in a world of their own.

Sipping cappuccino coffee laced with Amaretto, Hutch paid the bill for dinner and the waiter returned with the receipt back. "Thank you, señor. Have a nice evening."

The spell broke. Hearing the waiter say *señor*, Hutch immediately thought of tomorrow's mission, crowding out the magic of the evening. "Well, my lady, I'd better get you home," he said.

Hutch put his arm around her as they returned to the car and then again as he walked her to her door. "Thank you for showing me your studio."

"You're welcome. I wanted you to have a peek into my world. I'm glad you liked it. Will I see you again?"

He took her in his arms and kissed her deeply. Breaking his lips away from hers, he held her close. "See me again? All of Florida's manatees and alligators couldn't keep me away."

— ••• —

CATHERINE ENTERED HER home. She turned and waved goodbye to Hutch. Then she shut the door and leaned back against it. What a beautiful evening, she thought.

Catherine wasn't sure what happened at the restaurant when the waiter gave Hutch the bill, but she knew the balance of the evening was shared with something else. *Probably his work.*

Chapter 42

❧

THERE WAS NOTHING unusual about Friday morning in the Sullivan home. Bert had already left for work, and Shirley was enjoying her second cup of coffee. The telephone rang just as she was about to call Wendy to come down and join her for breakfast.

"Hello," Shirley said.

"Hi. My name is Ann Bell, Human Resources at Bradshaw Architects and Building Corporation. Is Wendy Sullivan there?"

"Just a minute and I'll get her." Shirley called to Wendy, letting her know Ann Bell was on the phone. *Now what's going on,* she muttered.

Wendy came down to the kitchen and picked up the receiver. "Hi, Mrs. Bell. What's up? I hope it's regarding a job assignment," she said, crossing her fingers.

"Hello, Wendy. Sorry for the early morning call. Yes, it is regarding an assignment. I wondered if you could work for Mr. Bradshaw for a few days. Monique's mother needs her help. Can you take a temporary job? If you have school or other plans, I can call an agency. Mr. Bradshaw asked me to try you first."

"I have a couple of classes this morning, but that's it until Monday afternoon. I'd love to take the assignment. If I get there by eleven, is that okay?" Wendy asked.

"That would be great. Just go on up to the office and sit at Monique's desk. She said she'd leave a note of instructions and her cell phone number in case you got stuck."

—•••—

WENDY LEFT SCHOOL quickly after her last class and made a beeline to Bradshaw's office. Douglas was talking on the telephone when she arrived, so she just gave him a wave through the open door to let him know she was on duty. She found Monique's instructions. It appeared Wendy just had to answer the telephone.

Tapping a pencil on the calendar desk pad, Wendy looked around to see what she might do, other than just sit. After all, she did want to make a good impression. She went over to the large bank of plants, some as tall as a small tree. Taller than her five-foot-two, that's for sure, she thought. The fake leaves were a little dusty. Looking in a cabinet nearby, she found a bottle with a label, "Keep your plant leaves shiny." She could at least use this on the ones she could reach. Wendy read the directions and began wiping the leaves of one of the bushes.

— • • • —

A MAN CAME RUSHING through the door and burst into Douglas' office. "Douglas, we need to talk. Now!" he yelled.

"Juan, what's the matter?" Douglas said, disconnecting his call and giving his office door a shove; however, the door failed to shut completely, remaining slightly ajar.

"Someone squealed to the Feds that they should check our labor force. Douglas, we're up to our necks with illegals."

"Calm down, Juan. How do you know the Feds are investigating?"

"Because I had a strange call. It was a man, and he spoke in a whisper. He said to expect a visit from the law. That they would ask all kinds of questions and demand to see payroll records—names, dates, when they worked. Douglas, we could lose our license or worse, big fines, maybe even jail."

"Juan, if someone does pay you a visit, tell him to see me, that you don't know what he's talking about. Tell him all our operations are open and above board. Go back to the site now and check what records you have in the office trailer. Anything to do with the workers put in a box and put the box in the trunk of your car. If he asks to talk with the employees, tell him he can't do that without my okay."

"Do you want me to send some of the guys home, just in case?"

"Not yet, we don't even know if this was a real tip or just someone trying to scare us. Now get back to the site. If someone does come and starts to ask questions, be sure to ask him for identification. Then call me on my cell, immediately, before you say anything. Got that?"

"Yes, boss," Juan said. He was shaking, but appeared calmer as he left the office. He didn't see Wendy behind the bank of plants.

"Wendy," Douglas called, as he emerged in the doorway to his office. He was pleased to see Wendy was not near his office door. She didn't appear to be alarmed, probably not hearing Juan.

"I'm going to work from home today," Bradshaw said. "If anyone calls, take the name and number and what they're calling about. Then call me at home. Monique has a list of numbers in her top drawer. If for some reason I don't answer, leave a message. Thanks again for coming in on such short notice."

"Sure, Mr. Bradshaw."

"Oh, and Wendy, call me, Douglas."

"Sure, Douglas," Wendy said with a smile.

— • • • —

DOUGLAS GRABBED HIS briefcase and laptop and headed for home. *I sure don't need any trouble from the Feds,* he muttered, as he wove his Mercedes through traffic. He entered the parking garage of the high-rise where he lived, parked the car, and took his private elevator to his penthouse. He always felt better when he was encased in his home. It felt like a fortress that protected him.

He grabbed a beer and set up his laptop on the glass-top desk overlooking the ocean across the highway. He kept this desk free from clutter, preferring to keep any paperwork on the desk in his guest bedroom.

"Damn, I didn't bring the new condo project file with me." He called Wendy and told her about the file he needed, which he'd left on his desk.

"Tell you what, Wendy, I already have more than I can do today. Would you mind bringing me the file tomorrow morning to my penthouse? I know it's Saturday, but I promise you'll be paid overtime."

"No problem, Douglas. I see your address on the sheet Monique left for me. I know how to find it."

"Good. Let's say about nine. Is that too early?"

"No, nine is great."

"Why don't you stop and get us a couple of muffins and coffee on the way over. There's an envelope in Monique's top drawer with petty cash. Take what you need."

— ● ● ● —

WENDY FOUND THE file and the petty cash. She glanced around the office to be sure she had put everything away, closed the door, and drove home. She was excited about going to Douglas' home tomorrow. *Maybe there will be an opportunity to tell him my big news.*

Chapter 43

❧

FRIDAY CAME TOO quickly for Roberto. He knew he had to muster up his courage. Señor Hutch had promised a new life for his family. He must keep his mama in the front of his mind today. He had to be brave for her.

He pulled on his jeans and a red T-shirt. It was the same outfit he had worn all week. His hand automatically checked his left pants pocket for the listening device, rubbing his fingers over the smooth surface. It had become a good luck charm, keeping him from harm, at least he hoped it would continue to do so. He finished dressing, packed his lunch pail, picked up the suitcase, and left for work.

— • • • —

THE DAY WAS A SCORCHER. Daytona Beach was experiencing a late-spring heat wave. The men working on the construction site were at first lethargic, and then they became surly. With forty-five minutes before the end of the shift, Roberto went to the lavatory and retrieved the suitcase he had wedged behind the bushes next to the toilet shed. He entered the office trailer through the back entrance, carefully walked down the hall, and opened Señor Juan's office door.

"Shit, Roberto, don't you ever knock?" Juan grumbled.

"Sorry, señor. I'm just so scared. Here is the suitcase."

"All right. All right. Go sit out front. I'll be with you in a minute." Juan took the suitcase and filled it with the phony money. He placed ten $50 bills on top of the stacks just in case Red Dog opened it before he was taken out by the hit man. Juan closed the suitcase and went to find Roberto.

"Okay, Roberto. The suitcase is set for the drop. Do just as the man asked and then leave, *fast. Don't look back.* Do you understand?"

"Si.

"I want you out of here with that suitcase. Don't go back to work, just leave. The horn is about to blow anyway. Here's your week's pay."

"Thank you very much, señor."

Roberto left the construction site and walked back to his room. He was too nervous to eat dinner. He opened the suitcase. He cut a slit in the lining and inserted the small disc. He closed the case setting it at the foot of the bed. Apprehensive the device might fall out, he jiggled the case, sat it down twice very hard on the floor, and then opened it to check. The wafer was exactly where he had put it. He closed the case again.

He just wanted to lie down, close his eyes, and think how happy his mama and brothers and sister were going to be when he told them of Señor Hutch's deal. He had to be brave and was glad he'd practiced taking the bus to the beach road.

At eight o'clock, he picked up the suitcase and left his room for the bus stop. The bus pulled up to the curb at exactly eight-twenty, just like it had the day before. Roberto went to the back and took a seat in an empty row.

There were only a few people on the bus. A man and a woman with beach towels under their arms were seated three rows in front of him. They're probably going to the beach to cool off from the heat of the day, he thought. There were also a couple of men, one sitting in front, and one midway back in the bus.

The two men left the bus at the stop before where Roberto was getting off. When Dunlawton Avenue came up, the two beach goers got off in front of Roberto and headed down the access road to the water. Roberto stepped off, and he too headed down the access road.

He had twenty minutes to spare so he slowly walked a short distance south down the sandy beach then wandered up to the marsh grass. Sitting down he leaned back on the warm sand where it curved up to meet the grass. He could see the pier. He estimated it would take him about five minutes to walk to the drop site.

The beach was almost empty. Only a few hardy souls were wading in the shallow water. A short distance from the pier, a small group of four people were lying down, looking up at the stars. He hoped one day he too could look at the stars without a care in the world. He noticed the couple who were on the bus with him walking hand-in-hand toward the pier.

Finally, it was time to go. Roberto stood, brushing the sand off his pants. He picked up the suitcase by the handle and headed for the pier. He hoped he didn't look nervous, hoped not to attract any attention, prayed it would be over soon. He reached the structure and immediately could see where Red Dog wanted him to leave the suitcase. Night had descended, the moon giving just enough light to see under the narrow structure.

Roberto walked up under the platform as far as he could. The trash can with yellow stripes was there, stuck behind a piling. He put the suitcase into the barrel and then turned and started walking as fast as he could back to the beach access road. He ran up the road to the bus stop.

Luckily, a bus was just pulling to the curb. As the bus door opened, he found himself sandwiched between two men, one in front and one in back. The three climbed up the steps of the bus, shuffled to the back of the bus, and sat down. Roberto had no choice—the two men almost carried him to the back seat.

"Roberto, be calm. Hutch sent us. In two stops we will get off the bus. We have a car waiting to take you to a safe place. By the way, you did great back there," one of the strangers said.

Roberto did as he was told and tried to breathe again.

—•••—

THE SCENE ON THE beach remained as Roberto had left it. The stargazers continued to gaze and the waders waded.

While Roberto was starting to relax on the bus, a large man dressed in black jeans and a black long-sleeved shirt walked north to the pier. Before he got to the structure, he sat down on the sand, seemingly to enjoy the cool air, taking in the quiet night. A few minutes later, he resumed his trek. Once he was under the platform, there was just enough light from the moon for him to see the barrel.

He hustled the short distance and grabbed the suitcase from the top of the trash.

"Drop the case," said a voice behind him, "and don't turn around."

Red Dog could feel a gun in his back. "Don't shoot," he said. "You can have the suitcase. There's money in there. $8,000. Take it. It's yours."

"You stupid son-of-a-bitch, trying to pull a blackmail job. You think they're going to just give you $8,000 because you asked for it?" the man said, jabbing the gun into Red Dog's back a couple of times to make his point.

"Who are you?" Red Dog asked.

"Where you're going you won't need to know who I am."

— • • • —

THE SAND MADE IT easy for Hutch's SEAL team to silently sneak up behind the two men. In a swift action one SEAL disarmed the gunman and quickly cuffed him; the second tackled Red Dog as he tried to flee. Turning him on his stomach, the lawman clamped the cuffs around his wrists. Both struggled and cursed, but to no avail. They had been outmaneuvered.

"Hutch said this job could be dangerous," said SEAL one. "Shit, we could have had a real picnic on the beach and these two thugs wouldn't have noticed us."

The couple who got off the bus with Roberto joined the SEALs. They opened the suitcase and retrieved the transmission device Roberto had placed in the lining when he went back to his room to rest.

"We're heading to the van with our cargo," SEAL two said. "We should be at the department within twenty minutes. Do we get beer and pizza when we get there?"

The SEALs and the two other officers smiled. They knew Hutch could hear them but could not answer back.

Chapter 44

IT WAS A usual Saturday morning at the department—DUI bookings of those who celebrated the weekend early at a bar and those who simply celebrated a paycheck. Unfortunately for the latter, it meant empty pockets until the next payday.

The bullpen was a stark contrast to the bedlam of the booking desk. Chairs faced the case board, and bodies leaned forward as the ICE agent filled them in on the previous night's sting operation.

"Last night went down as planned," Hutch said. "Roberto kept his nerves in check and followed Red Dog's instructions perfectly. The blackmailer picked the suitcase out of the trash, and the triggerman arrived as we suspected he would. The one difference is that we extricated Roberto safely."

Hutch took a pause in his report for a sip of strong coffee that Dani bought for him.

"The two SEALs I brought up from the Miami field office got both perps. They nabbed the gunman as he was threatening Red Dog. Then, almost at the same time, they cuffed Red Dog, the blackmailer. All was accomplished with no more than a few cuss words. However, neither one is forthcoming with information. Red Dog is asking for a lawyer, and the gunman has clammed up altogether. The gunman had no ID on him.

"Where are they now?" Manny asked.

"They are both behind bars in the holding cell. I'll start the interrogation here at the department after today's operation with Bradshaw. Manny, your team can use any information that pertains to the murder of Julie Stone. After the interrogation is completed, the two will be transported to either Miami or D.C."

"Where's Roberto now?" Fred asked.

"We're holding him in protective custody. He's our star witness. We sure don't want anything to happen to him. Some of his illegal buddies would probably like to silence him, afraid he might name names."

"Okay," Manny said, "our plan to arrest Bradshaw is ready for execution. Hutch, I take it you're leaving now to go to the construction site. From our surveillance of the place, no work is done on Saturday, but the head guy, Juan Ortega, is usually there."

"I'm on my way after your briefing," Hutch said.

"Fred and I will go to Bradshaw's penthouse," Manny said. "George will go to Bradshaw's office. Hutch, you and George rendezvous with us at the penthouse once the construction site and the office are secure. Remember, we still need to find more evidence. Dani will be on deck here to keep us in sync as changes occur. Any questions?"

Eager to get started, no one said a word. They wanted Bradshaw. The group broke up, each person concentrating on his piece of the assignment.

Manny, Fred, and Peaches left by way of the department's holding cell to take a look at Red Dog and the gunman. They then left the department for Bradshaw's penthouse.

Chapter 45

A SOUTH-WEST breeze carried warm humid air over the city. Wendy snuggled deeper under her covers and then sat bolt upright. "Oh my gosh, I have to go to Douglas' home this morning."

She quickly dressed, grabbed her purse, and left the house. Wendy pulled into the coffee shop's drive-in window and placed her order. The errand accomplished, she shortly found herself ringing Bradshaw's penthouse doorbell, juggling her purse, the file, and a sack with the muffins, coffee, sugars, and several little creamers.

"Hey, I see you found me," Douglas greeted her. "Come on in. That coffee smells good. You can put it out on the counter next to the pot I brewed earlier."

"This is a beautiful penthouse, Douglas. The view is incredible," Wendy said, emptying the bag.

— • • • —

NO SOONER HAD she said those words then the telephone rang. Douglas went to answer it only to hear a very distraught Juan on the other end.

"What do you mean, they're here? Whose they? Hang on a minute I have to go in the other room. Wendy, help yourself to the coffee and muffins. I'll be with you in a minute."

Douglas went into the guest bedroom. He used the room as an office when he needed more space.

"Okay, Juan, start from the top," Douglas said, shutting the door. He started to pace in the small room. "Who came to see you?"

"An agent," Juan said, nearly in hysterics. "A *federal agent*. His name is Stephen Hutchinson. He knows about Miguel."

"Juan, get a hold of yourself. I can hardly understand you. Where is the agent now? Can he hear you?" Douglas said, digging through the pile of papers on the desk to find the blackmail letter to Miguel.

"No. I'm in a closet in the storeroom, on my cell phone. He has a search warrant. He wants all my files. But I did as you told me yesterday. They're all in the trunk of my car."

"Good. Just play dumb. Tell him you know nothing. Tell him he'll have to talk to me at my office."

Douglas cut the connection, stood staring at the phone unit. Now what was he going to do? So, Juan wasn't kidding about the Feds. They've connected my construction site with Miguel, he thought. That's not good. Not good at all. Where did I put that damn letter? Searching the desktop in vain, he opened the door and returned to the living room.

—•••—

"WOW, CALLS FOLLOW you everywhere," Wendy said.

Douglas had forgotten she was there. He looked over at her. "Nothing to worry about, Wendy. They're always calling to check something or other. Now let's have those muffins. I've got work to do."

"Douglas," Wendy said, twisting a lock of her dark brown hair around her finger, "I do have something I'd like to talk to you about."

"You know, Wendy, there is only one other woman I've ever known who twisted her hair around her finger like that, my mother. She always took a lock of hair when she was frustrated or puzzling something through."

Wendy was shocked by what Douglas told her. "Douglas, that's what I wanted to talk to you about. I'm pretty sure your mother is my grandmother. Douglas, I'm your daughter," she blurted out. She stood on wobbly legs waiting for his reaction.

Douglas looked at her. Stunned. Then he really looked at her. It was as if he was looking into his own eyes. "Wendy, that's not possible. Your mother was married to Bert when you were born."

"I know, but I asked mom about you after I saw your birthmark in front of your right ear. I noticed it when you were hurt at the ball.

I have one just like it," Wendy said, her fingers touching the mark on her face.

Douglas automatically put his hand up to his own face and touched the mark she spoke of. He looked at Wendy as she lifted her hair and showed him the identical reddish blotch.

He tried to think back, almost seventeen years. The day Shirley moved out, he had thrown her on the bed, telling her he would show her what she was going to miss if she went through with the divorce. He remembered she was crying, but he took her anyway. She left their bed sobbing and walked out. He signed papers that were served him the next day. Two weeks later she got a divorce in Mexico. She married Bert almost immediately. He could remember wondering if she had been cheating on him. Then along came Wendy. It was said that she was premature.

Breaking into his thoughts, Wendy said, "I'd like to have a DNA test if you don't mind, just so we both know for sure."

Douglas looked up at her again, leaving his thoughts behind. "I guess we should do that, Wendy." He walked over and gave her a peck on the check. "Yes, we can do that."

Too much is happening too fast, he thought. Maybe it's time to blow this town. The law is closing in. Events are spiraling out of my control. Time to put my new life into action.

"Douglas, are you all right?" Wendy asked.

Douglas looked at Wendy but turned away, his thoughts spinning. Money has been transferred to my bank account, or rather Walter Romero's account, in Cancun. My plane is serviced. No point in dealing with all these shitheads. Her father? No way. She probably wants to shake me down for some cash. My head hurts again. Too much tension around here.

— ••• —

HIS MACHINATIONS WERE interrupted by the doorbell. "This is a regular three-ring circus today," Douglas said with a shaky smile. He went and opened the door to find Catherine standing there.

"Catherine, this certainly is a day of surprises. What brings you here?"

"Well, actually, I wanted to see Wendy," Catherine said, swiftly walking in then moving around Douglas. "I was cleaning out Julie's things for Russell, and I saw a perfect gown for Wendy next time she sings for an audience." Catherine was talking rapidly, her eyes darting around the room as she talked.

"So, I called Shirley, and she said Wendy was temping for you today at your home. Since I wanted to talk to you as well, Douglas, regarding a donation to the charity auction next month, I decided to pop up. I was in the area. How are you, Wendy dear?"

"I'm fine, and the gown sounds interesting, Catherine. Are you okay?"

"Yes, yes, I'm okay. My, Douglas, this is some view you have," Catherine said. Walking toward the window, she suddenly felt a lump under her foot. She stooped down to pick up the item embedded in the tight twist of the carpet. She had to dig into the fibers to free it. "Well, this is interesting. It looks like the dangle from an earring. Look, Wendy, do you recognize this?"

"It's kinda familiar. It looks something like the gold earring Julie made the first day of class. Remember we kidded her about creating a dangle the first day because we were going to do a whole class on them later."

They both looked up at Douglas. "Let me see that," he said. Catherine stood by the window as Douglas approached her. As he did so, he looked down through the large expanse of glass and saw a squad car pull up in front of the building. Captain Salinas with a dog in tow climbed out of the car.

Douglas snapped. Too much. Too much. Miguel, dangles, shake downs. No time to think. Put the plan into action. Yes. Yes. Action!

Douglas went to his desk drawer, pulling out a revolver and a roll of duct tape. "Ladies, we're going to take a little ride. Get down on the floor, both of you, on your stomachs," he hissed, waving the gun around, motioning them to lie on the floor. "Anyone wants to play like a hero will be shot first. I've already killed so a couple more dead bodies won't make any difference." He quickly taped their hands behind their backs and put a strip of tape over their mouths. "Okay, now get up. Come on, faster."

He had to help Catherine because she couldn't quite get her balance. Wendy was already on her feet. Once again flashing the gun, he said, "Go over to the kitchen. There's a door beside the refrigerator." Douglas shoved them along, then reached through and opened the door. He pushed a button and his private elevator opened, a direct shot to the garage below.

Shoving them, he said, "Hurry up and get in." He pushed the button marked *Garage*. Within a few seconds, the elevator stopped the door sliding to the side. The garage was cool and damp. He again shoved the ladies over to his big black Mercedes.

Opening the trunk, he ordered Wendy to get in and to make it fast. He pushed her body and then her legs into the trunk and slammed it shut. He then opened the door to the back seat and shoved Catherine head first into the car pushing her feet down so he could close the door. Catherine lay on the floor of the car wedged behind the front seat.

With his hostages safely out of sight, Douglas jumped into the car. The engine roared and the car barreled out of the back entrance of the garage.

"You girls are going to go for a big ride," he said loud enough for Catherine to hear him. Douglas headed for the New Smyrna Beach Airport. *I should be able to get the bitches into the plane without anyone seeing me. Good thing I have a space under cover far away from the terminal building.*

His temples were pounding. Chuckling, he muttered, "I'll head out over of the ocean and give these broads a chance for a little swim. That's it. I'll dump the bitches and then head for Jamaica. Ditch the plane, then to Cancun and my new life."

His mind still racing, Douglas reached under his front seat and patted the suitcase he had hidden for the moment when he put his escape plan into action. It was filled with cash, hundreds and twenties, totaling $20,000, along with a set of ID's for Walter Romero. The big stuff was already in Cancun, just waiting for Romero to claim it.

Douglas pulled into the airport and headed for his plane's parking stall. There sat his Cessna sheltered nicely from the weather, but more important, sheltered from view. The stall next to his plane was empty. Plenty of room to park the car, get his cargo on board with no one the wiser.

"Okay, Catherine, my love, you and I are about to continue our little journey." Douglas got out of the car and hurriedly walked to his plane. He opened the door. Flipped down the staircase. He climbed aboard and started the plane, allowing it to warm up. Then he had a thought. It would be much easier if he only had one passenger to contend with. "I'll leave Wendy in the trunk. That's it. Leave her in the trunk." Hustling back to his car, he gave a thump on the back end and said, "Wendy, I don't think I'm your father, but no matter, our relationship ends here."

He retrieved the suitcase from under his front seat as well as his gun. He didn't like guns much, even though he was a military-trained marksman. But he didn't hesitate to use one when he felt he had to. Douglas quickly stashed everything in the plane's ample storage compartment and went back for Catherine.

"Come on, Catherine, out you come," he said, pulling her out from behind the back seat. He got her upright and then walked her quickly to the plane. Standing in back of her, he shoved her up the four stairs and into the plane. She stumbled into a passenger seat in the back. She tried to say something, but the tape over her mouth only allowed muffled sounds.

With Catherine in the plane, and the plane's engines humming nicely, Douglas went back to the car and locked it. He gave another thump on the trunk. "So long, Wendy." He turned away from the car and climbed into his plane.

Douglas buckled himself in. Then he carefully guided the Cessna out of the hangar and began to taxi down the runway.

"This is CS548 to control tower. I'm going up for a couple of hours sightseeing, asking for clearance to take off."

"This is NSB Tower to CS548. You are cleared for takeoff. It's a beautiful day for a ride, CS548."

Once in the air, Douglas headed east toward the ocean and then made a sharp turn south. "Catherine, I think I'll keep you with me for a little while. It might be nice to have some company. Ever been to Jamaica? I bet a rich bitch like you has been there many times. Cancun, Daddy's coming," he said gleefully.

Chapter 46

৵

"COME ON, Fred, let's go pay a visit on our friend Mr. Bradshaw," Manny said, as he stepped out of the squad car, snapping a leash on Peaches.

"Lorna's heading back to the department," Fred said. "She told me Bradshaw hasn't budged out of the building all morning."

Having already alerted Manny he was done at the construction site, Hutch pulled up in back of the squad car. He joined Manny and Fred as they entered the building through the revolving doors.

"Thanks for the call, Hutch. Sounds like Bradshaw alerted his construction site to ditch all the files," Manny said. "We do have a potential problem. Lorna recognized a young woman entering the building a while ago. She said she had some files in one arm and a bag in the other, like a fast food bag. Lorna ID'd her as Wendy Sullivan."

"I called Wendy's house," Fred said. "Her mother told me she was working for Bradshaw today at his home. Wendy's probably in the penthouse now. Lorna saw her entering the building so we have to assume that's where she went."

— •••—

THE DOORMAN, Orly Sanchez, returned to his post after relieving himself in the men's room. He was having one of those days when his stomach was balking at the refried beans and eight tacos with hot sauce he had eaten for dinner the night before. He was beginning to think he had food poisoning with the number of trips he had taken to the bathroom. When he saw the three men in his lobby, huddled in conversation, he became very nervous. Ever since he was questioned by Detective Anderson, he hadn't been sleeping well. He wished he'd ignored the Channel 13 news bulletin.

Fred saw Orly return to his desk. He went over to him. "Excuse me. You're Orly Sanchez?"

"Yes, sir."

"Have you seen this woman here this morning?" Fred asked, as he sorted through the pictures on his cell phone to find the one of Wendy.

Oh no, it is trouble, Orly thought. He knew they were going to ask him more questions about people coming and going from the building. "Yes, sir. That girl came in. She didn't say anything, but she had some papers in her hand."

"Do you know who she went to visit?"

"Yes, sir, I wasn't busy, you understand. I watched the lights on top of the elevator door. She went to the penthouse, Mr. Bradshaw's penthouse."

"Thank you, Orly. Has she left?"

"Not that I see."

— • • • —

"THIS COMPLICATES THINGS," Manny said. The three went to the elevator. Fred punched the button and the elevator door opened after descending several floors. Manny pushed the top button for Bradshaw's penthouse. "Here's how it's going down. When Bradshaw opens the door, Hutch, you take him. Fred and I find Wendy. Once we have Bradshaw under control, Fred, you search the penthouse." Fred and Hutch nodded in agreement.

The elevator stopped. The door opened and the men exited the car. It was just a few steps to Bradshaw's front door. Hutch pushed the doorbell. Nothing. They positioned themselves on either side of the door, guns drawn. Hutch pushed the bell again. Nothing.

"Bradshaw, open the door. Come out with your hands up. Come out and nothing will happen to you," Hutch commanded. The door remained shut.

"Okay, boys, let's go in," Manny said.

"Let me do the honors," Hutch volunteered. Within seconds they were inside.

"Bradshaw," Manny yelled.

The three fanned out, guns drawn, doing a quick room-to-room search. "It appears our boy isn't here, and neither is Wendy," Fred said.

"Uh-oh. Look what I see—two purses," Hutch said. He opened the little pink flowered purse and pulled out the wallet. "Here's a driver's license for Wendy Sullivan." He opened the second cream-colored leather bag. "This one belongs to Catherine Jane Hainsworth. How did she get in here?"

"What? Let me see that," Manny said, grabbing it out of the agent's hand.

"Manny, the coffeepot is full and cold," Fred called out. "There are a couple of foam cups—half full. One has lipstick on it. I'd say the coffee klatch was interrupted."

Manny looked over at Fred, and then down at the leather bag in his hand. *Bradshaw better not harm Catherine or he'll never see the light of day.* "I wonder when Catherine came up here," Manny said. "The doorman didn't mention another woman coming in, and why would she come to see Bradshaw anyway? She knows he's the prime suspect in Julie's murder. Fred, quiz the doorman again," Manny said, flipping open his cell phone. He punched Catherine's code number. After three rings, her answering machine picked up. "Catherine, this is Manny. Give me a call on my cell as soon as you receive this message."

Fred snapped his cell phone shut. "The doorman didn't see any woman come in this morning except Wendy, and he didn't see Bradshaw leave."

"He must have taken the elevator to the garage," Manny replied.

"Hey, Manny. There's a back door in the kitchen," Fred shouted. "And, there's an elevator."

"Shit, a private elevator. Hutch, check the garage. He has a 2008, four-door, black, Mercedes."

"Do you have the license number?" Hutch asked.

"Yes." Checking his notes, Manny said, "License number is FL39524. I'm putting out an APB on the bastard. Signal if you need help. Fred, keep searching the place. See if you can find the digitoxin. When you're done, call me. I'm heading down to the car to call in the APB."

Manny and Peaches took the elevator down to the lobby floor. He radioed Dani from the car and told her to put out an all-points bulletin on Douglas Bradshaw and that it was believed he had two female hostages. Anyone spotting Bradshaw was not to engage him but to call in his location to the department. Manny was going to handle Bradshaw personally.

— • • • —

EVERY POLICE OFFICER in the county, plus the adjacent ones, were instantly on the alert for the black Mercedes.

Manny figured Bradshaw had a forty-five-minute head start, an hour at most. He called Dani again. "Dani, do a search on Bradshaw. See if he has any other vehicles. Although we believe Wendy and Catherine are hostages, check to see if you can find Wendy. Call her home and Bradshaw's office. Also, call Catherine Hainsworth, house number, see if she's home yet. Above all, keep me posted."

Fred darted out of the building, joining Manny. "I found the digitoxin in the medicine cabinet. Just as the pharmacy had listed, there were two bottles, one for his mother, purchased a month ago. It was empty. The other was a prescription in his name, thirty tablets to be taken as needed. Three were left. Bradshaw's prescription was purchased the same day as his mother's."

Manny's radio crackled. "Yah," he barked.

"Dani here. Douglas Bradshaw rented a plane six-months ago. He is a licensed pilot. The records indicate that he parks it at New Smyrna Airport. The plane's call numbers were not listed. Over."

"Good work, Dani. Call George and tell him to meet Fred and me over at the NSB Airport. Tell George I have the warrant for Bradshaw's arrest. Hutch is looking for Bradshaw's car in the garage, but I'm sure he's given us the slip. Out."

Manny screeched away from the curb. "Fred, call Hutch and tell him where we're headed. Give him Dani's number if he needs directions."

Fred already had the agent on his cell phone. He put it on speaker and held it out so Manny could hear.

"No car in the garage with those plates or description," Hutch reported. "I did have a call from the department. The gunman my

SEALs took into custody last night finally talked. He was hired by Bradshaw. I want Bradshaw as bad as you guys."

"We believe he's headed to the New Smyrna Airport," Fred said. "Call Dani. She'll give you directions. See you there." He flipped his phone shut and grabbed the roll-bar handle above his head. Peaches braced herself in the back seat. The squad car raced down the street, siren blaring. Cars pulled over to curbs to get out of the way as the police car hurtled through traffic.

Chapter 47

DOUGLAS PULLED back on the Cessna's throttle. She climbed easily into the clear blue sky over the east coast of Florida. In seconds, he was above the ocean. Banking the plane south, he headed for Jamaica.

"Settle back, Catherine, and enjoy the ride. We'll be at our destination in about two hours. Then you'll be as free as a bird."

Douglas couldn't understand Catherine's muffled protestations through the duct tape covering her mouth and over the hum of the small plane. For the first time today, he began to relax. He looked over at the compartment where he stowed the case with cash and a new passport—the case holding his future. A smug smile crossed his face.

He began to plan how he would proceed to Cancun once he landed in Kingston, Jamaica. He had flown to Kingston a couple of times over the last few months to become familiar with the airport's procedures. He knew he would be required to go through Customs, so he must leave the gun in the plane. He would be without a weapon for only a few hours because he planned to buy a replacement in town. He didn't want to draw any attention to himself, so he'd park his plane wherever the tower directed. He'd tell them he would be in the country a few days.

Time passed quickly. It was a beautiful day to escape. The sun was now low in the sky, but it didn't bother him. Catherine stopped trying to get loose and looked to him as if she was taking a nap. Two hours and forty-five minutes later, he landed at Kingston Airport. Like the other times he had flown to Jamaica, the control tower welcomed him and then directed him to a parking area way south of the terminal. This reception, of course, was perfect for his plans to be as inconspicuous as possible. He taxied as directed and pulled into the designated area. He shut down the plane's engines and breathed a sigh of relief.

"Well, Catherine, I'll give you a chance to freshen up," Douglas said, yanking the tape from her mouth.

"Ouch! That hurt. You'll never get away with this, Douglas. Manny knows you slipped Julie something. He'll find you."

"Now, now, Catherine. Such anger. And here I treated you to a nice ride. See how thoughtful I am? I'm even going to let you freshen up before getting off the plane."

Douglas pulled her out of the seat. "Stand up and walk over to that door." He guided her into the small lavatory. "Stay facing front and I'll undo your hands," he instructed.

Douglas ripped the tape from her wrists, shoved her into the lavatory, and pulled the door shut. The door handle was in the shape of a small ring protruding from the door. The hole in the ring was large enough to receive the screwdriver Douglas took from the toolbox next to the door. He forced the tool through the ring. The make-shift lock was enough to imprison Catherine in the lavatory.

"I'll leave you now, Catherine. Have a nice day," he called, through the door.

Douglas stuffed all of his "Bradshaw" identification into the case and twenty-thousand dollars mad money. He retrieved the rolling suitcase he had previously packed and placed in the plane's closet. With any luck, customs employees would not open either of the two cases. *Kingston officials are not like the nosy bastards in the States,* he thought.

Taking the roll-along suitcase, he grabbed the small case in his other hand. Ready to face his future, he disembarked the Cessna, folded the set of stairs back up into place, closed and locked the plane's door. Pocketing the plane's key, he strode nonchalantly to the terminal.

Once in the terminal, he became part of the crush of passengers who had just deplaned from a large jetliner. The customs agents were swamped and checked only the baggage of about every tenth passenger. Bradshaw sailed through.

He broke away from the passengers heading to get their baggage and walked to a bank of storage lockers. Taking the key from locker number twenty-seven, he deposited the small case with the Bradshaw ID and cash into the locker. He removed half of the bills and stuffed them into his pants pockets. Just in case I ever want to resume my old identity, I'll have a little money, he thought. He pocketed the number twenty-seven key with the plane's key.

He exited the terminal through the automatic doors of the baggage area. The Hilton airport shuttle stood at the curb ready to take guests the one-and-a-half miles to the hotel. The shuttle was full of chattering people. Some had squealing children, and one was trying to quiet a wailing baby. He lifted his roll-along suitcase and slid it into the open storage area behind the driver. Finding an empty seat, he sat down.

Across the aisle and up one row from him, Bradshaw observed a young girl wearing a pink dress. His mind returned to what Wendy had divulged to him. "I'm your daughter."

Can't be, he thought. Yet, I wonder if she cried like that little girl. I bet she did. To Douglas, the girl looked like she was spoiled rotten. I wonder why Shirley and Bert never had any other children. Probably one screamer was enough.

"Hilton Hotel," the driver called out. The van rolled to a stop and the door opened, letting in a gush of hot humid air. "Watch your step."

Bradshaw was eager to get out of the confinement of the shuttle van and to leave the noisemakers behind.

Slipping into the men's room at the hotel, he entered the stall designated for the handicapped and opened his suitcase. The stall afforded him plenty of room for the birth of Walter Romero.

He took out an eight-by-ten inch mirror with double sided tape on the back and stuck it to the wall. He stripped down to his shorts and jammed the discarded clothes into a black plastic bag he'd packed for this purpose.

Next he pulled out a new cream-colored suit, cream alligator shoes and belt to match, and a sky-blue shirt, along with a couple of hangers. Hanging the clothes on the hook provided in the stall, he smoothed out the wrinkles. The fabric he had selected allowed the wrinkles to fall away quickly. He then dressed in his new attire, leaving the top three buttons of the shirt open.

The facial disguise was next. He took out his new passport, which was hidden with a few other items for his new identity in a secret pocket in the suitcase. He studied the picture and then retrieved a small zip-lock bag, also from the secret pocket.

The bag contained a mustache and a watchband of cream-colored leather. Looking in the mirror, he positioned the mustache, checking several times to be sure he matched the picture exactly. He replaced his watchband with the alligator band to match his belt. Then he took a last look at his image in the mirror. *Perfect!*

He put Walter Romero's passport, his Mexican driver's license, and a wallet with ten-thousand dollars cash into his pocket. He had traveled to Cancun the year before when he opened the Walter Romero bank account. The account contained two million dollars—no wire transfers, no record.

Before stepping out of the stall, he repacked the roll-along suitcase holding his toiletries and a change of underwear. Opening the stall door, he grabbed the handle of the suitcase and the black plastic bag with his old clothes. Again, Lady Luck was with him. No one else was in the lavatory. He stuffed the black-plastic bag down into the large trash barrel, fluffing up some of the debris to cover it. "Goodbye, Douglas Bradshaw III," he whispered.

Then Walter Romero exited the lavatory.

—•••—

ROMERO MADE A RESERVATION at the hotel for one night. He followed the directions to his room and put his suitcase into the closet. Romero returned to the hotel lobby and exited to the street. The hotel shuttle soon arrived and transported him back to the airport.

All he needed was a one-way ticket to Cancun and his new life. He sauntered to the Air Jamaica counter. There was a young woman behind the counter who had just finished ticketing a passenger. Her badge displayed her name—Marie.

"Hello, Marie. How are you today?" asked Romero.

"Very well, and you, sir?" Marie asked.

"Fine, thank you. I'd like a ticket to Cancun on tomorrow morning's flight number twenty-one. I believe it leaves at six thirty-five."

"Yes, sir. The price is $482," Marie replied.

Romero counted out four one-hundred-dollar bills, plus the eighty-two dollars in small bills.

Marie scheduled the flight and printed out his ticket. "I hope you have a nice time in Cancun, sir."

Romero took his ticket and exited the airport terminal. Hailing a cab, he told the driver to take him downtown. "Can you recommend a good pawn shop?" he asked.

"Yes, sir. Carl's Pawn Shop has many things."

"Please take me there. I'll see if they have what I want."

After the trip to the pawn shop, he retraced his steps to the hotel thinking all that was left to start his new life was a nice meal, a good night's sleep, and the flight to Cancun. He would then melt into the over one-hundred-nine million Mexicans.

I'm glad I went into town after making my airline reservation, he thought, smiling. That pawn shop had just what I wanted, a nice little .38 Special. I probably won't need it, but I can't be too careful. I'm so close to making my new life a reality.

Chapter 48

SIREN BLARING, tires squealing, Manny and Fred, followed by Hutch, arrived at New Smyrna Airport. They pulled to a halt in front of the small building that served as a terminal. The three officers went in and quickly found the man in charge.

"Hello, gentleman, how I can I help you?" The name on his shirt identified him as Hank Greenfield.

"Hello, Mr. Greenfield," Manny said, flashing his badge. "My name is Captain Salinas. This is Agent Hutchinson and Detective Watson. We're looking for a Cessna leased to Douglas Bradshaw III. We understand he parks it at your airport. We have an APB out on him and have reason to believe he may be planning to take a trip on this plane. Have you seen him?"

"Yes, he does park it here, but I saw him take off about an hour ago. His car is still here though."

"Did he file a flight plan?" Manny asked.

"Let me check with Rick. He's on duty in the tower." Hank Greenfield went over to a desk phone and punched a few buttons. "Rick, this is Hank. Did Bradshaw give you a flight plan? ...No? Did he give you any indication where he was going? ...Thanks. He told the tower he was going sightseeing and would be back in a couple of hours."

"Can you take us to his car and also give us the call numbers on the plane?" Manny asked.

Greenfield again called the tower. "Rick, do you have the call numbers for Bradshaw's plane? CS548. Thanks. Oh, and Rick, if by any chance Bradshaw radios you, let me know. Did you get that, CS548?" Greenfield said to Manny.

"Yup, now let's go to his car."

"Follow me. The car is under the plane's covered parking stall." Greenfield jumped into his Jeep and took off down a utility road alongside one of the runways. Hutch jumped into the car with Manny and Fred. They pulled out behind the jeep.

— • • • —

PEACHES WAS HAVING a heck of a ride. Her master was driving crazy, so she bounced all over the back seat, tail wagging, slurping her new seat companion when she bumped into him.

"Peaches, cut that out," Hutch said, wiping his cheek with his handkerchief.

Wendy and Catherine's purses slid to the floor of the backseat and Peaches, landing on top of them, sniffed them. New toys?

Manny pulled in behind Bradshaw's car and jumped out along with Fred, Hutch, and Peaches.

Bradshaw's car was locked. Manny looked in the front seat and the back seat. Empty. Peaches raced around the backend of the car, barking. She sat then ran around again, all the time barking.

"What the heck is the matter with you?" Manny yelled at his dog. "Knock it off." He rubbed his head in frustration, feeling in his gut that Bradshaw had gotten away. He patted his breast-pocket and drew out a cigarette he kept as proof he didn't need to smoke. He looked at it and then jammed it back in the pocket.

"I could be wrong, Manny, but I think Peaches is trying to tell us something," Hutch said. "She's alerting on the trunk."

"Can you crack it open?" Manny asked Hutch.

Hutch was already digging in his pocket. He pulled out a small blade and within seconds he had popped the trunk's lid.

Wendy laid unconscious, her wrists tied and her mouth taped. "Good Lord, what has that bastard done?" Manny said, as he carefully lifted her out of the trunk and laid her on the grass next to his car.

"Dani, get the EMTs out to New Smyrna Airport ASAP," Fred ordered over his cell phone. "We found Wendy. She's unconscious."

"I'll go back to the terminal to meet them," Greenfield said, jumping into his car.

Manny carefully turned her over so he could remove the tape from her wrists. He and Hutch then carefully shifted her onto her back again. Manny felt her carotid artery under her chin. "Her pulse is weak but she's alive. Much longer in this heat, we would have lost her."

—•••—

THE WAIL OF SIRENS could be heard approaching fast. The medics were parked at the New Smyrna Beach police barracks down the street. They responded to the scene within minutes and took over the life support.

There were three medics. One administered to Wendy and another retrieved a stretcher. They lifted her unconscious body onto the stretcher and into the van. Fred jumped into the van alongside Wendy. He would be with her in case she could tell him where Douglas was headed and if Catherine was with him. The EMT siren wailed again as the ambulance pulled away from the airport, heading for Halifax Memorial Hospital.

—•••—

Manny and Hutch turned from the departing EMT van and looked down at Peaches. She was sitting by the trunk of the car, ears back, tongue hanging out from exertion. "I'd say that dog has been trained to track given a scent," Hutch said. "Where did you say you found her?"

"I didn't find her. She found me at the Daytona Beach Farmer's Market," Manny said. "I learned later she served in the military. She'd been trained to track, but we didn't give her anything to sniff."

"In a way we did. The purses were on the back seat of your car and with your wild driving they landed on the floor. Peaches was falling all over them," Hutch said.

"Well, I'll be. I guess the guy at the VA hospital was right."

"What VA guy?" Hutch asked.

"I'll tell you later when we have more time," Manny said, as he knelt down, lovingly stroked Peaches' head. "You're a mighty fine dog, my girl, and I see a steak in your future." Peaches loved every minute of the praise and gave Manny a quick kiss in return.

"Hutch, Bradshaw is probably going to cross state lines or worse yet, leave U.S. territory," Manny said as he stood up. "What can you do for us in tracking that plane?"

"I'll call the agency and ask them to check all airports within the plane's range. I would think we have a shot at finding him within a couple of hours. If we're lucky," he added.

"Okay, get on it. I'll drop you off at your car and then head back to the department. Call me there with your progress. When you do find him, or the plane, let me know," Manny said. "I want to go with you to arrest the SOB for murder and kidnapping. It's a good bet Catherine is with him."

"If he's out of the country, we'll have to get extradition papers to bring him back. But let's not get ahead of ourselves. First, we have to find him," Hutch said.

Chapter 49

࿔

MANNY LEFT THE NSB Airport, dropped Hutch off at his car and returned to the police department. The bullpen was quiet. Everyone was out on assignment except Dani. With Manny pacing like a caged lion, Peaches followed on his heels every step of the way, but she knew to keep her mouth shut.

Manny's phone rang. He grabbed it before the second ring.

"Manny, Fred here. Wendy is conscious and talking. She's severely dehydrated, but the doctor says she just needs some fluids."

"That's great news."

"Wendy said Catherine is with Douglas. She said she detected the engine of a small plane start. She heard Bradshaw tell Catherine that they were going to go for a little ride. He thumped on the trunk lid, and then she could hear the plane taxi away. That was it. From the time they left the penthouse, she guesses she was passed out for less than thirty minutes. There's more, but I'll fill you in when you get here."

"I'll catch up with you later," Manny replied. "Right now, I'm waiting for a call from Hutch. He said he'd call when the agency finds the plane. When they do, I'll be joining him. Hopefully, we'll be as lucky with Catherine and find her alive."

— • • • —

TWO HOURS LATER, Manny got the call he was waiting for. "Manny, we found the plane. It's parked at the Kingston Airport in Jamaica. I have a jet ready to take off from Daytona Beach. As soon as you can get here, we'll head to Kingston. It should take a little over an hour."

"I'll be right with you, and thanks, Hutch."

For the next hour and a half, Manny agonized over how he was going to find Catherine. "God, please let her be okay," he prayed. Peaches seemed to understand her master's agony. She laid her head on his shoe to comfort him during the flight to Kingston. He pulled the slightly bent cigarette from his pocket, struck a match, putting the flame to the tip. He inhaled deeply.

When the plane finally touched down at the Kingston airport, the two men and a dog hurried into the terminal. They were greeted by Kingston Police Chief, Dennis Grant.

Manny and Hutch introduced themselves and handshakes were given all around. Hutch excused himself from the group, telling them he wanted to call the department to check on the progress of the interrogation of Red Dog and the gunman and also to be sure Roberto was safe.

—•••—

"WHAT HAVE YOU GOT, Chief Grant?" Manny asked.

"I think we have some very good news for you," the chief said smiling. "After we got the notice about your missing plane, we found it right here in our hands. I went over to check her out. It appeared the pilot had left, so we, shall I say, let ourselves in. The very good news I have is sitting over in the VIP lounge. She asked to see you as soon as your plane landed."

The chief was already walking toward a huge oak door labeled "Guest Lounge."

As soon as the door opened, Catherine flew into Manny's arms. "I thought I was going to die," she said softly. Peaches sat whining at her feet.

"Cat, thank God you're safe," he said, holding her tightly. "Are you all right? Did he hurt you?"

"No. No. I'm fine," she said, regaining her composure. "But Manny, you have to get Wendy. She's in the trunk of his car at New Smyrna Airport. I heard the tower identify our location when Douglas took off. You must hurry."

"She's okay. We found her. She's at the hospital. Fred called and she's doing fine, just dehydrated." Manny guided Catherine over to the big overstuffed couch so they could sit down. "Do you have any idea where Douglas is?"

"No. Once in awhile he mumbled something when we were flying, but I was too far away to make out what he said. His last words to me were, 'I'm just beginning my travels, but your journey ends here.' He left me in the plane, and I could hear him lock the door. A little later Chief Grant found me. Did Douglas get away?"

"Hutch is with me. Douglas can't be too far ahead of us. We have to track him down quickly before he gives us the slip. When we have him in custody, I'll let you know," Manny said. "Will you be all right here for a little while? I'll see about a hotel room. We can get you a flight back to the States in the morning, but nothing is flying out of here tonight."

Hutch interrupted the two on the couch. When Catherine saw Hutch come through the door, she instantly stood up and stepped forward to receive a friendly hug from him. "There's a Hilton hotel down the road, Catherine," he said, quickly releasing her. "I have a cab out front that will drive you there if you like. There's nothing out of here until morning."

"Thank you, Hutch. Manny said as much. I will do just as you both suggested. Do you think I'll see you two later?" she asked, looking from one to the other.

"You can bet on it," they said, in unison. The two men turned to look at each other, their eyebrows raised.

Catherine had witnessed tension between her two friends before. She suspected she might be the cause and was also realizing that relationships can bring complications. "Please let me know when you find Douglas or if there is anything I can do."

The two men, Peaches, and Chief Grant walked Catherine to her cab and saw her on her way to the hotel. Then the lawmen and the dog piled into the chief's car.

Chapter 50

ॐ

THERE WERE NO flights out of Kingston for the rest of the day. The three lawmen had to act quickly to find Bradshaw before dawn.

"I think the airport is our best bet," Manny said. "Catherine heard Bradshaw say he was just starting his journey. He's definitely on the run."

"I agree," Hutch said. "Chief, when we met you at the airport, I saw only three airlines—American, Delta, and Jamaica Air. Are there leasing companies or pilots for hire?"

"Yes, there are five leasing outfits," Chief Grant said. "I will send an officer now to start checking. It's late so I don't think he'll find any attendants, but he can start calling their offices to see if any had inquiries from Mr. Bradshaw in the last twenty-four hours. You and Manny check the ticket counters, will you please. The earliest flight out is six thirty-five in the morning to Cancun—one on Jamaica Air and the other with American. You might find an agent on duty."

— • • • —

MANNY AND HUTCH stopped at an all-night café to grab a sandwich and some coffee, which they devoured in the car on the way to the airport. When they reached their destination, they went to the American Airline ticket agent. No one was on duty, and a sign read, "Open at three AM."

Air Jamaica was a different story. There was a young woman, Marie, putting the counter in order so she could leave. Her shift was over, and she looked tired.

"Hello, Marie. We're looking for this man." Manny showed her his badge and Bradshaw's picture. "I wonder if you have seen him.

He might have booked a flight, possibly to Cancun, in the last four to eight hours?"

Marie looked at the picture. "No, he doesn't look familiar. What's his name? I can check the bookings this evening."

"Douglas Bradshaw," Hutch replied.

"No one by that name has booked anything in the last several days. I can look back further if you like."

"Not yet. Can you give me a list of passengers you booked in that timeframe leaving on your first flight out? I believe it's scheduled for departure at six thirty-five tomorrow morning?" Manny asked.

"There are four. Mr. and Mrs. Roger Avery, Helen Hunt, and Walter Romero," Marie answered.

"Do you have contact information for these passengers," Manny asked.

"I don't have anything for Romero, but the other three are at the Hilton, just down the road."

Hutch and Manny looked at each other and then turned together and headed out the doors to the Hilton hotel. It was now two in the morning. Traffic at this hour of night was non-existent, so it took them only a few minutes to drive there. They drove up under the hotel portico and parked. They both jumped out of the car and headed into the lobby's reservation desk. The clerk was leaning back in his chair, snoring softly. When Manny hit the little knob on the bell, the clerk jumped to attention, almost knocking his chair over.

"Excuse me. What can I do for you gentlemen?" the clerk asked, blinking wildly.

"We'd like to see your reservation log for the last twenty-four hours," Hutch said, displaying his ID along with Manny.

"Sure. Sure. Anyone in particular?"

"Yes, a Walter Romero, Helen Hunt, and Mr. & Mrs. Roger Avery."

The clerk scanned the reservations. "Helen Hunt made her reservation a week ago. The Averys booked through a travel group about five months ago, and Romero booked his reservation this evening."

"By any chance, were you on duty when Romero made his reservation?" Manny asked.

"No. Patrick was working at that time. His shift ended at midnight."

"How did Mr. Romero pay for his room?" Hutch asked.

"There's no credit card listed, and the record shows the room is paid in full. It must have been cash."

Manny dug Bradshaw's picture out of his pocket and asked the clerk, "Is this Romero."

"As I said, I wasn't on duty."

"Can you give us Patrick's telephone number? Better yet, what's his address?" Manny said. "We'd like to ask him a couple of questions regarding his shift last night. How far does he live from here?"

"Sure, but he won't be too happy." The clerk wrote down the number and the address on a Hilton pad of paper. He drew a diagram showing how to find where Patrick lived. "His house isn't too far from here. I'd say no more than two or three miles."

Hutch and Manny took off down the road in the car Chief Grant had provided to them. "This isn't hard. Just two turns," Manny said, looking at the make-shift map.

"What do you think about the four people? We could be missing someone," Hutch said. "Bradshaw could have made reservations to go on the lam awhile back."

"I doubt it," Manny replied. "He didn't act like he was leaving until you came into the picture. Looks to me like he was prepared in case he had to run, but my guess is today we spooked him into action."

"My thoughts, too," Hutch agreed. "This Romero looks like a possibility. If Bradshaw's using an assumed name, he may have changed his identity. I'll call Grant and ask him to have some officers do a sweep of the airport—the hotel lavatories, the dumpsters in each facility and outside."

Hutch made the call to the chief as Manny pulled up to the address the clerk had given them for Patrick. The two men got out of the car and walked up the dark path to the front door. Manny knocked on the door. Knocked again. Knocked again louder. A light came on and a very grumpy male voice on the other side of the door asked, "Who is it?"

"Patrick, we're police officers," Hutch said. "We're looking for a fugitive you might have seen today. You've done nothing wrong. We just want to show you a picture. Please open the door."

The door opened slowly and a short, sandy-haired, pudgy man with a mustache peeped out. He looked at the IDs of the two men in front of him and then opened the door wide enough for the officers to enter the little stucco house. A dim light on a table next to a couch was the only illumination.

Manny pulled out Bradshaw's picture and showed it to Patrick. "Have you seen this man?"

"No. I've never seen this man. I'm sure."

"Do you remember a gentleman named Walter Romero?" Hutch asked. "He made a reservation at the hotel about eight-thirty last evening, staying just tonight."

"Yes. Yes. Very nice. Paid cash. I remember because most people pay by credit card."

"Can you describe him, please?"

"Yes. He was about your height," Patrick said, looking at Hutchinson. "He had a mustache and wore a light-color suit. He had a straw hat on." Patrick smiled, pleased with himself.

"Very good, Patrick. What time do you come on duty today?" Manny asked. "We may have more questions."

"I will be at the desk at three o'clock in the afternoon."

—•••—

THE OFFICERS RETURNED to their car and drove back to the hotel. Manny called Catherine's room from a lobby phone. "Catherine, I'm so sorry to wake you," Manny said.

"It's quite all right. My head is a bit foggy though."

"Catherine, do you remember what Douglas was wearing when you last saw him?"

"Oh, dear, let me think. He had on a pair of dark slacks, and oh, yes, a light green golf shirt. I don't know about his shoes. Have you found him?"

"We're not sure, but your information is very helpful. I hope you can go back to sleep. Goodbye for now."

Just then Chief Grant entered the lobby. "Hello, gentlemen. Let me bring you up-to-date. My men canvassed all charters at the airport and the marinas. I can tell you we have some very unhappy Jamaicans. They were not thrilled about being awakened at this time of night. Anyway, nothing turned up. Most of the charters were booked weeks ago by tourists for the weekend. Nothing turned up in the way of clothes being dumped at the airport. I'm waiting for a report from the hotel here."

Grant was interrupted by one of his officers. "Hey, Chief, I just found this black bag in the barrel in the men's room down the hall," he said, handing the bag to the chief.

Grant opened the bag and dumped the contents on the chair beside where the men were standing. Manny picked up a green shirt and looked at Hutch. "It appears our man changed his clothes here. What's the schedule for the maintenance crew to empty trash?" Manny asked the officer.

"The last trash pickup for the day was six o'clock last evening. The trash in the barrel has accumulated since then. This bag had some stuff on top of it."

Hutch addressed Grant. "Chief, you have jurisdiction here. We're carrying a warrant for Bradshaw's arrest. If Romero is our man Bradshaw, can you detain him and then turn him over to my custody to return him to the States?"

"Well, yes. But there is a protocol I have to follow and, of course, paperwork. If you can identify him, I should be able to have everything in order so you could take him tomorrow. Of course, you are assuming this Romero is your man."

Chapter 51

৵

IT WAS THREE O'CLOCK Sunday morning, and most of Jamaica was still asleep. A calm lay over the community. Not so inside the Hilton Airport Hotel. The hotel desk clerk told Chief Grant that Walter Romero had left a four-thirty wakeup call. Grant relayed this information to Manny and Hutch.

"Stupid bastard," Manny said under his breath.

At three-thirty, Manny, Hutch, and Chief Grant began the stakeout of the lobby.

"I think we should grab him in his room," the chief suggested.

"We can't knock on the door," Hutch said. "He would be alerted that something's up. With the wakeup call in less than an hour, chances are he's already getting ready to leave."

"If we bust the door down, and if he has a gun, we would be easy targets," Manny replied. "He's already going to be nervous trying to get out of town."

"If we wait for him to come off the elevator, he's not going to be expecting trouble," Hutch countered. "The lobby is empty. Everything will look peaceful, and we have the element of surprise."

"Okay, Agent Hutchinson and Captain Salinas, you win. The lobby it is," the chief replied.

The three law enforcement officers continued to scout the lobby for the best vantage point to get the drop on Bradshaw, if in fact, Romero was Bradshaw.

Marble pillars delineating a wide aisle from the elevator through the lobby to the hotel exit door looked ideal for a cover. The pillars started about twenty feet from the elevator. Lush bushes stood shoulder high between each pillar. Grant was positioned on one side of the aisle and one of his officers dressed as a bellhop stood nearby the elevators. If someone should happen into the lobby, who did not fit the description he was given, the officer would quickly divert them away and out a side door. Hutch, Manny, and Peaches were on the other side.

— ••• —

WALTER ROMERO OPENED his eyes before the hotel wakeup call. "This is going to be a great day," he said to himself. "I'm a new man."

He jumped into the shower, letting the warm water beat down on his body, washing all vestiges of Douglas Bradshaw down the drain. He got out of the shower, dried off, and went into his room to dress. The light on the telephone was blinking, indicating a message. He lifted the receiver and listened to his wakeup call.

Replacing the phone, he finished dressing. With the aid of his passport, he again positioned the mustache to match the picture. The last thing he put on was his Panama hat. By five o'clock, he was packing his few things into the rolling suitcase. He put his passport into the inside pocket of his jacket, a few dollars into his pants pocket and more into his wallet. The gun went into the waistband of his slacks. The gun, covered by the jacket, did not show a bulge. Taking a look in the mirror and satisfied with the result, he left the room and headed down the elevator to the lobby.

Romero stepped off the elevator, his sight set on the lobby doors to the street. He did not spot Manny or the chief, or Hutch crouching behind the bushes. Neither did he see Peaches standing at attention, not moving a muscle beside her master.

"That's Bradshaw," Manny mouthed across the aisle to Grant.

On signal, Chief Grant and Hutch approached Bradshaw from both sides, guns drawn. Grant moved quickly in front of Douglas, blocking his path to the lobby door. "Douglas Bradshaw, you are under arrest—"

Before the chief could finish his statement, Bradshaw grabbed him around the neck in a hammerlock hold. He spun the chief around like a rag doll putting his gun to the chief's head.

"Drop your gun, you SOB," Bradshaw snarled into the chief's ear, pressing him hard against the temple with the barrel of his .38.

The chief did as he was told and dropped his weapon.

Bradshaw started inching backward toward the lobby doors. "You want to be a hero?" he yelled to Hutch. "You'll have to kill this fat ass first."

Bradshaw waved his gun around erratically, back and forth between the chief and Hutch. "Lay down your gun," he demanded of Hutch. "Now. God damn it, now, I said."

Hutch carefully bent forward and laid his gun down on the marble floor.

Bradshaw's head hurt. What do I do? What do I do? he thought. I have money in my pocket. Hijack a cab? Grab a boat? I'm outta here. Yah. Get a cab, get a boat, and get out.

Bradshaw didn't see Manny a few feet behind him. He was still in back of the bushes but inching forward very slowly. Because Bradshaw was backing out of the lobby, Manny and Peaches were on his right side. Bradshaw's gun side. He was still waving his .38 around.

"You guys do as you're told and nobody gets hurt," Bradshaw shouted. With Bradshaw waving his weapon in the air, he was no longer pointing it at Grant's head. The hammerlock on his neck, however, was like a vise.

Manny lightly tapped Peaches on the back and whispered the command to attack. A black streak, muscles taut, racing on padded feet, then airborne, sank white fangs into Bradshaw's shoulder tissue.

Bradshaw went down as Peaches hurled herself against him. His gun fired wildly and then dropped to the floor. Peaches stood on his chest, fangs bared, guttural growls warning him not to move.

Manny came forward and saw that Hutch was hit. When Peaches landed on Bradshaw, his arm jerked up pointing at Hutch when the .38 fired.

"What the heck?" Hutch muttered. Blood dripped from his face and neck.

Grant shouted in the direction of the desk clerk, "Call the medics. Tell them to get over here ASAP."

The frightened clerk quickly did as he was told. However, he kept his head down, not sure if the gunfire was over.

Manny called Peaches off of Bradshaw's prostrate body. The chief rolled him over on his stomach, jerked his arms back and cuffed him.

Hutch was trying to wipe the blood from his face. He couldn't figure out where it was coming from. He felt fine. He wiped his neck then his ear.

"Youser," he yelped, as a jolt of pain hit his head.

Manny came over to take a look. "Agent Hutchinson, it appears you have a notch in the top of your ear. It will most likely require a team of surgeons, and nurses I might add, to put you back together," Manny said, with as serious a face as he could muster.

Chief Grant, his foot pressing down on Bradshaw's back, tried to catch his breath and settle his nerves. "As I was saying, Douglas Bradshaw, you are under arrest for attacking a Jamaican officer and as a fugitive from the United States."

Manny joined in. "Douglas Bradshaw, you are wanted for the murder of Julie Stone, Miguel Marquez and Raul Santiago and for the kidnapping of Wendy Sullivan and Catherine Hainsworth."

It was then Hutch's turn. Pressing a blood-soaked handkerchief to his head, he said, "Douglas Bradshaw III, you are under arrest by the Government of the United States for the hiring of illegal immigrants and the planning and commission of murder. Douglas Bradshaw III, you have the right to remain silent. If you give up the right to remain silent, anything you say can and will be used against you in a court of law. You have the right to speak with an attorney and to have the attorney present during questioning. Do you understand your rights?"

Bradshaw, face down on the marble floor, bleeding where Peaches punctured his skin, muttered, "Yah, you bastards. I hear you." As he said the words, the fake mustache slipped off his upper lip onto the cold marble floor.

—•••—

THE HOTEL ELEVATOR came to a stop, emitting a soft ping, signaling that the door was about to open. The door slid back, and Catherine stepped out, ready to go to the airport for her six-thirty flight to Miami.

Startled at the scene before her, Catherine's hand quickly touched her lips. "Oh, my," she said.

Chief Grant had his foot on the back of a man lying face down on the floor. Peaches was also on the floor in front of the man, fangs bared. Hutch, while talking to the prostrate person, was wiping blood from his neck.

She hurried over to Hutch. "What happened to you?"

"Our agent here had the tip of his ear blown off," Manny said with a smile.

"Manny, I don't think this is very funny. He's losing a lot of blood," Catherine said. "Here, give me that handkerchief."

"I'm okay. It's just a little flesh wound," Hutch said, apparently pleased that Catherine was tending to his ear.

"Well, it may be what you say, but you're losing a lot of blood."

"Cat, he'll be okay," Manny said.

"Well, I will need some attention," Hutch said, obviously enjoying Catherine's sympathy.

"Of course you will," Catherine said. "Come sit down before you faint."

"Faint? Come on, Cat," Manny said.

"*Really*, Manny. I just want to apply a little pressure to see if I can stop the bleeding," she said.

Sirens announced the EMT van as it drew up to the front door. Two men jumped out with medical kits in hand.

"Gentlemen, over here, please. This is Agent Hutchinson. It appears his ear has been winged," Catherine said, backing away so the medics could tend to Hutch.

"Manny, who is that on the floor? Shouldn't you tell Peaches to stop growling?" Catherine asked.

"That, my dear Miss Cat, is none other than Douglas Bradshaw III."

Catherine walked around so she could see the man's face. His neck appeared to be bleeding as well as his shoulder.

Chief Grant, his foot still on Bradshaw's back, looked up at Manny. "What was that you said to your dog when she charged this guy?"

"Chief, that was dog speak. She's been trained by the military, and one of the words she knows is a Dutch word which means to attack."

"Well, I'll be. She certainly acted on your command."

Catherine looked at Manny, "Thank God you got him. You must tell me all about how you and Hutch managed to find him so quickly."

What's all this you and Hutch stuff, Manny thought. "Cat, I have a plan to do just that, fill you in on Bradshaw's arrest. Can you stay in Jamaica a few more hours? How about we meet for coffee out on the patio, say about ten o'clock. Then we'll see about a flight out of here mid-afternoon."

"That sounds wonderful. I haven't checked out yet, so I'll go back to my room, but before I go, let me see how Hutch is."

— • • • —

THE MEDICS HAD PLACED a bandage around Hutch's head. Gauze was wound around from under his chin to the top of his scalp to hold the compress in place on his ear. The gauze was tied with a bow on the top of the agent's head. He did not look happy.

However, what his unhappy face did not reveal was the depth of his emotions toward Catherine. If she had entered the lobby a few minutes earlier, she could have been in the line of fire, he thought. *No, I cannot, and will not put her in jeopardy. I've always felt that my job was bad for a relationship, and I was right. An occasional fling with someone like Sherry is one thing. An involvement with Catherine is out of the question.*

Chapter 52

✑

HALIFAX MEMORIAL HOSPITAL was beginning to see activity following the weekend. Fred got off the elevator and headed for Wendy's room.

The nurses had alerted the kitchen to prepare two extra lunch trays so the Sullivans could eat together. Shirley and Bert had just finished lunch with their daughter and were making plans for her homecoming while they waited for the doctor. He indicated the evening before that Wendy might be released today.

When Fred entered the room, their conversation stopped. They looked up expectantly for the latest news on Bradshaw.

"Good afternoon, everyone, Wendy, Shirley, Bert," Fred said, nodding to each in turn. "I have good news. Captain Salinas just called. Douglas Bradshaw has been arrested."

Bert and Shirley immediately stood up. Shirley leaned over Wendy's hospital bed and drew her daughter close. Bert quickly walked over and shook Fred's hand.

Wendy drew away from her mother's embrace. "What about Catherine? Where is she? Is she okay?"

"She's just fine, Wendy. Seems Bradshaw locked her in the plane when he landed in Jamaica. The Jamaican police found the aircraft at the Kingston airport. They boarded the plane and released Catherine."

"Detective that is the best news I've heard today. Where is Bradshaw now?" Bert asked.

"He's in the custody of the Kingston police. They're working out jurisdiction issues with Agent Hutchinson, Homeland Security.

"When do you think Douglas will return to Florida?" Shirley asked.

"The trip could happen anytime from a couple of hours to a few days. He'll be bound over to the agent for transport back to the States for arraignment."

As Shirley again cradled her daughter, Wendy began to sob uncontrollably, her body shaking, the pressure finally released through her tears.

Looking over at Bert, Wendy said, "Daddy, please come here." She extended her hand beckoning to him to join her.

Bert went to the side of the bed across from his wife. As Shirley released Wendy, Bert stepped in and put his arms around the girl he had always considered his own.

"Daddy, please know, you may not be my biological father, but you are my dad in every other sense of the word. I will be forever grateful that you are the one I know and love as my father."

Bert held her close as his tears spilled onto her cheek. "Thank you, Wendy. Those are beautiful words."

Chapter 53

❧

CATHERINE SAT out on the hotel veranda. She was surrounded with beauty—sounds of gently splashing water cascading over three cherubs, punctuated with tropical birds communicating with their morning songs. It was a good day to be alive.

A waiter came over to Catherine's table and laid out the coffee service she ordered, complete with cream and sugar for Manny. She poured a cup of the rich black coffee for herself.

Going over the events of the last forty-eight hours, her thoughts drifted to the day Douglas had offered her a job. *Thank goodness I didn't take him up on his offer,* she thought. *What a mistake that would have been, and I would have been disloyal to Russell at a time when he needed me most. The new development is going to stretch thin his company's resources once it gets underway.*

Catherine took another sip of coffee, but she couldn't let go of a plan developing in her mind. *My dream of one day owning my own firm, taking projects I feel are challenging, seems like a goal that is in my reach.*

"You look deep in thought, Cat. May I interrupt?" Manny asked, walking up beside her.

"Oh, Manny, today is wonderful. I'm so glad you're safe," she said, standing up to greet him. She went to Manny, put her arms around his neck, and gave him a friendly hug. Peaches gave a slight whine, looking for attention as well. "Yes, pretty girl. You are very special, too."

"How beautiful you look, Miss Cat, a brilliant jewel in this paradise setting," Manny said. *The only trouble is,* he thought, *she treats me like a brother. I desire a warm kiss but she only gives me a hug. Well, I'm not going to give up.*

"You wax poetic, Captain, and poetry is very fitting with all these flowers." Catherine returned to her chair and put the exact amount of cream and sugar in his cup and then added the coffee, just as he liked it. "Now tell me what's new with the case. How did you find Douglas?"

Manny sat down, took a sip of coffee, and retrieved a cigarette from his pocket. "Cat, do you mind if I have a quick smoke?"

"Of course not. We're outside so you won't bother me, but I thought you kicked the habit."

"Well yes, I did, too. After you went to your room yesterday, Hutch and I interviewed people who might have seen Bradshaw. No one had. Then we got a break. Only one man made a reservation yesterday evening for a room at this hotel, a Mr. Walter Romero. Turned out Romero was Bradshaw in disguise."

"I bet there's a lot more to the story. You and Hutch must have gone through many contortions trying to track Douglas down."

"You're right. I'll leave that tale for a time when we have a glass of wine in our hands on the deck of my boat."

"That's a deal. Who has him now?"

"Bradshaw is with the Kingston police. Chief Grant and Hutch are working out all the jurisdiction issues to transport him back to the States. There's a pile of paperwork and dozens of signatures needed to complete the transfer. It could be a day, a week, but probably not months."

"Did Hutch see a doctor?" Catherine asked.

"Yes, he did," Manny said, showing a slight annoyance. "I guess he had to have a few stitches to close the wound. He'll have a souvenir from this job for the rest of his life. Instead of a notch in a gun grip, he'll have a notch in his ear."

"At least he's alive to see the notch," she said with a smile. "Does Wendy know you have Douglas?"

"She will shortly, if she doesn't already. I called Fred before I came down to join you. He's headed to the hospital now. He's pretty sure she'll be going home today. Her mom spent the night in the hospital with her, so I guess she's snapping back fast. The intravenous fluids are doing the trick. We found her soon enough that it doesn't appear she suffered any damage other than the dehydration."

"It's such a relief to know he's been caught," Catherine said. "I have a hard time grasping all the evil acts he did. He was always a bit of bore, but murder? How does a person who appears to do so well with his business end up committing murder?"

"I'm sure the trial will be front page news for months to come," Manny said, taking a sip of his coffee. "There will be salacious testimony regarding the affair between Julie and Douglas. I guess he killed her because she was breaking off their relationship."

"Their affair just doesn't seem to rise to the level of murder," Catherine said.

"We'll find out at the trial, but I believe Julie let Douglas know she was going to confess to her husband that she had given Stone & Associates' draft of the tower project bid to Douglas. Did you know Douglas was preparing a lawsuit against the board for not choosing him?"

"Yes, I heard rumors to that effect. What will happen to Douglas' employees?" Catherine asked.

"I don't know. His Chief Financial Officer, Philip Longwood, will probably continue to handle company issues until someone takes over. I suppose another corporation could buy the company, or it may be dissolved. Any money realized from a sale would go to creditors. If there is money left over, the funds would belong to Douglas. He'll need it for legal fees."

"I just can't help thinking of all the people affected by Douglas' actions. The hurt, the anguish, to say nothing of the cost of lost lives. What will happen to the illegal immigrants and all the sub-contractors who did business with Bradshaw?"

"They will come under Homeland Security, ICE," Manny said. "The illegals will be rounded up and ultimately be deported back to their home countries. Many of them will slip away and work someplace else. The employers face a stiff fine and, in some cases, jail time."

"You know," Catherine mused, "at the time Douglas started down this road of self-destruction, he didn't realize where his chosen path was going to lead him. You might say that petty crimes perpetrated by petty people can result in huge consequences."

"Well said." Manny finished his coffee and put his cup down. "Now, Cat, there is the matter of you and me getting back to Florida.

I talked to Hutch about the plane he commandeered that brought us down here. He offered to fly you and me back early this afternoon, sometime after two o'clock. He's returning to Washington to move the process of extradition along on that end. The plane could drop us off at Daytona Beach on the way to Washington. How does that sound to you?"

"Like music to my ears, Captain."

"Good. I'll go let him know. When he has a definite time, I'll call your room."

— ● ● ● —

MANNY LEFT CATHERINE in the garden. He had already told Hutch they would take him up on his offer. He headed for the bar. With all the action in the past twenty-four hours, he felt he deserved a drink, maybe two. He thought about relaxing on his boat when he got home, a glass of scotch in his hand.

Epilogue

⁊

AS CATHERINE WAITED for the traffic light to turn green, she looked at her list of things she had to do in the next few days. *Never enough time,* she thought, adding another item to the list. The light turned green, and she quickly turned into the plaza and parked in the shade of a stately palm tree directly across from the House of Beads.

Tillie had called a few days before to ask if she could drop by the shop. The ladies who attended the class the day Julie died wanted to hear her tale on being taken hostage. Wendy was going to be there, as well as Barb and Susan. How could she turn down the invitation when the saga had begun in the little bead shop?

Catherine slipped out of her BMW, clicked the button on the car key to lock it, and quickly strode to the store. The crystals hanging in the window sparkled brilliantly in the afternoon sun, and the familiar silver bell tinkled softly as she entered. She was immediately surrounded, bombarded with questions. Everyone spoke at once.

Tillie stepped in front of the small group and gave Catherine a fierce hug. Releasing her grip, she stepped back. "I read all about your harrowing story in the *News Journal*. Thank God you and Wendy are safe. I just can't believe what a monster Douglas Bradshaw turned out to be."

"I'm glad you came through your ordeal unscathed," Susan said, stepping up and giving Catherine a quick squeeze in spite of herself.

Catherine and Wendy gave each other a brief embrace. One of the first things Catherine did when she landed back in Daytona Beach was to visit Wendy at home. She wanted to see for herself, that her young friend was okay.

"Dear, dear, come on, everyone, into the classroom," Tillie said. "I have a surprise for you. I bought a new espresso machine for the occasion. There are sugar cubes on the table," she said as she fixed each of the ladies a small cup of the hot, thick coffee.

"Really, Catherine, I couldn't believe what I read in the paper, that you actually went to Douglas' penthouse knowing he probably killed Julie," Susan quipped, adding two cubes of sugar to her cup.

"Well, when I tried to find Wendy that Saturday morning, and her mother informed me she had gone to tell Douglas she was his daughter, I was concerned for her safety. As it turned out, it was lucky I did."

"It sure was," Barb said. "You saved Wendy's life."

"I also happened to step on something hard in his living room carpet. When I dug it out of the wool, the object turned out to be Julie's earring. When Douglas panicked and pulled out his gun, I put the earring into my pocket. Manny told me later it will serve as a key piece of evidence when Douglas goes to trial. The earring places Julie in his penthouse."

"Where is Mr. Bradshaw now?" Barb asked.

"He's in prison up in Tallahassee awaiting the court proceedings. From the account in the paper the other day, that probably won't start until January or February of next year," Catherine said.

"Wendy, have you recovered completely?" Barb asked. "You could have died in that car trunk. It was a very hot day."

"I'm perfectly fine, but I can tell you I was scared to death when Douglas pulled out that gun," Wendy said. "At first, I was glad I was in the trunk. I thought I was safe, at least I couldn't see him. But then I was frightened for Catherine because I heard her fall on the floor of the backseat."

"It must have been terrifying, dear," Tillie said, giving Wendy a little hug.

"When he stopped the car," Wendy said, "and I heard him thump the trunk and say goodbye, I didn't think I'd ever be found. I guess I passed out. I wasn't aware of anything that happened until I woke up in the hospital."

"He actually said goodbye?" Susan asked. "How awful. The scoundrel. What do you think of him being your father? At least that's what everyone is saying."

"They're all wrong. Bert is my father, always has been and always will be. He would never treat me the way Mr. Bradshaw did." Wendy got up from the table and went to the window. Her eyes misted over, her hand shaking as she willed herself to regain her composure. "I wish people would stop asking me about Douglas," she said softly. "I never want to talk about Douglas Bradshaw again. As far as I'm concerned, he has ceased to exist."

Catherine sensed her young friend's distress. She went to her and gently encircled Wendy in her arms. "People will talk until the trial is over, dear," she whispered. "You and I share a special bond now, and I'll always be here for you even if you just need a sympathetic ear."

Returning to the others, Catherine changed the subject. "Tillie, I brought a swatch of cloth from a new aquamarine dress I had designed for the charity auction in a couple of months. I thought I'd have a look around to get some ideas for jewelry to complement it," Catherine said.

"I have some beautiful pearls you should take a look at," Tillie said.

"Thank you, I will. The auction should be quite an event. Peaches was a real hero in capturing Douglas. She's going to get a special award. There will also be a tribute to Julie for all her charity work. Many of her designer gowns will be auctioned off at the event, and I think Agent Hutchinson may come down from D.C. to attend."

"Ah, the handsome agent I read about," Susan said, with a devilish grin. "Coming all the way from Washington, is he?"

"Oh, yes, Catherine," Tillie said. "You must tell us more about that wonderful Captain Salinas and his dog. I saw you and the Captain at the ball. You were a handsome pair."

"Wait a minute, Tillie. I want to hear about the agent who flew our Catherine back home from Jamaica," Susan retorted.

"Now, ladies. There is nothing to tell," Catherine said. "They are both very nice gentlemen, but right now I have no intention of entering into a relationship with either one of them. I have more than I can handle with my work at Stone & Associates."

Catherine didn't like the way the conversation was going, and she especially didn't want to field any questions about Hutch. She took her cup to the tray by the espresso machine signaling that the coffee klatch was ending.

Hutch hadn't called since that day he dropped Manny and her off at the Daytona Beach Airport. Just as well, she thought. I guess my intuition was right...he pulled away...he doesn't want to get involved. Well, I have my own plans to work out...maybe my own firm some day.

"The charity auction sounds like a lively occasion," Tillie said, breaking into Catherine's thoughts. "But there won't be romantic dancing like at a ball."

"No, there won't," Catherine replied.

But, she thought, smiling to herself, one doesn't need a ball to dance!

The End

REVIEW REQUEST

Dear reader, I hope you enjoyed meeting a new friend, Elizabeth Stitchway. If you have the time, it would mean a lot to me if you wrote a review, your honest appraisal. What did you like most? It's super easy. Go to Amazon. Log in. Search: Mary Jane Forbes Choices

Thank you!

Meet the Author

Mary Jane Forbes is a computer geek and a news junkie who believes in the law. The pathos produced in applying the law, there's the story. Her novel "Murder in the House of Beads" is set today in Daytona Beach, Florida, a paradise near where she lives.

Murder in the House of Beads is the first bead in a string of four. The paths of the three protagonists and a dog crisscross as they fight the bad guys. Look for the following three books in Mary Jane's House of Beads Mystery Series: *Intercept, Checkmate, and Identity Theft.*

Website:

www.MaryJaneForbes.com

Books by Mary Jane Forbes

DroneKing Trilogy
A Toy for Christmas, A Ghostly Affair
Love is in the Air

Bradley Farm Series
Bradley Farm, Sadie, Finn
Jeli, Marshall, Georgie

Twists of Fate Series
The Fisherman, a love story
The Witness, living a lie
Twists of Fate, daring to dream

Murder by Design, Series:
Murder by Design
Labeled in Seattle
Choices, And the Courage to Risk

Elizabeth Stitchway, PI, Series
The Mailbox, Black Magic,
The Painter, Twister

House of Beads Mystery Series
Murder in the House of Beads
Intercept, Checkmate
Identity Theft

Novels
The Baby Quilt … a mystery!
The Message...Call Me!

Short Stories
Once Upon a Christmas Eve, a Romantic Fairy Tale
The Christmas Angel and the Magic Holiday Tree

Visit: www.MaryJaneForbes.com